Contents

Lord of Rouen
Book 8 in the
Norman Genesis Series
By
Griff Hosker

Lord of Rouen

Published by Sword Books Ltd 2018

Copyright © Griff Hosker First Edition

A CIP catalogue record for this title is available from the British Library.
Cover by Design for Writers
Thanks to Simon Walpole for the Chapter Headings.

PART ONE
The Land of the Saxons

Prologue

I am Göngu-Hrólfr Rognvaldson. I was once called Rollo but
that was before I was reborn. My brother, Ragnvald, killed our
father and I had been sent to the bottom of the sea. The gods had
saved me and I had been reborn into another clan. I had been
adopted by the jarl and, when he died, I should have been jarl but
there was treachery in the clan and I had been denied my title. I did
not mind. I did not wish to remain in Norway. I had a home in the
Land of the Horse. My brother ruled there now, allied to King
Salomon and his treacherous Bretons.

I looked astern at *'Fáfnir'*. She was my threttanessa and Sven
Blue Cheek, who was my lieutenant, sailed her. She was under
crewed for we had fought and captured a larger drekar of Man. I
now sailed that ship. The crew were dead and we did not wish to
rename her for that was unlucky. Then we noticed the figurehead.
It was not a dragon. It was a warrior riding a horse and his head
was that of a dragon. Sven Blue Cheek knew then that she was
named after a god, Hermóðr, who had ridden Odin's horse,
Sleipnir, into Hel. We were happy with the name. She was
'Hermóðr' and it was *wyrd*. She became my drekar and served me
well.

We were heading for Dyflin. We had captives to sell and more
crew to find but I was inordinately happy for I had been able to
save the life of my grandfather, Hrolf the Horseman. The ship in
which we sailed was his knarr, *'Kara'*. He had spent two years
searching for me. One of his old oar brothers, Erik Green Eye had

1

died in the search and my grandfather laid low but he was tough. He and the most loyal of his men had never given up as they searched the seas for me. He had not believed that I had drowned. He knew that I was alive. As Dyflin hove into view I thought of the webs spun by the Norns.

I now had two families. One was in Norway: that was my adopted mother Gefn and her sister Bergljót and the last member of my other family lay sleeping at my feet. My birth mother had died when my father had failed to return from our raid. I was told she had a broken heart. Had she known that my father had been murdered it might have tormented her in the other world. My grandmother, Mary, a Frankish noblewoman, had slowly succumbed to a wasting sickness. Her death had been a reason why my grandfather had set sail to search for me.

I now knew that I had a task set for me. I had to find enough drekar to sail to the Land of the Horse and fight my brother for my birthright. It would tear the Clan of the Horse apart and I did not want to do it but if I did not then I would be letting down my family and, most of all my grandfather. My father needed vengeance. The dead men who had died as a result of Ragnvald Ragnvaldsson's treachery needed revenge. I would be the instrument that would bring justice. We would trade and sell the captives. We would sail back to Norway and I would take my new family to a home in the Land of the Franks.

Lord of Rouen

Chapter 1

Dyflin harbour was largely empty as we sailed in and that disappointed me. I had hoped for more ships. More ships meant men who might follow me and my grandfather. As the smallest ship, we had entered the channel first. My grandfather was awake. He stood with me as we watched the wooden walls draw closer. "I thought there would have been more drekar in the harbour."

My grandfather nodded, "As did I. There were many here when we arrived and that was just a few days ago. I wonder where they have sailed."

The answer was simple. Three sons of Ragnar Lodbrok had landed in the land of the East Angles. It was said that they had more than three hundred and fifty ships at their command. Every Viking had sailed to join in this attempt to take all the treasure that was known to be in the churches of the Saxons. It was said that they had already begun to take Northumbria and East Anglia was theirs. The good news was that with so few slaves being brought to market we achieved a higher price for ours but the bad news was that there were fewer men seeking an oar. It was my grandfather's name which secured twenty men for us. All were Vikings who had rowed a drekar but all had one thing in common. They had fallen out with their captain or their fellows. None had mail and only half had a helmet. What they all possessed was a sword along with a shield. As Sven Blue Cheek and my grandfather pointed out, that would have to do.

Sven Blue Cheek was an older warrior but he saw things in me I did not, "Göngu-Hrólfr, you are young but you are a mighty warrior. You are like Thor; you will be the smith who beats their raw metal into swords! We now have crew enough to row back to

3

Norway. Who knows, there may be more there who wish to join us. Bjorn is not a popular jarl. When two drekar enter the fjord his *'Dellingr'* will not seem as powerful as it did when we left." He stood. "I will go and use some of the coin to buy supplies for the voyage home. Now that we are rich we can buy spare sails."

When Sven Blue Cheek left us, my grandfather nodded his approval, "I like him. He is a good man. He reminds me of Ulf Big Nose. He speaks plainly. Men like that are good to have around a young leader like you. He is right; better to have a crew which you make your own. It will take some time for us to sail to your home. That will make them your men."

We sailed on the evening tide. "Grandfather, what of my father's jarls? Did all of them support my brother?"

He looked sad, "Some did but most of them chose not to. Folki took his folk south to try to build a home south of Carentan. I have not heard of them for some time. Others went to Denmark to join Ragnar Lodbrok and his sons. They may be in East Anglia. Some sailed to Miklagård to seek their fortune there. With your father gone few wished to follow Ragnvald."

"What of Gilles? And my father's horsemen?"

"Gilles' sons still raise horses but the clan does not ride them. Stephen of Andecavis took the last six horsemen with Folki when they went south. Your brother did not think that horsemen were of value. He went to hire out his sword. He was sad to leave. Gilles died. I think his sons moved to better grazing. As Ragnvald did not wish the horses they had to sell them somewhere and they sold them to Franks."

"But we are the Clan of the Horse!"

"We were. Your brother changed it to the Clan of the Sword."

I shook my head. "You founded the clan. You are Hrolf the Horseman."

"I am a relic of the past. I know not why your brother allowed me to live. He did not like my opinions. We were cursed because of the priest and my grandson Ragnvald. When the priest watched your brother being born it changed everything. You are the last hope of the clan." The family curse had destroyed not only the

4

family but the clan. The priest who had witnessed my brother's birth had much to answer for.

My adopted father had said much the same. He had adopted me to save his clan. My adopted mother Gefn had spoken of the hope that I might save my new clan. I had much to do and many miles to sail. My grandfather and I did not return on *'Kara'*. She was laden with goods we had bought. We were going to make a new start. Harold Haroldsson was happy to sail her. I was aboard *'Hermóðr'*. Sven Blue Cheek sailed *'Fafnir'*. I think the men of Man must have captured the drekar I sailed for she was far too well built to be a Manx ship. With sixteen oars on each side, double crewed she could easily hold sixty-four men. We had but forty on board. Half were new men and the other half were men like Sámr, Bergil and Ragnar who had sailed with me from Norway. It was a long journey and, as we were sailing at the speed of our knarr, it was a slower journey. It served two purposes: I got to know my new men and my grandfather improved day by day. When I had first seen him, I had thought him close to death. We spoke of the past and of his search for me.

He was interested in the sword I had had made. It was longer than any other sword he had ever seen. He confessed that he would have to use it two handed. I shrugged, "I can use it two handed but I use it one handed normally. Years of rowing and my long arms make it easy. I have to wear a scabbard across my back. I keep a shorter sword there too. Sometimes, in the shield wall, a shorter sword is best."

He was impressed by the runes and he ran his finger along them: 'I am Long Sword, Göngu-Hrólfr is my master'. "This sword will end the life of your brother."

"How can you be sure? He is a cunning warrior."

He smiled, enigmatically, "The sword tells me."

That pleased me.

He told me, as we turned east to sail around the rocky coast of the lands of the Pictii, that he did not know how many summers he had seen but that it was more than sixty. He did not look his age. True his beard was white and his hair growing thin but his body still had the hard, lean look of a warrior. He had received his

5

wound because of sheer numbers of pirates who had attacked the knarr. I told him the truth of my adventures since I had been knocked overboard off Cent. He had heard the rumours. They had been exaggerated versions. He had not heard of the tale of Jarl Rognvald Eysteinsson and his wife Gefn.

After I had told him he said, "That is not unlike the story of Jarl Dragonheart. The difference there was that Prince Buthar did not perish in his own land. He was in Man. You have been chosen, as I was. My work is done. I founded a foothold in the land of the Franks but I was told, by the Norn, that my blood would make it their own. You are that blood."

That was a great responsibility. I had but a handful of men. True I had two drekar but it would take many more than that to wrest my home back from my brother. From what my grandfather said his allies, the Bretons, had increased their power. When my father had been alive we had almost defeated them.

Our Norwegian home, Møre lay up the fjord. My grandfather had grown up as a slave in the land of the Franks and, to him, this land of rocks, snow and ice was a wonderland. I had told him of Bjorn Eysteinsson and his treachery. He had nodded, "It seems that our family is not the only one to have a good son and a bad one!"

I wondered if Bjorn Eysteinsson had returned from the meeting with the chief of the tribe. Jarl Halfgrimr Halfdansson had been surprised that he now led our clan. Haraldr Finehair would one day lead the tribe. He had ambitions to rule Norway and I did not think that he would be happy with Bjorn Eysteinsson as a jarl. I had my answer when we neared the settlement. His drekar, *'Dellingr'*, was tied up to the quay. The mast had been stepped. She was not going to sea. When last we had hove to and spoken I had told my captains that I would be the one who would land first. I was not certain of our reception. I wanted Bjorn to know that I was not afraid of him. I had not run away. Every man who had mail wore it. I assigned Sámr to watch my grandfather.

We slid next to the quay and the ship's boys swarmed ashore to make us fast. Gefn and Bergljót came down from their hall to meet us. There were no others who greeted us. Had I not seen smoke coming from the halls and homes of the settlement I would have thought it deserted. Were we being treated as some sort of pariah?

Gefn threw her arms around me. She squeezed me tightly and I felt the salt tears coursing down her cheeks. Bergil was the second ashore and his mother gave him the same welcome. Gefn kissed my cheek and then looked up at me and said, "You have been away forever."

I nodded, "We have had an interesting time. I found my grandfather even though he had spent two years seeking me."

Her eyes lit up. "Then surely you are a chosen one."

I put my arm around her as I led her up the path to her hall, "What is going on here?"

"Bjorn has been back for twenty days. Haraldr Finehair asked him to supply two drekar to fight in the war to gain a kingdom."

"And he only has one. What will he do?"

She stopped. "I fear that he means you harm. It is the witch, Ailsa, he has married who has put him up to this. I am certain she poisoned Gertha. Son, I beg you to go back with your ships and sail to this land of yours. You have your grandfather. This is *wyrd*. If you stay here I fear that there will be bloodshed."

I shook my head. "Would the jarl have run away? I think not. Besides many of my men have families. They wish to take them with us to the … to our new home. I have a family. There are you and Bergljót. I will not leave you here. It takes two to fight and I will avoid it if I can."

"There was a time I believed that might have happened but Bjorn has now backed himself against a mountain. He needs your drekar and he needs your crew."

I nodded. I understood that. What Bjorn did not know was that we now had more men. If he chose to fight us then it would not be so easy as it would have been before we left. "I have two drekar now and two crews. He will not find it quite so easy." I stopped, "I will fetch my grandfather. He was wounded and is only now recovering."

She looked aghast, "I am forgetting myself. I have beds and food to prepare." She turned and rushed back to the hall.

I went back to the drekar. Sven Blue Cheek was waiting for me. I told him what Gefn had said. He nodded as though he had expected nothing less from Bjorn. He had served with the brothers for many years. There was bad blood between Sven and Bjorn.

I lowered my voice, "We need a good watch on our drekar and the men should be warned of treachery."

"I can slit his throat for you, lord. It would not trouble me. I have killed far more worthy men than Bjorn Eysteinsson!"

"No, Sven, if blood is to be shed let him be the cause." I waved Sámr over, "Come, let us take my grandfather to the warm. He is not used to these northern climes."

My grandfather scowled, "I am not yet ready to go to the Otherworld! I am still a Viking albeit an old and grey one." I smiled. His complaint showed that he was becoming better. I left Sámr to take him to the hall.

Harold Haroldsson had just tied up the knarr. "Where do we take our supplies lord and where do we sleep?"

I had not thought of that. Most of my men had families and homes. The warrior hall would be filled with Bjorn's men. That would invite trouble. "Follow Sámr and take them to the large hall. It is my hall. We will sleep there. Make sure that there is someone to watch the knarr. We have enemies here."

"I thought this was your new home?"

"It is but there are problems. Let us just say that I will sleep with my sword close to hand."

We set more guards than we would have done had we landed at a lonely beach. There was mistrust and there was danger. Had it just been my warriors then it would not have been a problem. We could have handled any violence but we had women, children and, in my grandfather's case, the old. Gefn fussed around my grandfather while Bergljót organised the thralls who served us our food. Between them, they told us of events in the village.

"There is bad blood between those who follow," I could see Gefn had a problem saying the word, "the new *'jarl'* and the others."

"Aye, when they sailed to the Chief's home Bjorn was humiliated. Halfdan the Black is getting old but he was still sharp enough to demand to know why your adopted father's wishes had been ignored."

Gefn made certain that my grandfather had enough ale in his horn, "And that is when Bjorn became foresworn. He told Halfdan and his son, Haraldr Finehair, that just a few of the men in the village followed you and that the rest waited with *'Fafnir'*. They believe that there are two ships waiting here for Haraldr when he begins his quest for a kingdom." She scurried off to fetch some more pickled herrings for my grandfather appeared to be enjoying them.

"There was bloodshed. Some men did not like the lie." Bergljót's hand went to her amulet. "Erik Three Fingers was slain on the voyage back and his body dumped overboard. It has further divided the men of the clan."

Gefn returned and placed the herring in front of my grandfather. "Thank you, lady. This is a veritable feast." He was getting old but he was still sound of mind and showed that he had been listening. "Then this Bjorn will have a problem when he has to return with two drekar. When do they muster?"

"At Þorri and they sail in Gói."

"Then he does not have long to persuade men to his side."

"But he cannot crew two drekar. Even if we gave him *'Fáfnir'* he would not have enough men!"

"After Erik died he sailed along the coast picking up any who would join his crew. They were the sweepings of the coast. He now has more men than when you left. Girls have been abused." Gefn shivered.

All eyes were on me. Sven Blue Cheek was watching me particularly closely. I was aware of his scrutiny. I was used to it but I also saw my grandfather's keen eyes upon me. I emptied my horn and I stood, "Mother, ladies, I will not stay here and serve a foresworn murderer. Tomorrow we tell all who wish it that we are sailing for the Land of the Horse to begin a new life." I saw Gefn look up at the ceiling of the hall. This had been her home for as long as she could remember and she would be giving it all up. I put my hand on her shoulder, "It will be a long voyage. If we are taking so many of the clan we will need to stop often. We might have to overwinter somewhere. When we reach my home, I will have to fight my brother. I know it is much to ask and I would not blame any who refuses to follow but I believe that the Norns have a web and it is spun around me. I did not choose this fate but from the moment I died and was reborn, I have seen purpose in my life. My grandfather has returned to me and that is a sign too for he has met a Norn. What say you, mother, Bergljót?"

Gefn smiled and put her hand on mine, "We are Vikings. We are neither soft Saxons nor fey Franks. No matter what Bjorn says you are jarl of this clan for my husband willed it so. We will follow you." She turned to my grandfather, "There is greatness in you. I see here a great warrior who sailed the seas to find his grandson. That alone tells me that we are bound to follow you and if we perish on the way then I will join my husband and son in the Otherworld. What I will not do is to stay here and be subject to the whims of a murderer and his whore wife!"

There was an enormous cheer at that. I had made certain that the ones on sentry duty were the single men or the ones who had joined us in Dyflin. The agreement came from those who would have families to take. We then had to talk of how we could transport half of the clan first to the land of the Saxons and thence to the land of the Franks. We had two drekar and my grandfather's knarr. Sven Blue Cheek remembered another old knarr. It had belonged to Erik Three Fingers. His son, who had seen but sixteen summers, was no longer willing to stay in the fjord. Gefn said that he did not wish to stay with the clan. With four ships we might just be able to take our families and enough animals to help us start anew.

My grandfather listened and then said to Gefn, "And this hall?"

She patted his hand and gave my grandfather a tight-lipped smile, "If Ailsa the witch thinks that she will get this home then she is in for a shock. I will burn it before we go." We spent some time making plans and then most retired to bed.

When all had left the fire to us I sat with my grandfather and Sven Blue Cheek. Sven looked particularly pleased with the outcome, "You have shown that you are a leader but where will we go first? Winter is coming and we cannot sail far with so many women and children. The ships will be overcrowded."

I had thought of this. "I know that it may seem reckless but when we raided Streanæshalc we destroyed most of it. We were told, in Dyflin, how it had become an empty place. With the monks and the nuns gone there are just fishermen who remain. The river there is like our fjord here. We could stay in the ruins of their church. It would make a warmer temporary home for us. There is little snow in the land of the Saxons. The abbey we destroyed has a good position high above the river. We could defend it and the land is ripe for raiding."

Sven Blue Cheek stroked his beard, "And we know that the King of the Northern Saxons was killed in battle. It is a bold move but it might succeed. We could build a knarr or a drekar on the river." He turned to my grandfather, "Your grandson is a clever and bold warrior."

My grandfather's eyes began to fill, "Aye. He is just like his father."

Sven rose, "That still leaves us with the problem of Bjorn."

"I know but I have a plan for that too. If he will not let us leave peacefully then I will challenge him."

Sven laughed, "He is a coward! He will not fight!"

"Then we will have won. There is dissension already amongst his men. If many were humiliated by the visit to Halfdan the Black then this may just persuade the others to quit him. We cannot stay here for to do so means that we serve Haraldr Finehair. I like the man but my destiny lies in the land of the Franks!"

I did not sleep well. My mind was filled with what might go wrong and problems I had not foreseen. In the end, I fell asleep through sheer exhaustion. It meant that, when I awoke, I was not refreshed. Gefn had prepared much food. I think that she and Bergil's mother had been up most of the night preparing food. She would be leaving her home forever. Each meal she now prepared could be the last.

Sven Blue Cheek had also been up early and he came back from the quay. "Our two drekar and knarr are unharmed. I spoke with

Ulf Eriksson. He and his mother are more than happy to come with us to a new life. We have the second knarr."

"Then when we have eaten you and I will go and visit Bjorn, the jarl. I will tell him to his face what we intend."

"I will have armed men close by."

"Not too many, Erik. I do not wish to be seen as the aggressor. If we can do this peacefully then so much the better."

Sven shook his head, "I have spoken this morning with those who are disillusioned with the jarl. He is in a bad place. He is between the fjord and the ice of the glacier. It is hard to see how he can survive this catastrophe. He has to provide two drekar. At the moment he can barely crew one. He will try anything he can."

A picture drifted into my head. It was of Gefn and Bergljót. They were in danger. "Have men guard the hall. I would not harm come to my grandfather and the women. This Bjorn and Ailsa have shown that they are both treacherous and capable of poison."

Sven smiled, "I have done so already. Sámr and Ragnar have six men watching the hall. There will be no poison there."

After we had eaten, Bergil, Sven and I went from the hall to the hall of Bjorn. We did not take shields and we wore no helmets. I had my Long Sword and my short sword in scabbards across my back and I wore my byrnie. We took just eight men with us. As we neared the hall I saw that outside the hall were gathered the worst of the warriors of the clan. There were others I did not recognise and as we drew closer Sven said quietly, "The ones you do not recognise are the scum he picked up when heading home."

We stopped some twenty paces from the hall. I recognised Haldi Ship Breaker. He was a huge and powerful warrior but I saw that now, he had run to fat. He and the other warriors had been enjoying the good life with the new jarl. Gefn had told us how the clan produced less and there was hunger. A good jarl provided for the clan. Haldi sneered as I waited, "The giant returns with his tail between his legs. What do you wish, boy? Do you beg the jarl to take you back?"

I turned my gaze to him. "I do not come to bandy words with a lump of lard such as you Haldi Ship Breaker, I come here to speak with Bjorn Eysteinsson."

His hand went to his sword, "That is the jarl, boy and I will trust you to keep a civil tongue in your head."

Sven Blue Cheek said threateningly from behind me, "Or what? Would you challenge Göngu-Hrólfr Rognvaldson? Pray do so for that I would like to see. It is a while since I have seen a pig butchered."

Before he could say more the man they called the jarl appeared. He was mailed and he wore his helmet. Behind him, he had four oathsworn. They too were ready for war. "So Göngu-Hrólfr, you return. Have you brought back the clan's drekar?"

I shook my head. I was aware that the men before us were spreading out. This was a trap. "No, for the ship is mine by right. I come here to collect Gefn, Bergljót and the families of our men. We are leaving the clan."

"And what if I say that you cannot leave; that I forbid it. What then?"

I saw that he was preparing to step back. I smiled and stretched my arms up, "This is a fine fjord but it is not my home. I would sail to the land of the Franks and besides none of us can stomach living so close to a man who is foresworn. You told Halfdan the Black two lies."

I saw him step back and, even as his oathsworn rushed at us I drew my Long Sword. Bjorn's twenty men had shields and they had helmets but they had neglected their practice. We had not. We were killers all. Haldi Ship Breaker rushed at me and I used the full length of my sword. I swung it in a wide arc. It tore through his throat. His eyes widened and his hands went to his throat but he was dead before he touched the ground. I twisted the sword and lunged at the oathsworn warrior who ran at me. My sword had a tip which was sharp. I am a strong man and I used the speed of the warrior to let him run on to my sword. He was already swinging his sword at my unprotected head. My sword killed him before his blade reached me.

Bergil and Sven had old scores to settle with Bjorn's oathsworn. Their swords were a blur. Both used a sword and a short sword. Sven flicked away the shield of Aðalbriktr Aðalbriktrson. The oathsworn had often butted heads with Sven. Now their enmity would be settled - in blood. As soon as the shield was turned aside Sven stepped in close and he hooked his leg behind that of Aðalbriktr. The warrior tried, ineffectually, to hit Sven with the pommel of his sword. Sven leaned in and pushed his foe to the floor. As he lay there Sven rammed his sword into his neck.

Bergil too showed that his skills had improved. Facing Landbjartr Persson he used his speed and quick feet to evade the flailing sword of his opponent. He whipped around the back of Landbjartr and brought his sword into the man's back. The crack as his spine was shattered could be heard above the cries of the wounded and dying.

My other men had been chosen well by Sven. Six more Bjorn supporters lay on the ground. I shouted, "Stop! Or you will all be slaughtered where you stand!"

More of my men had run up and it was obvious that Bjorn had lost. He nodded and his men sheathed their weapons. Just then there were cries from my hall. I pointed my sword at Bjorn. "You will stay away from me and my men or risk death!" I was angry and I saw men recoil. I shouted, "Any who wish to sail with me are free to do so. I leave this clan for a new life!"

We backed away for none of us trusted these warriors. Sven said, "And if they all choose to come, what then? We have little enough room as it is."

I smiled, "In light of this treachery I am more than happy to take *'Dellingr'*."

Sven Blue Cheek laughed, "And I would dearly love to see how he explains that to Halfdan the Black!"

When we reached Gefn's hall I saw four bodies laid outside. None were my men. Sámr was cleansing his blade. "They came like murderers in the night. They were going for your grandfather and the two matriarchs!"

I looked and saw Hrolf the Horseman smile as he too cleaned his sword on the cloak of one of the would-be killers. "It is good to know, Rollo, that I have not yet lost my touch."

I cupped my hands, "Begin to load the two knarr and the two drekar! We leave as soon as we are loaded." I turned to Sámr,

"And you, my friend shall now be known as Sámr Oakheart for you defended that which I value more than the world.

As the morning progressed men and their families arrived. They all said the same thing, "Göngu-Hrólfr Rognvaldson we would sail with you. There is no honour here and no life. If we stay then our families will starve."

It became obvious that we needed the *'Dellingr.* I waved over Olaf Two Teeth and Bergil. "We are going to take *'Dellingr'*. Find ten more men. Lounge close to the drekar as though you are just waiting for us to leave. When the other ships are loaded we will make a shield wall while you step the mast and warp her into the fjord. We will load her closer to the sea. Have your men take bows. We will board when we have bought us time."

They were both more than happy to do so. I turned to Sven as they hurried off. "This time we will need our shields. Choose well the men for the shield wall. I will go and see to my drekar." Old Æbbi Jorgenson had been hurt during the raid on Streanæshalc. His left arm would not support a shield and yet he was as keen to serve as any. His son Petr Æbbison was a strapping warrior and he more than made up for Æbbi's disability. Æbbi was helping, as best he could, to load the knarr. I said, "Æbbi, I have a task for you."

"Yes, lord."

"I wish you to watch Bjorn and his men. Let me know if they make any moves which threaten us. I suspect there may be treachery being plotted. Pretend your arm aches."

He grinned, "Aye lord, I will play the cripple. They mocked me enough when you were away and I was healing."

"That will soon be in the past."

'Hermóðr' was the largest drekar. I would take Hrolf the Horseman, Gefn and Bergljót with me. I waved over Pétr Tallboy. He had been a ship's boy and with Olaf Two Teeth now committed I needed someone who could steer while I was busy. "Rig an old sail just behind the figurehead. Hrolf, Gefn and Bergljót will use that while we sail. We will need as much storing beneath the decks as we can. I will be busy. You can sail her to the sea?"

"If you trust me to then aye, Göngu-Hrólfr Rognvaldson. It would be an honour."

"When it is ready, fetch the three of them. I would have them aboard first."

As the afternoon passed the four ships were loaded. I saw smoke and looked up the side of the fjord. The hall was on fire. Gefn's face was covered in tears as my grandfather and Bergljót helped her to the drekar. She was burning her old life. Bjorn and his wife would not have her home.

Sven came to me a short while later. "Our four ships are loaded. I would say overloaded for they cannot sail on the open sea as they are."

I nodded. The fjord was one thing but I would not risk my people on the open sea. "Then tell them that when the horn is sounded they sail and wait for us in the channel. When that is done fetch the shield wall."

I went over to Æbbi. He had been pretending to drink from an ale skin. "Well?"

"They are gathering, lord. I counted thirty of them. They have been drinking. I think they are building up the courage to attack you."

I saw that my four ships were almost ready. "Go to Bergil, tell him now is the time. Join him on the drekar." He hurried off. If Bjorn and his men wondered at the sudden speed of the old man it was too late now. I turned, "Sven!"

Sven Blue Cheek and my shield wall were ready. All had had their shields about their backs as they loaded the ships. I waved Sámr Oakheart over. He had the horn. "Sound the horn now!"

Everything seemed to happen at once. As the strident notes of the horn sounded Olaf Two Teeth and Bergil led my men to the *'Dellingr'*. Sven ran to me with my shield and helmet. My men formed up alongside me. We were between the *'Dellingr'* and Bjorn's hall. They were, as Æbbi had observed, gathering but we had been so quick that we were ready before they were.

I heard Bjorn's voice, "Treacherous monster! They steal our ship! Get them!"

Our shields locked and Long Sword peered over the top. Sven had chosen just twenty men for the shield wall. Thirty enemies ran at us. This time they were desperate for they knew that if we took their drekar the would be forced to stay in the half-deserted settlement. The exception was Bjorn who stood and watched his men hurl themselves at us. They came at us wildly. Even though we were unsupported their reckless attack availed them nothing. A spear came towards my head. Had there been one or two others I might have been in trouble but Arne Pétrsson was alone and my shield came up to send the spear's tip above my shoulder. I rammed my sword forward. His speed killed him. My sword tore into his screaming mouth. I ripped it out sideways for Beorn Long Toe hurtled into me. He had an axe and he tried to take my head from me. I was too tall for him. My shield took the blow. It shivered and shook but it held. An axe is not the weapon for close in fighting. I slid my sword over the top of his shield and caught the side of his helmet. He had not fastened it correctly or perhaps it had poor leather straps. It came off. I brought my head back and used my helmet to butt him. He fell in a heap at my feet.

Ten arrows flew overhead. The men on the drekar were doing as I asked. I saw that Bjorn had to bring his shield around to save himself. Five warriors lay dead before us and when the arrows began to descend the rest raised shields. More than half of them did not have mail. "Walk back to the drekar!"

We strolled backwards. Just as we did so Þióðkell the Silent suddenly threw away his shield and began to bite the edge of his sword. He took it and a second sword and ran at us with a sword in each hand. Sven said, "That is all we needed; a berserker!"

Two arrows hit him but did not even slow him down. I slid my shield around my back and took my sword in both hands, "Sven, get the men aboard. I will deal with this!"

There was the slightest of pauses and then he said, "Aye lord! Back to the drekar!"

I stepped forward to meet the berserker. A berserker seemed impervious to pain. I had seen few of them but Folki had seen many and he had told me that you needed to kill them quickly. There could be no half measures. Þióðkell stepped on to the body of Beorn Long Toe to launch himself at me. I swung my Long Sword before me. I watched as the sword of Þióðkell came down towards me. If I misjudged my swing I would be either badly wounded or dead. I trusted in my sword and my skill. The sword bit so deeply into his side that I felt it scrape, first off his ribs and then his backbone. He was knocked to the side. I saw his frothing lips and wild eyes and then he died. He fell in a heap. There was a moment's silence and then cheers sounded both behind me and on the fjord. I walked slowly back to the drekar and climbed aboard. Bergil used an oar to push us off and the current took us downstream. Bjorn Eysteinsson was left to rue his treachery.

Chapter 2

It took longer than I would have liked to rig the sail. The drekar had not been well cared for. Bjorn was not a sailor nor a warrior. It was his brother who had made the clan successful. We sculled her to the other ships which awaited us. We were unable to lift her decks and so we loaded the deck cargo from the other drekar. It meant she was not as well balanced as she ought to be. We would have to sail her carefully. I returned to my ship along with Bergil and Sven. The rest stayed aboard the drekar. Once I was aboard we headed slowly down the fjord to the sea. When dawn broke we were moored by one of the many islands which littered the coast. Leaving the knarr on the water we rowed our three drekar to the beach and spent the rest of the morning loading cargo on the *'Dellingr'*. With the ship beached we were able to lift her decks and load the cargo correctly so that she was balanced and lithe. By the time we had finished all of our ships rode higher in the water. That made me feel happier. We could cope with a lower freeboard in the fjord but not on the open seas. With even number of crews on our ships we left, in the afternoon, to head down the coast. We would make camp at another deserted island we knew of before we began the long and risk-filled voyage to the island the Romans had called Britannia, the next morning.

We made many miles south. The wind was a cold one from the north and enabled us to sail further than we might have expected. After our camp, we headed west. It was always a strange experience. As soon as the land disappeared in the east the vast expanse of the sea opened before us. If we had not had the two knarr then we would have taken to the oars and made quicker time.

As it was we used the wind to head west. With the wind coming from the north-west we crabbed our way towards land.

Gefn and Bergljót along with the majority of women and children had never sailed on the open sea. To them, it was both strange and exciting. My grandfather made it easier for them. He kept them by the steering board. He explained how the compass worked. He told them how the sail was worked. He reassured them about the vast seas. They feared sailing off the edge of the world. "There are two enormous islands between us and the edge of the world. We cannot miss them. When you see rocks and land, fear not, we will be almost there.

I was getting used to the new drekar. Pétr Tallboy and I learned together. Each ship is like a horse. There are differences. They may be subtle but a good captain, like a good horseman, learns them. *'Hermóðr'* was more sluggish than *'Fafnir'*. She did not respond to the helm as quickly but she made up for that with her straight-line speed. She could fly. I stored that information. When we had oars to propel us then we would be a powerful weapon. I guessed that the men of Man had not looked after her as they should have done. There would be weed and sea life clinging to her hull. When we reached Streanæshalc we would clean her and coat her hull.

We hove to when darkness fell. It would have been too easy to try to sail and then become separated in the vastness of the ocean. I wanted all of our people to stay together. We tied the five ships together. The wind moved us south and east, away from our destination, but it was not a great distance for the wind was not that strong. When dawn broke we raised our sail and headed west once more. It was noon when we spied the coast. I suspected it was the coast of the land of the Pictii. It did not matter overmuch. We would just sail down the coast and look for the rivers. There were three or four mighty rivers before we reached Streanæshalc. The last one was the most important and would be easy to spot. There was a large muddy estuary on which seals basked. We knew, from our raids, that, on the way south, there were plenty of empty beaches where we could land and camp without fear of an enemy. Din Guardi was the exception. It had been the home of the kings of Northumbria. Whichever lord lived there would be a formidable foe. We would avoid it.

Each day my grandfather grew stronger. He took to leaning by me at the steering board as I looked for familiar landmarks. He had rarely sailed down the east coast of the land of the Saxons and was interested in what he saw. As we watched he spoke of our home. He elaborated on what my brother had done.

"He has left the way of the horse. I know that I was the one who helped to make us into horse warriors but we were able to fight off the Franks by using them. Instead, he has allied with the Bretons. You would not recognise our home. The Haugr is almost deserted. After Rurik One Ear died he took over Valognes. He splits his time between there and Ćiriċeburh. The tower of the Haugr fell down in a wild storm. The sea is reclaiming the sea defences. None repaired it. The church which your grandmother took such pride in is now the hall of one of his warriors. They used some of the stone from the Haugr to make it defensible. Gilles' sons left with their horses and they went to find better land for horses south of Carentan."

I nodded and thought on my brother. To me, he had always been someone I did not like. I put that down to simple fraternal rivalry. "You believe that it was all down to the curse?"

"I do. You are not the same man as your brother. The spell which Kara cast was a powerful one. Look at you. You are a mighty warrior. There has never been such a Viking. Your brother has badness in him. It came not from your father nor your mother. It is not in our blood. It must be the curse. When you have something malignant you cut it out to stop the rest of the body from withering. Your brother must die." He shook his head. "I find it sad to say so for he is of my blood. He came from your father's seed and yet…" He stared ahead as though he could see all the way to Frankia. "I just pray that I am there when you defeat him and take the clan on the right course."

I was silent. When I spoke I measured my words, "Grandfather, when we reach the land of the Franks I will have three under crewed drekar. Half of my men do not have mail nor helmets. I will need to build up my forces first. I had thought to go to Raven Wing Island. You built up the clan when you lived there."

He shook his head, "That is out of the question. The Bretons have made that their own. We showed them its importance. It would be a battle to take it. You are right you cannot take the Haugr back; the battle would be too difficult. Now the Issicauna is a better place for you to make a base and a home for your people. It has been raided so much that the Franks no longer regard it as their own. The Franks have fled to the inland areas. There are empty places where we could make a strong home. The Saxons build burghs to defend their shore but the Franks do not. They rely on their horses."

"We have no horsemen. There would be but you and I."

He laughed, "There was a time when there was just one and that was me. That matters not. Make a home. Make a strong home. Raid the Franks and use their treasure to attract more men. When you are ready it is not far to go to raid and then fight your brother. You will become stronger and he will become weaker. He is the lapdog of the Bretons. He lives from the crumbs from their table. The Bretons believe that by controlling Ragnvald they have provided a buffer between them and real Vikings. When you are strong enough the Allfather will help you to defeat your brother. Time is on your side, if not mine."

Two days later we passed the sands with the basking seals and saw the high headland. Soon we would be at the river they called the Esk. It was late afternoon when I moored us at the tiny fishing port which lay to the north of Streanæshalc. I knew that it was a risk. The fishermen could send men to warn those at Streanæshalc but we needed to be ready. I would not land and fight a battle with families aboard. We landed. The men fled and left the huts empty. I chose ten warriors to guard the families and the two knarr. They occupied the Saxon huts. I smiled at Gefn and Bergljót for they staggered as they stepped ashore, like men who had drunk to much ale. We put on our war faces and then took *'Hermóðr'* and *'Fafnir'*. We had seventy men on the two ships and that, I hoped, would be enough. We left the third drekar moored in the small port. We stepped the mast and put the chests as benches for the oars. We were no longer a transport. We were a ship of war.

We were sailing into the relative unknown. The rumour was that there were just fishermen there but we did not know. We had been the clan who had destroyed the abbey and the priests. This was where the jarl had fallen. Were we caught in the web of the Norns? I led us into the river. The tide was on the turn. The river was incredibly narrow. A drekar could barely turn around, even in the mouth. The last time that had almost cost us dear. I saw the fishing boats dragged upon the southern bank of the river. Tendrils of smoke came from the huts there. It was dark; there was no moon and we had no sail. They did not see us. The sound of the river and the sea hid the creaking of the oars.

I took us to the upstream side of the settlement. We ground on to the sand. The ship's boys tethered us to the shore. Sven led the men ashore. I had told them that, if possible, no one was to be hurt. It would make our stay here easier if that was the case. By the time I jumped into the water we were tied to two large tree stumps and my men were ashore. When I reached the huts, Sven was there and he had taken off his helmet. It was a good sign. There were Saxon men before him. None was armed.

"This is Ethelbert. He is the headman. I told him that we mean him no harm."

He looked up at me, "You are the giant who came last time. What else is there to take from us? The priests are gone and the men who guarded them are gone. We are just poor fishermen."

I took off my helmet and I smiled, "Then the warriors are back to protect you." I pointed up at the ruins of the abbey. "We will be spending the winter there. I promise you that no Viking will dare to attack you while we are here. We will buy fish from you. What say you?"

He still looked suspicious, "When the wolf says he will be the friend and will not eat you then you just look at the teeth and you do not hear the words," he shrugged, "but, it seems we have little choice."

I nodded, "Good. You will not regret this decision. Olaf Two Teeth, when the tide turns take a skeleton crew and row back for the knarr, the other drekar and our people. We will head to the abbey and see what remains."

Ethelbert said, "Very little, lord. What you did not take or destroy was taken by Thegn Athelstan." He pointed, "He lives thirty miles to the west of us."

"We will see."

He was right. However, the stone walls of the church and the post holes of the sleeping quarters remained. As we walked around it I worked out that we could put a roof over us and build up the sides with turf. There was plenty. We could build a hall by using the post holes. It would not take more than a few days. We had a new home.

By the time the knarr and our drekar arrived, we had a roof on the church. My men had had to march a few miles to find sufficient trees but by the time Gefn, Bergljót and my grandfather climbed up the steep path there was something which looked like a hall. There were stone walls and crude timbers across it. When it was covered in turf it would be warm and keep out the rain. After three days we had a second hall, turf huts and enclosures for the few animals. Leaving most of the men to dig a ditch around our new home Sven and I led our men to find animals to augment that which we had brought. It would also serve to show us where our new neighbours lived.

We knew that there was a village, Staithes, to the north of us. That was where we had landed. It was a fishing village. Other than that, the nearest settlement we knew of was a Saxon stronghold thirty Roman miles away. In a perfect world, we would have taken horses and ridden there to assess the danger. That was not meant to be. There were few horses and none of the ponies would have accommodated me. We went on foot. The first day we headed up the Esk valley. We found farms. Our helmets, mail and shields made every Saxon flee and hide. They feared us. We took the animals they left. There were not many. We travelled for half a day and saw no sign of an enemy who might threaten us.

We rested for a day and added a palisade to the ditch my men had dug then we headed south along the coast. Ethelbert had said that there was another fishing village there but it was very small.

He also said that there was another Roman signal station. If it was close enough I thought we might use the stone. Sometimes you do not know what the Norns have in store. The path along the cliff was well worn. That, in itself, made us wary. To our left and the east were cliffs which plummeted down to the sea. I felt more secure. To the west were farms dotted along the sloping turf. We did not take anything from them. We would have to come back. That would be the time to raid.

Then we emerged at the top of a wide sweeping bay. There were just four huts there but, on the rocky ledge which ran from the beach to the sea lay a drekar. She was Danish. I could see that she was wrecked. I had never seen such a long stone ledge. With the tide in it would be a dangerous place for a large ship to land. There were channels of water between the rock but none were large enough for a drekar. Out to sea, I could see two more drekar. I wondered why they did not attempt to come to rescue the Vikings who were stranded on the rocks. There were not many. It did not look like a full crew. The warriors held their shields and their weapons and faced the other two drekar. Then it came to me. The two drekar had driven the wrecked one here. They were the hunters and she was the prey. The rocky shelf was unique. I had never seen the like. It was as though the shelf made up very low islands. The Vikings were on one such island and the drekar could not get close because of the shelf. There was water but it was too narrow for the drekar and too deep for the Vikings to ford. I realised that we could help because there were channels and inlets on the landward side of the shelf.

The fishermen in the hamlet were not going to help. They wished the wolves from the sea to drown. I saw them outside their huts watching. They would probably salvage what they could from the warship when the battle was over. The tide was on its way in. Once it did so then the two drekar would swoop on the men floundering in the sea and kill them. Sven Blue Cheek said, "The three ships are all Danes. Do we let them kill each other?"

Something made the hairs on the back of my neck prickle. I shook my head, "I was rescued by the clan when I was in their position. I cannot allow them to die. Go and fetch some of the fishing boats. We will rescue them. At the very least it might increase our numbers." And as we descended the cliff path I could hear the Norns spinning. At the sight of a giant leading Vikings towards them, the fishermen fled. The nature of the rocks was such that the Danish warriors, the survivors of the wreck, were trapped against a deep channel. We clambered aboard the fishing boats. The Danish drekar would have to wait until the tide was high to reach their victims.

As we approached I saw that the men we were going to rescue numbered just eighteen. While we negotiated the channels I wondered what had occurred to leave such a small crew left alive. Few had mail upon them. Once we found the channel we made good time. I hailed them as we approached, "Come to the fishing boats and we will take you ashore."

Their leader fingered his sword, "And what would be the price for such a rescue?"

"None. It is offered freely. I am Göngu-Hrólfr Rognvaldson and I am never foresworn."

I saw that he had heard of me, "We will take you up on your offer then. I fear our comrades have a more sinister end planned for us."

After wading through the shallower water they clambered aboard. I saw that four of them were wounded. We had an easier journey back for the tide was rising. We had reached the Danes just in time. With a rising tide, they would either have drowned or been killed. We reached the rocky beach and climbed from the fishing boats. I pointed north. "We have three drekar beyond the headland. Come and we will give you food and you can tell us your tale."

As we headed up the beach he said, "I am Guthrum Ragnarsson. I thank you Göngu-Hrólfr Rognvaldson for our rescue." He pointed to the two Danish drekar bobbing just beyond the rocks. "We had been raiding and the two captains with us decided that we did not deserve any of the treasure we had taken. There was a battle and our ship fell foul of the rocks. We barely made the stones which were above the water. They may come to your home for they will want us dead."

I laughed, "Then they will find us a hard nut to crack."

"I hope you have more men than this then, Göngu-Hrólfr Rognvaldson."

I said simply, "We have." As we headed up the slope to the cliffs I said, "We have heard that there is a Danish army led by Ragnar Lodbrok's sons. Are you part of that army?"

"We were but Knut Knutson decided that we would be better off raiding the abbeys. He was wrong for others had beaten us to them. We took treasure but it was not enough for three crews. Mine was the smallest. They decided to take our share. We fought. I lost twenty of my men. I do not forget such hurts."

We reached the top of the headland and the ruins of the abbey could be seen ahead. "I should warn you Guthrum, that we only overwinter here. Come the spring and we head to the land of the Franks."

"We can build a new drekar in that time. You are certain that there will be enough room for us with your people?"

"We made a hall from the old church. There will be room."

"As soon as we have a ship I will return to the Land of the East Angles. To the west lies Wessex and they are rich! I have had enough of raiding from the sea. The sons of Ragnar Lodbrok have the right idea. Take horses and attack the weak heartland of the Saxons. Since Egbert died the men of Wessex are weak."

I nodded, "But they have burghs. They defend what they have."

"And while they defend we plunder the land. I have spent long hours on deck watch working out how to become rich."

We reached my new home. In the short time, we had been away much work had been completed. The clan were hardworking. Gefn made Guthrum and his men welcome. I sent Sven to mount a watch on the headland in case the two Danish drekar chose to finish their work and take Guthrum and his men. I walked with the Dane and showed him our defences. He was impressed. I told him why we had made them so strong. "We learned how to make strong defences in the land of the Franks. I fear the strength of defences is one reason raiders do not fare well when they land."

The wounded were attended to and then the Danes enjoyed a hot meal. Gefn could not help being a hostess. While we ate we exchanged stories. I learned that Guthrum had been raiding since he had been a ship's boy. He was a hardened warrior. When he heard of the land of the Franks he was intrigued. "Many of my people raided the land thereabouts. Some were on the Great Paris raid. They came away rich but it is a long way to sail. They said that it was a rich one but the land of the Angles and the Saxons is even richer. I have an idea to make money from the Saxons. They fear us so much that if we asked them to pay gold to stop us raiding then they might so do. Think of that, Göngu-Hrólfr Rognvaldson. We could drink and whore. We would not even need to fight! The gold would come to us for the Saxons are like sheep and we know how to shear them."

"You are right. The Franks were happy to pay us to leave them alone."

My grandfather leaned forward, "There is another way. You get them to give you titles and land."

I turned in surprise, "Does that not mean that you owe them, what do they call it? Fealty?"

"It does but the Saxons and the Franks have one thing in common. They all have relatives who seek to take their crowns and their thrones. You are both warriors. You sell your sword to the highest bidder and gain land and power that way."

My grandfather was wise and he set us both thinking. We both imagined a life when we were lords and living an easy life. We had had a good drink and I went to bed slightly drunk. Bergil awoke me. "Lord the Danish ships are entering the river."

I was awake in an instant, "Rouse the men."

I grabbed my mail byrnie and slipped it over my head. I woke Guthrum. "It seems your friends have returned for you. They are entering the river."

He rose, "I am sorry to have brought this upon you, Göngu-Hrólfr Rognvaldson."

"It is the Norns. Come they will find that this river is not quite as easy to navigate as they think. My men are already descending to the river. We will use our drekar as a fighting platform."

I did not bother with my shield and I left my helmet in the hall. It was dark and I had found it better to fight bareheaded. Guthrum

had no mail. He wore a leather jerkin studded with metal plates.
He had a long Danish axe. We went down the path together. "No
matter what happens, Göngu-Hrólfr Rognvaldson, my men and I
owe you much. If we survive then the debt will be repaid without
question whenever you ask."

"Let us just deal with these raiders first, eh Guthrum?"

Our drekar had neither mast nor sail. They would be hard to see.
The two Danes, in contrast, were using the wind to enter the
narrow river. I waved our men aboard the three drekar. The Danes
would have a shock for I guessed they thought we would not keep
a good watch. The fires on the clifftop would tell them where we
had camped. We kept hidden beneath the sheerstrake and listened
to the two Danes as they approached. Their ropes and sails
creaked. Orders were passed. It was not a silent approach. I knew
that my men would wait for the order to attack but I was not so
sure about Guthrum's men.

I heard the order to lower the sail and then watched as the hooks
were thrown to secure them to our three drekar. We waited. My
two swords were both ready to plunge into an unsuspecting Dane.
I was on the middle drekar, *'Fafnir'*. I could smell the Danes.
Their drekar were never the cleanest and these two appeared to be
particularly pungent. I waited until the first Dane stood on the
sheerstrake and then I plunged Long Sword into him. He had a
look of surprise on his face as he slipped into the river between the
two drekar. My men rose as one. Swords found flesh Guthrum was
close to me and I saw that he was in a vengeful mood. He led his
men on to the deck of the Danish drekar.

I heard the captain of the second one shout, "Pull back! It is a
trap!"

That was easier said than done. They had to sever the ropes
which tied them to our ships and the very wind which had brought
them close to our three drekar now fought against them as they
tried to escape. I joined Guthrum on the deck of the Danish drekar.
The chief had realised he had made a costly error. He too was
trying to extricate himself. His companion ship had managed to
get his oars run out but he had fouled the dragon on the other ship.
It pulled his stern around. Guthrum and his oathsworn hacked and

cut their way along the deck to the steering board. We had far more men than the crew of the drekar.

I watched as Guthrum worked his way to the chief. He faced him. Guthrum had his two-handed axe. The chief had a sword and a shield. In theory, the man with the sword and the shield was favourite to win. However, Guthrum had dead oar brothers to avenge. He bought his axe over from on high and demolished the Danish shield. The Dane lunged with his sword. It slid along the leather armour which Guthrum wore. He then punched the chief with the top of his axe. It knocked him to the deck. Guthrum was in no mood for mercy and his axe split his skull.

As the last of the crew were slaughtered I looked at the second drekar. The narrow river which had almost done for us now did for the Dane. It caught on the sandbank on the north shore of the river and that pulled its stern around. It broached. We had discovered the dangers when we had raided. It had cost my adopted father his life. We watched as it seemed to fall over in slow motion. The mast shattered on the north bank as water began to flood in to the hull. Many of the Danes had been wearing mail and they drowned. Even the ones who had leather mail were dragged beneath the black and icy water. In the darkness, we saw perhaps twelve Danes make the bank. They scrambled up it, grateful that they were still alive.

Guthrum had been hurt by the sword but he would take the wound as a badge of honour. He had lost three of his oathsworn but he had gained a drekar. He would not need to build one. More than that the hold would be filled with the treasure denied him.

He turned to me, "Göngu-Hrólfr Rognvaldson it was *wyrd* when you rescued us. We were waiting to die. Now we have a ship, we have treasure and we have a new friend."

I clasped his arm, "The Norns were spinning, Guthrum!"

Our sudden attack meant we did not lose any men but we had a problem with the wreck in the river. The next day every man was ferried across. We would salvage what we could and then destroy the rest. The crosspiece, sail and the oars were all sound. The mast fish was usable. We let the figurehead remain where it fell. It would be buried by the mud of the river. We did not wish ill luck.

Lord of Rouen

Guthrum insisted on sharing the treasure from the wrecked drekar with us. By the time evening came most of the timbers were gone. For the next six days, bodies were washed ashore. The fishermen in the village saw this as a good thing. Their bodies would feed the fishes and the shellfish on which they relied. The twelve Danes who survived disappeared. Perhaps they stole a fishing ship or became brigands. All I knew was that we did not see them again.

Guthrum and his crew stayed for a month. During that time Guthrum questioned me long and hard about how my grandfather's Clan of the Horse had used horses and carved out a land in the Land of the Franks. He seemed to absorb all that we told him. He was keen to learn. He had been betrayed and he would ensure that he was never betrayed again. They left at the end of Haustmánuður.

"We go to the Land of the East Angles. I know I have just one drekar and a small crew but give me time and I will rule the land. I will join the rest of the Vikings. I have heard that the anchorages are so full of ships that you can walk from one side of the bay to the other on drekar! Farewell, my giant friend. I wish you well on your venture." They rowed from our river and headed out to sea.

Many of my men had overcome their dislike and distrust of Danes during the time they had spent with Guthrum and his Danes. As Sven told us; there had to be good and bad Danes just as there were good and bad Norse. He cited Bjorn as an example. The settlement was quieter without Guthrum. His men were always lively.

The next month or so saw us settle into a routine. Life went on even though we were far from the land of the fjord. Babies were made and babies were born. Some of the old died and that was sad for they were far from the land of their birth. We buried them in the graveyard of the nuns and the monks. Gefn and Bergljót made certain that we were comfortable with enough food for all. This was their clan. We were all better off than in the land of snow and ice. One chilly day at the end of Ýlir I found Gefn sitting on top of the headland. It was a raw cold day. We had learned that while this land did not have much snow it could be as cold as Norway.

I saw that she was weeping, "What ails you, mother?"

She was well wrapped against the cold and she waved an irritated hand at me. "I am just a silly old woman. I will be fine." She took my hand and patted it, "I am just thinking of your adopted father. He would have approved of this. You have made new allies and given us a home. It is just that this is where he died and that has made me think of him. I miss him."

"He will be in Valhalla. He died well."

She shook her head, "I would rather he had not gone on the raid and then he would be alive. It is you warriors who yearn for a glorious death; not your families."

I squeezed her, "Then he would not be here for he would still be alive and living in the fjord. His brother would be plotting and I would be heading south to the Land of the Horse."

She stopped and nodded, "You are the cleverest man I know Göngu-Hrólfr Rognvaldson. Of course, this was meant to be and he will be with me when I close my eyes and hear his voice. Come let us go indoors. They have raw winds hereabouts. When I was growing up we called them lazy winds. They do not go around you, they go through you!"

It was in Mörsugur, after the winter feast when the Saxons came. There were eight of them, and they rode the short ponies they favoured in this part of the world. Three of my men were hunting in the woods at the head of the Esk Valley. Sensibly they stayed hidden and followed the eight Saxons. One was a thegn. Arne recognised the seal around his neck which glinted in the winter sunshine. They noted that they carried shields, wore helmets and had long spears. They also noticed that they did not have stiraps. I was a horseman and I knew what that meant. The eight of them kept hidden in the woods which bordered the small river. When they reached the Lar Pool they stopped. Within the protection of the trees, they were able to observe our ships and yet remain hidden. After a short time, they turned and retraced their steps. My men followed them back to the head of the valley.

They spoke to Sven Blue Cheek and to me when they returned. "It was inevitable I suppose. We knew there were Saxons nearby. Our presence could not remain hidden. The men from Staithes would have sent word to the thegn about our drekar."

Sven nodded, "And the weather is milder than one might have expected. There is neither snow nor rain. We will prepare. We have a palisade. If we have the men dig a ditch then by the time we have worked up a sweat we will be surrounded. The monks picked a good site. The land is steep as it is. The weakness is from the south along the road from the beach with the rocks."

I nodded, "Just so long as our ships are ready to sail when it comes to Einmánuður. It may take a month to edge south and I would be at the Issicauna by Harpa."

I joined my men and we toiled at the ditches. The Saxons were not the only visitors. Other knarr called in. Sometimes they had no choice for they had been damaged at sea but one or two were curious to see the three drekar in the Saxon river. One of them told us of the fate of Bjorn Eysteinsson. "Haraldr Finehair is now chief of the tribe. He sailed north and gave Bjorn the blood eagle. He also swore enmity towards you, Göngu-Hrólfr Rognvaldson."

"You have heard of me?"

The knarr captain smiled, "I have and I confess I did not believe in the legend of the giant. Now I have seen you and I do."

"Do you think that this Haraldr Finehair will come here?"

He shook his head, "His priority is to gain the throne of Norway. I will say that there are some of the tribe who do not agree with Haraldr. They think that Bjorn reaped the reward for his treachery."

"You are of the tribe?"

He shook his head, "I am married to one. It serves me well. I can trade with the tribe and yet I am not bound to them and can sail where I like. I will tell those who wish to join you where you are."

"Thank you."

"The war will cause problems. I can see many Norse leaving their homes and doing as you do. We will tell them about this place. When you leave it would make a good home for others fleeing Finehair."

After he had gone Bergil asked if it had been wise to allow him to sail away, "He could tell Haraldr Finehair."

"He probably will but that changes nothing. If he comes then he comes but I believe our knarr captain. Haraldr Finehair would be King of Norway; the first King of Norway and until he achieves that then I am a minor irritation. Besides we will be long gone by then."

With the ditches complete we turned our attention to the ships. The advantage of the small beach on the south side was that the drekar could be easily drawn up and the hulls cleaned and the protective coating we had brought with us applied. Weed and the worm were greater enemies than any other ship. We cleaned Bjorn's old boat. It was covered in weed, limpets and barnacles. It was no wonder she had been so sluggish. While we toiled in the water the women turned the fish which the fishermen traded with us into supplies for the journey south. They were preserved in salt or vinegar. The river and the bay teemed with fish. The larger cod were salted while the mackerel and herring were pickled. Now that we knew there were Saxons close by we had even more men hunting and keeping watch. We had deer and wild boar to salt. The beach to the south of us proved a perfect place to make salt and also keep watch on the approach from the south. We also began to build a third knarr. In a perfect world, we would have built a drekar but we were limited in the timber we had and a knarr was quicker.

The Saxons came at Gói. It had been a mild winter and we expected them. They had seen us and then organised men to hunt us. Our own hunters heard their approach. While we had waited we had made arrows. The Saxons did not use many bows. We had dug pits in unexpected places and covered them. My aim was to disrupt any attack. As soon as we heard of the approach of the Saxons I went to the headman, Ethelbert. "The thegn is coming with a warband. I can offer you shelter in the abbey."

He shook his head, "When you are gone we will have to live here." He smiled, "Do not worry, we will vilify you and make up such stories that will make your hair turn white. We will take our families to the northern bank. There we will be safe from the fighting and can say that we had no part in the defence of the burgh."

It was a good answer and I could expect no more.

We had expected the attack and there was no panic. Boys who had left Norway as boys were now young men. Some would use bows and others, slings. We had twenty warriors who wore mail although everyone had a shield and a helmet. The Danes who had attacked us had given us the means to protect ourselves. We had spears too. We had a smith and he had turned some of the poorer swords into spearheads. We waited.

The Saxons made a slow and cautious approach. I wondered if they remembered our earlier fight here. That would explain their caution. They had a hundred warriors. This was a wapentake. The thegn had called together all the men who lived close to his hall. I wondered at the wisdom of such a decision. If I wanted to rid myself of a pest I would have employed my neighbours too. Most of the men had a shield and a spear. Only one or two had helmets. The thegn rode a horse as did the man who carried his standard. They halted two hundred paces from our palisade. I saw a debate ensue for they were well below our defences. One of the Saxons hurried off east, towards the cliff.

Sven Blue Cheek nodded, "They are no fools, lord. They go to find a better approach."

"I know but we have fine defences there too. Be ready to shift our mailed men to face the greatest threat. If they move it may be a trick. There might be others close by."

"I doubt it, lord, but you are wise to prepare."

When the man returned the whole warband moved east. Bergil asked as they did so, "Why do we not send arrows at them?"

Sven Blue Cheek answered for me, "Let that come as a surprise. We could have sent arrows when they stood before us but we would not have killed as many as when they move across the killing ground. We have pits there and they will not have such an easy time of it."

We marched our mailed men around to match the Saxons and left just ten men to watch the steep western slope. The thegn appeared satisfied with the land and he began to array his men. I had seen it many times before. They used three ranks. The ones in the fore all had shields and helmets. Spears protruded from over the tops of the shields. Sven Blue Cheek had never fought Saxons. "They always fight like this? They do not use archers?"

"They have one technique. They try to batter down our defences. Their warriors do not train as we do. Man for man they do not have as much skill. The thegn and his standard-bearer will watch from behind the lines and shout orders. In the centre of the front line will be the hearth-weru. Do you see how two or three have metal plates sewn on to leather? They are his best warriors. He is wary else he would have used a wedge. He keeps his best warriors to break through the heart of our defence."

The standard-bearer sounded a horn and the line banged their shields and all shouted. They began to move towards us. It was slow and ponderous. They did not march in time. Sven turned, "Archers and slingers wait for my order. Choose a target."

He waited until the Saxons discovered the first of the pits. It was just one hundred and twenty paces from our ditch. It caught them out for they were not expecting it. As the first men fell Sven shouted, "Now!" Arrows and stones flew. At least two of the men who fell had either broken legs or had been stuck by the stakes in the bottom of the pits. The hearth-weru were lucky and they came on but it meant that the ones on their flanks were behind them. They would hit our ditch first.

The relentless arrow and stone storm took their toll. Most did not kill. They were hunting arrows but an arrow in a shield had an effect. A stone which struck a helmet could hurt the warrior. It was the pits which did the most damage. When they neared our ditch they stopped. A Saxon voice in the front rank gave orders. The hearth-weru were in command.

Sven shouted, "Archers, concentrate on the men without armour!" The Saxons were less than thirty paces from us. Although their shields were held high the less experienced warriors were looking at the ground, fearful of another ditch. They began to fall.

Then a Saxon voice shouted, "Forward!"

They stepped down into the ditch. The unwary found the stakes but the hearth-weru managed to make it across and to clamber up the other side. I shouted, "We hit them and we hit them hard!"

Lord of Rouen

The Saxons attempted to break down the palisade. While they attempted to do so, spears and swords jabbed through to cause real wounds. The hearth-weru used their weight to break through the wooden wall. When they did so then they would face us. I saw that they had spears. Many of our men used spears. I relied on my long sword. As the hearth-weru burst through we launched ourselves at them. I swung my sword before me. It chopped through the shafts of three spears. A fourth was taken on my shield. In the time it took for the Saxons to reach for their swords two had been slain. One took my sword blow to the neck. Bergil and Sven caught the other two. One died and one lay with a bad wound to his side.

Sven Blue Cheek shouted, "Push them back into the ditch!"

Only the hearth-weru had broken through the palisade and with half of them wounded or dead the other Saxons began to flounder as stones and arrows were hurled at close range and spears, sometimes taken from the dead Saxons, were hurled towards them. A horn sounded three times and the wapentake began to move backwards. Two of the hearth-weru attempted to make a fight of it or perhaps they sought a glorious death. I know not. One threw himself at me. He swung his sword at my head. He miscalculated my height and my shield easily blocked it. I swung my sword at his shield and he was knocked backwards. Bergil fought the other hearth-weru. His opponent had an easier time for he was the same height as Bergil. Bergil had, however, improved since first I had met him. He feinted and then the Saxon brought up his shield he stabbed him in the thigh.

My opponent was brave but he was reckless. Realising that he could not hit my head he went for the biggest target, my body. He battered at my shield. I had padded the inside with leather-covered wool and the blows were absorbed. I allowed him two or three strikes and I saw him tiring. As he swung back for the fourth blow I punched him in the face with the boss of my shield. He tumbled backwards, over the damaged palisade and into the ditch. I took two steps and saw that he had found one of the stakes which lay there. He was impaled and dying. I turned in time to see Bergil lunge at his opponent and his sword entered the man's chest. As the Saxons fell back arrows and stones continued to hurt them.

When they were beyond the arrows' range Sven Blue Cheek said, "They will not be back!"

"Perhaps but there are other thegns. They may not like our presence. The sooner we can leave the better." I pointed to the handful of men we had lost. "We can ill afford to lose brave warriors."

The bodies of the Saxons yielded little treasure. We gained eight mail byrnies and fifteen helmets. Their swords were good ones and they replaced the poorer ones some of my warriors used. We burned their bodies and we buried our own. We replaced the palisade and dug the pits once more. After four days there was little sign of a battle.

Two days later and a rather leaky drekar limped into the river. We were not worried that it might be an attack; it came during daylight and was but one ship. In addition, there appeared to be animals, women and children on board. We went down to the river to meet them. They tied up next to *'Fafnir'*.

A greybeard stood and said, "Göngu-Hrólfr Rognvaldson?"

"I am. You look to have had a rough time of it. Bring your people ashore before your vessel sinks."

My grandfather said, "I think, Rollo, that it might be better for them to land at the beach and they can land easier and repair their ship."

"Thank you. I fear we take more water than we can remove."

While they rowed down to the beach we walked down to meet them. "They wish to join you, Rollo."

"How can you tell grandfather?"

"You do not sail with wives and family in such leaky vessels unless you are desperate."

He was proved right. Magnús Magnússon brought the last survivors of Haraldr Finehair's attempt to unify Norway. They had fought against the would-be king and they had lost. Magnús had escaped after a fierce battle which saw the rest of his clan and their ships destroyed. "The jarl died along with his oathsworn. I was charged with escaping." He shook his head. "I would rather have died with a sword in my hand but the jarl was my brother and I obeyed him."

"And you came here."

"We heard that you did not bow the knee to Finehair. Our own land is gone and a passing knarr captain told us that you intend to make a new home. He told us to look for the seals on the beach and then find the river which lay to the south. Is this your new home?"

"No, Magnús, this is a temporary camp. We sail soon for the Land of the Horse. You are welcome to join us but we will need to make your ship seaworthy. We have many leagues to travel."

"We will make her whole once more. We had thought she had seen her last voyage. We were wrong."

Later that night as Sven, Bergil and my grandfather sat and spoke with me Hrolf the Horseman suddenly laughed, "The *wyrd* sisters weave strong webs, Rollo, my grandson. Haraldr Finehair swears vengeance and the first result is that we gain a ship and warriors!"

Chapter 3

Every man helped to make *'Dragon's Teeth'*, Magnús Magnússon's drekar, seaworthy. We all knew what it was like to lose your home. We now had four drekar. None were fully crewed but the Norns appeared to be working toward remedying that situation. The next day a second drekar arrived. Magnús recognised it. "That is a drekar from one of the neighbouring clans, *'Wolf's Tongue'*, Ubba Long Cheek is a fierce warrior. He would not have fled unless all was lost."

This time the drekar was not about to sink and looked seaworthy. Nor did they wish to join us. Ubba Long Cheek asked merely to use the river for one night on their way south. "We have our women and children. We have news for the sons of Ragnar Lodbrok and we hope to join them. King Ælla of Northumbria has captured and killed Ragnar Lodbrok. He had him thrown into a pit of wolves. His sons will want that news. It is said he views it as a sign that their White Christ is on their side. If I were you, Göngu-Hrólfr Rognvaldson, I would make plans to move away from here. We saw an army to the north of the sands where the seals bask."

"Thank you I will heed your advice but we have a drekar to repair."

Ubba left the next morning. Magnús seemed upset that his poor drekar might be the reason we would be attacked by vengeful Northumbrians. My grandfather shook his head, "This is the work of the Norns, Magnús, you are not the cause. If they come, then they come. This is a well-fortified place. We can defend it."

Even as he said it I wondered about the thegn we had defeated. Would he bring King Ælla of Northumbria and the Saxons to punish us? Only the drekar *'Dragon's Teeth'* was not ready, the rest of our people were ready to set sail. It was almost a race to see if the repairs could be completed before the Saxon army descended upon us. In the end, we lost, but it was not by much. *'Dragon's Teeth'* had new pitch applied and the damaged strakes had been replaced. She was drying on the beach and so we began to load the holds of the knarr and the other drekar. I had not been so foolish as to pull in our hunting parties and they reported an army approaching from the north-west. It had to be Saxons.

We held a council of war while the ships continued to be loaded. My grandfather showed his experience, "We cannot wait and fight behind walls this time. If we do then this King Ælla of Northumbria will be able to cut us off from our drekar. Our families, our animals, our goods all must be on the ships when we fight."

"We risk losing men!"

I smiled at Bergil. He was the least experienced warrior at the council. "There is much in what my grandfather says. We leave men to guard the ships and the rest make a battle line between the river and the higher ground. The slopes are steep and we can fill the ground with a shield wall. We make them come at us and use the narrow pass to make them bleed. They will be confident."

Sven smiled, "And perhaps we can make them less confident. We could infiltrate their camp and slit a few throats." He turned to Magnús, "When can you refloat your ship?"

"We could do it on the high tide tonight."

"Then, if we are able, we raid tonight. If they are not close enough for a raid then we can leave them unharmed."

"Come, Sven, we will go and view the enemy. We can do little if we do not know where they are. Bergil, you and Hrolf the Horsemen continue loading the ships and making preparations."

We did not don our mail nor take our shields. We were not going to fight a war. We were going as scouts. Of course, my size made me a poor scout but my grandfather had given me enough tricks. I knew how to blend in with my surroundings. I could move slowly and silently. I knew how to darken my skin. The river had steep sides. For almost a Roman mile it was too wide to ford but there were a couple of fords higher up the river. We headed there. I was confident that a slow-moving Northumbrian King and his army would take longer to reach the ford than it would us. We did not head for the large one at Hrīs Wearp. There was another just one thousand paces north of our anchorage. If they chose the Hrīs Wearp crossing then we would be able to escape before they reached us.

We had not been hiding in lower branches of the willow long when four scouts appeared. They were lightly armed. Three of them took off their boots and waded into the river. They carried their boots above their heads. It was not yet low tide and the water came up to their chests. One said, "The one further north was a better crossing."

"Aye, but it would take the army longer to reach the Vikings. The King is keen for another swift victory. Egbert, go back and bring the army here. We will spy out their defences. Thegn Edward said they had ditches."

As the one called Egbert ran off the other three waded across the river. Sven and I drew our swords. We could not afford for them to see that we were at the river. They stood just fifteen paces from us. By now the fourth scout had disappeared. We were safe to attack the scouts. I nodded to Sven and we leapt down from the willow. They had not seen us. These three were scouts. My grandfather had told me that a scout was always prepared for danger. The three of them threw their boots at us as they drew their short swords. Long Sword swept through the arm and the side of the nearest one. Sven Blue Cheek hacked across the neck of a second. The third realised that he had to get back to the army. He turned and ran. Sven picked up the short sword dropped by one of the others and threw it like a knife. It plunged into the back of the luckless scout. The river took his body.

"We will have to get rid of these bodies too or they will be wary." We hurled the bodies and their swords into the river. Once we were certain that the current had caught and was taking them out to sea them we headed downstream. They were coming. We had no idea of their numbers but they would know ours. The thegn we had defeated was with them. This King of Northumbria would not fight us unless he was confident he had enough men to win. As we walked back Sven said, "Then we do not raid?"

"If they camp then it means we can sail on the night tide. I fear that they will just attack. We will defend the ships while they are loaded."

The men were standing ready to fight. Magnús and his men were still loading the knarr. The tide was on its way out. They had started to load the hull of their drekar. This would be a finely judged departure. I ordered the knarr into the river. They would moor safely in the centre channel. I made sure the old were on board and the pregnant women. Most of the children, too, were able to fit on board. Most of the boys, even the youngest, had their slingshots and they waited with us. They would use the drekar as a fighting platform.

I donned my mail as I shouted out the orders, "They will soon be here. We have merely delayed them and kept them uninformed about our position. As soon as *'Dragon's Teeth'* is refloated then we leave. This land is not worth dying for."

Sven said, "If a warrior goes to Valhalla we will have to leave his body but we will honour him in our new home." I saw nods as all men accepted that.

We took a chance. We were just two hundred paces from *'Fafnir'* but we were at the narrowest part of the valley. The river was on one side and to our left, the slope rose steeply and was covered in rocks. Men could climb it but they would struggle to keep their feet. Sven placed some youths with bows and with slingshots there. A man would find it hard to balance and to defend himself. It meant we had a frontage of just forty men. All of us were mailed. We stood three ranks deep. Realistically we did not need the last rank but if we posed just two then the Saxons might well seek to sweep us aside. Sámr Oakheart, much to his annoyance, was with the third rank. He wished to be with me in the front. Similarly, Ragnar was in the second rank. I had given them orders that when I commanded they were to retreat to the drekar and cast them off one by one.

We watched the water lower. Soon there was a gap between Arne and the sea. It was a muddy morass but it showed that it was low tide. The sun began to set. That also gave us an advantage as we would be hidden in the dark. All that would be seen would be a mass of men. Time passed and still the Saxons did not come. When Arne said, "Lord the tide returns." I began to hope.

"Take twenty steps closer to the drekar."

So far, the Saxons had not sent scouts out. Perhaps they still awaited the three we had slain. As darkness fell and the waters rose we moved slowly back until we were just forty paces from *'Fafnir'*. Then we heard the sound of bowstrings and the snap of slingshots. There was a cry and a body tumbled from the sides of the valley. Our youths had sharp eyes and they had seen the Saxons.

"They have scouts out. Stand to! Sámr Oakheart, back to the drekar! It is dark enough now so that our numbers do not matter."

"Aye, lord!"

The rest of my men presented their spears over our shields. The Northumbrian King was eager. He was too eager. He sent his men at us in the narrow pass hoping to sweep us away with sheer numbers. He should have used order. He had mailed men in his ranks but, instead, it was the lighter armed men without mail who saw the opportunity to be the heroes who killed the giant while their King watched. We had no ideas of numbers. We just heard the roar and the cheer as they launched themselves at us. The last light from the setting sun glinted down the Esk valley. It shone from spears and some helmets. With our left legs braced behind our shields, we waited. When the storm came it was like hailstones on a wooden roof as they hurled themselves at our shields. From the slope, our boys sent arrows and stones into the mass who were trying to get at us.

Two of the men trying to get at me were skewered by spears from behind me. Then a mailed warrior led three other similarly armed warriors purposefully towards me. I took in that they all had simple willow shields. They wore open round helmets. They carried spears and their mail was overlapping pieces of metal.

"For St. Oswald and St. Cuthbert!" Invoking their dead saints seemed to inspire them. I knew not why.

I took the blow from the first spear on my shield and swung my Long Sword from on high. It smashed into the willow board shield of the leading warrior. He reeled and, as he did so, Sven Blue Cheek rammed his sword under his arm and into his chest. I punched my shield into the next mailed warrior's face. I took a risk and stepped from the line to despatch him. A third Saxon thought he had me and tried to stick me with his spear but I had quick feet and I was back in line before he could hit me. Bergil swung his sword at the shield of another of the mailed men. Their willow boards were poorly made and he reeled.

"*'Dragon's Teeth'* is afloat!"

There was a temptation to return to the drekar. Instead, I took the offensive. "Ragnar, back to the drekar. Front rank on my command step forward! Now!"

We had thinned their front rank and most of us had space in which to step. Although more men were rushing to join the fray they were coming at us singly. It was as we stepped forward that I saw, on a white horse, King Ælla of Northumbria. He had holy relics and priests next to him and was exhorting his men forward. Our sudden attack caught the advancing Saxons out. They had not locked shields. They stabbed with their spears and their swords but my men wore mail. Even when they defeated the shield wall they did not penetrate mail. My sword came away bloody each time it was plunged into the body of a Saxon. When the press of men died Sven shouted, "Enough, lord! We are losing men."

I nodded, "Fall back! Boys! Get to the ships!" The boys with bows and slingshots scampered like goats across the steep ground. Stones skittered down from the valley side. We stepped back slowly and had moved ten paces before the Saxons realised what we were doing. We were thirty paces from our drekar. All were crewed and still tied up. As we moved back the Saxons rushed at us. From over our heads came the sound of arrows as our crews used the elevation of the drekar to loose into the mass of warriors racing to get at us.

As we neared *'Fafnir'* I shouted, "Ten men board!" I had to step forward and sweep my sword in a wide arc. With my long arms and long legs that made the killing zone greater. Four men fell back and my sword caught one on the shoulder. It allowed us to move back to *'Dellingr'*. "Ten men, board!"

The Saxons were now having to endure the arrows from three drekar. Already *'Fafnir'* was pulling into the middle of the river. There were few enough men before us for me to give the order to board *'Hermóðr'*. "The rest, board!" As we clambered aboard I saw that there were just fifteen of us left. We had left comrades behind. We cast off and I took off my helmet. I went to the steering board as the sail was lowered.

I saw King Ælla of Northumbria on his horse. He raised his sword, "I am King Ælla of Northumbria. I slew Ragnar Lodbrok! I have sent the Viking giant hence and now we shall go to Eoforwic and scour the last of your kind from this island!"

I said nothing but Sven Blue Cheek laughed as he lifted a pail of water from the river to cleanse the blood from his mail. "He has not heard then that there is a Danish Army heading north!" Had we wished we could have beaten him. I think this King Ælla will enjoy his victory for a brief time." There was something of the galdramenn about Sven for he was proved prescient.

When we were aboard I clapped Ragnar about the shoulders. He had held his men well and not lost a single one, "That was bravely done. From this day you are Ragnar the Resolute!"

It took time to arrange our sailing order. It was night time and the rocks along the coast were treacherous. We had to stand offshore. Once again, we were sailing at the pace of the slowest ships, the knarr. I made certain that we sailed close to the knarr with my family aboard. I waved to show them that I was safe. I knew that *'Kara'* was the most seaworthy of the knarr and Harold Haroldsson was the best captain. They would be as safe there as anywhere. Like Sven, I cleansed my mail with river water and then laid it in my chest in the sand-filled sack. I hoped we would not need it again. Some men slept. I could not.

We sailed slowly down the coast reaching the mouth of the Ouse just after dawn. I had thought of sailing up the river to Eoforwic but decided against it. The wind was from the west and aided us. It proved propitious. In the middle of the afternoon when we were approaching Lincylene, we spied four drekar leaving the old Roman port. We hove to for I recognised one of them.

Guthrum hailed me as we neared his drekar. He had fine mail and a magnificent helmet. He had converted his treasure well. "Hail Göngu-Hrólfr Rognvaldson, I am pleased that we have met. I have joined the army of the sons of Ragnar Lodbrok. We sail north to avenge his death!"

I nodded and pointed north, "King Ælla of Northumbria makes it easy for you. He has his army and they are marching to Eoforwic. He seeks to scour the land of pirates!"

"You fought him?"

"We did. Your four drekar crews could easily defeat him."

"We have more than that. Ivar the Boneless and the other sons of Lodbrok lead an enormous army north. They seek vengeance."

"Fare ye well."

"I have told all that Göngu-Hrólfr Rognvaldson is a true warrior and a friend to the brothers. When we have finished with this Saxon King, we can come to help you reclaim your land."

"That task is appointed to me but I thank you, Guthrum. You will ever be my friend."

We lowered our sails and continued south. These were the days before the Saxons had decided to use ships to scour the seas of Vikings and with four drekar we were too large a fleet for any but the strongest of foes. We were able to land in the land of the East Angles for it was now the land of the Dane. Guthrum's friendship meant that we were welcomed. The days of hiding on secluded beaches were gone. I knew that it would be different once we crossed the narrow stretch of water to the Land of the Franks but we enjoyed the journey down the coast of the Angles.

Once we crossed the water to the Land of the Franks we hung shields from our sides. On our last camp in Cent, we had held a council of war. My grandfather now looked years younger than when I had found him at the mercy of the men of Man. Gefn and Bergljót made a real fuss of him. They enjoyed feeding him up. His bright eyes and sharp mind were in evidence as he spoke. "Rollo, if we land anywhere close to the Land of the Horse we will be attacked as soon as we are seen. We will lose people we can ill afford to lose."

I nodded. He had been there more recently than I had. "What is your suggestion?"

"I have spoken with Harold. He knows of a deep anchorage, Djupr. It is a deserted fishing village. It has a place where we could build a citadel and use it as a base to raid. It is just half a day from the Haugr and Caen. That is our best tactic. We need to build up our numbers. We have four drekar. We need more."

It galled me to have to wait and to allow my brother to go unpunished but I listened to my grandfather. I would be patient. I agreed and we made the shorter journey to Djupr.

We reached Djupr in the middle of the afternoon. It was perfect. There was a jetty along with three huts. The Frankish fishermen who lived there fled when our fleet arrived. The river looked very similar to the Esk. By the high cliffs it was wide and deep but just a few hundred paces upstream it became very narrow. It was deep and we could easily fit in our fleet. They would be protected from attack by the citadel we would build on the headland. While most of the men began work on the walls I led my best men up the river to seek foes. Five Roman miles from our new home we found a forest. So far, we had seen no Roman roads and now we saw hunter's trails. We travelled another three miles before we saw the smoke of a hut. It was coming on to dark and we returned to our camp. There was no one close enough to threaten us. We had time to build.

Sven Blue Cheek was pleased with the progress made but worried about supplies. "The journey south has used up all that we bought and stored. We need to replenish and that means raiding. We have no treasure left to send the knarr and to trade."

"We do not raid blindly. We scout." I pointed to the abandoned fishermen's huts. "The fishermen lived here. We have knarr which can fish. We will take '*Hermóðr*' and I will show you the land in which I grew up."

I saw my grandfather frown. "You are not going to risk a confrontation with your brother?"

Shaking my head, I said, "We are a Manx made ship. He thinks I am dead. There must be other drekar plying the seas. If he sees us he may be worried but he will not see it as a threat from me. You know these waters as do the crew of *'Kara'* but the rest do not. If we are to make these waters our own we need every captain to know them as well as we do. And you, Hrolf the Horseman, can build us a home as strong as the Haugr once was."

"I can do and if you can get some horses..."

"Then I will do so."

The next morning as we sailed Sven asked, "Why horses, lord?"

"My grandfather was born with an affinity for horses. Sadly, there are few that I can ride but I too like horses. This land is not like Norway. This land has rolling and gentle hills. A horse can make travel much easier. We fought from the backs of horses. We had to because of the Franks and the Bretons. If we manage to claw a home here then it will need us to master the horse as well as the drekar."

I fully crewed the drekar. We went armed. I would not go too close to my former home but I knew that there would be drekar all along the coast. If we had to fight then we would. The wind was in our favour and so we used the sail. We would need to row on the way back. This would allow those who had followed me from Norway to see the home for which we would fight. As we passed the bay of the Issicauna estuary I pointed to the river. "That is where we will raid and if I do not regain my home, where we will settle. The capital of the Franks is there: Paris. It has more riches than Lundenwic for that is where their emperors left their treasure. One day we shall raid there and become rich men."

Sven nodded, "And glory."

"Of course. We will sail closer to the mouth when we have visited where I was raised. I would like to see what my brother has allowed it to become." We stood well off from Bárekr's Haven. The waters around it could be treacherous. There were just two drekar in the anchorage and I recognised neither.

Sven asked, "Will you still know the captains and warriors here?"

I shrugged, "Many died on the raid. Others like Rurik One Ear were old. Bárekr? I do not know. He may live. He was a good man. My grandfather would know." As we turned south the wind was still with us and was a little stronger. We were able to take in a reef or two. It allowed me to view the Haugr for as long as possible. My grandfather had prepared me but I still felt shocked at what I saw. The tower and the wall had been built well. My father and his men had toiled long and hard. Although it had been built close to the beach, men could have watched when the storm came. I saw now that no one had done so. A wild storm must have lashed the walls and the beach. Instead of repairing the damage done by the sea, it had been neglected with the result that the next storm had brought down the tower and part of the sea wall. It was a stronghold no longer. I saw my grandfather's hall. It still stood but the place looked run down.

My mother's church, in contrast now, had some of the stones from the tower around it. The church belltower had been replaced by a watchtower with a fighting platform. Even as we approached I heard a horn sound and men ran from within. They were mailed men. There was a drekar at the quay but there was no mast set. The warriors just stared at us as they tried to identify who we were. I turned away.

Olaf Two Teeth said, "Do we continue on this course, lord?"

I had started and so I had to finish. "Aye. I will see what else he has allowed to happen."

When we reached Gilles's farm it was deserted. Although it was some way from the sea there was no smoke from the hall and, more importantly, no horses. The fences were down. Grandfather said that Erik and Rollo had moved. Where had Gilles' sons gone?

When we neared the coast again I ordered the oars out and the sail lowered. We did not chant. Speed was unimportant. I saw a drekar in the water close by Carentan. That could be Folki or, perhaps his son, Folki had been of an age with my grandfather. I saw that there were now fewer settlements. Since my grandfather had first come there had been many raids and the coast was no longer an attractive place to live. Inland was safer, especially if you built a stronghold. When we neared the mighty mouth of the

Issicauna we slowed the oars so that my crew could see just how wide it was.

Sven Blue Cheek shook his head in amazement, "There is nothing guarding it! We are used to that in Norway but there we have nothing to defend. Here they defend an emperor's treasure."

As my men started to row again I said, "And that is where we have a chance. The King uses Counts to rule parts of the land for him. Not only that, the land we have just passed now belongs to a Breton Count. They bow the knee to the French King but they do not like to support him. They protect their own and leave the river to the Vikings. We shall make them rue that mistake."

Part Two
The Land of the Frank

Chapter 4

When we began to build our new home, the men seemed happy enough. The first time we saw it the potential was obvious. With two good beaches for careening and collecting shellfish as well as the piece of high ground we could use for a citadel, it was as close to perfect as one could get. As Sven pointed out we need not even raid using our drekar. We could take men across country and raid overland. I smiled to myself. He was realising the potential of horses. I wondered why we had seen so few. We spent the next seven days finishing off our ditches, walls and halls. We discovered mussel beds and some of our men constructed fish traps to catch fish travelling both up and down the river. I deemed that we could afford a raid. It was Skerpla and I knew that most of the farmers would be sowing crops. It was the perfect time to raid. With the sons of Ragnar Lodbrok making the land of the Saxons into a huge graveyard we would be the only drekar raiding. We could pick and choose our targets.

My grandfather asked me what I had seen when I had visited the Haugr. I told him and he nodded his head. "The warrior you saw in the old church is the brother of Arne the Breton Slayer. Ailmær the Cruel is well named. He sailed with us as a ship's boy. No one liked him. Your brother favoured him. He served with Knut the Quiet until Knut died suddenly. Ailmær said it was one of the other crew who had murdered him and had him killed. He now commands a drekar. He is no sailor but neither has he honour."

"And what of Gilles' sons, Rollo and Erik? I remember you said they had left their home. I saw no sign of them. The farm looked long deserted."

"When their father died they decided to find somewhere better to breed horses. The last we heard they were south of Carentan." He shook his head. "I sailed to search for you and the journey lasted two years. Almost another year has passed. The world changes in such a short time. I hope that they live and that Folki does too. He had most of the older warriors with him. Folki was a throwback to the real heart of the clan. Many of the braver ones died in the wars against the Bretons and now your brother is the ally of them."

I nodded. An idea was forming. "I thought to raid Caen and the land thereabouts."

He thought about my words and then said, "None of our folk had settled close to there and the raids from the Danes were along the Issicauna. Lisieux and Bayeux are both rich towns also."

"One target at a time, grandfather. As I recall Caen is or was rich. It lies along a river which means we could sneak in, attack and leave. We need supplies. We need weapons and my men need to fight Bretons. Times past they would have been Franks. The Saxons we fought were no opposition."

My grandfather nodded, "Charles the Bald now allies with the Bretons and tries to make them fight his foes for him. The Franks are weak. You do right to strike at Caen. It is exposed. You could use it as a stronghold."

"When I capture a stronghold, it will be Rouen!"

"That is a mighty target!"

"And it controls the river. If I am to claim the valley as my own then I need the strongest of its castles. That is Rouen. We will take small bites from the Bretons to make us stronger. Then we move on the Franks. I am patient. The Bretons will rue the day they allied with my brother. By hurting the Bretons, I hurt him."

My grandfather beamed, "And you make him come for you! When he hears of Vikings raiding his King it will make him seek you out."

53

I swept a hand around my new land, "And this will come as a complete surprise to him!"

We put a crew of warriors aboard *'Kara'* and sent her to Eoforwic. I was keen to know the progress of the Danes. I also wished to capitalise on the friendship I had with Guthrum. We still had some seal skins and some animal furs. There would be a better market for them in the land of the Angles than the land of the Franks. I also asked Harold to find more men for us. I hoped that there might be Norse who tired of a long war in the land of the Saxons.

We took just three ships on the raid. *'Dragon's Teeth'* still needed work. We did not use the mast nor the sails. We rowed and, for the first forty or so miles we chanted. We were new to fighting together. There was a wide mixture of men aboard and the chants brought us together. We sang a dark chant. It was deliberate. Our task was to wrest a land back from my enemy and I needed darkness in their heart.

Skuld the Dark sails on shadows wings
Skuld the Dark is a ship that sings
With soft, gentle voice of a powerful witch
Her keel will glide through Frankia's ditch
With flowing hair and fiery breath
Skuld the Dark will bring forth death
Though small in size her heart is great
The Norn who decides on man's final fate
Skuld the Dark sails on shadows wings
Skuld the Dark is a sorcerous ship that sweetly sings
Skuld the Dark sails on shadows wings
Skuld the Dark is a sorcerous ship that sweetly sings
Skuld the Dark sails on shadows wings
Skuld the Dark is a sorcerous ship that sweetly sings
The witch's reach is long her eyes can see through mist
Her teeth are sharp and grind your bones to grist
With soft, gentle voice of a powerful witch
Her keel will glide through Frankia's ditch
With flowing hair and fiery breath
Skuld the Dark will bring forth death

Lord of Rouen

Though small in size her heart is great
The Norn who decides on man's final fate
Skuld the Dark sails on shadows wings
Skuld the Dark is a sorcerous ship that sweetly sings
Skuld the Dark sails on shadows wings
Skuld the Dark is a sorcerous ship that sweetly sings
The witch's reach is long her eyes can see through mist
Her teeth are sharp and grind your bones to grist

We stopped singing as we headed across the open water towards the river mouth in the fading light from the sun. We had less than thirty miles to travel. I headed for the small settlement which had once been Folki's brother's. Long abandoned it was a marker. We slid down the river in darkness. There were fishing boats pulled up alongside the water but the fishermen were in their huts. They knew that they were too small a prey for Vikings. The river was wide enough for three of us to sail abreast of each other but I led the other two. I had raided here. I knew the river. My grandfather had offered to come with us but I had deemed it unfair. He had risked much on my behalf already. I remembered the river even though it was many years since I had sailed here with my father. The town lay on the north bank. Any defences they had had were destroyed in the raids before we had raided Lundenwic. If they had been rebuilt then they were in wood.

It would be almost dawn by the time we reached the town. A town watch would be tired. They would have expected danger to strike earlier. I was relying on the speed of my warriors. The ones with less experience of raiding were spread out in the three ships. Bergil led one crew, Sven a second and I the third. Magnús sailed with Sven Blue Cheek. He was happy to serve under such a famous warrior.

As we neared the newly erected wooden walls I gave the signal to ship oars. Olaf Two Teeth skilfully put the steering board over so that we ground gently next to the river bank. The ship's boys swarmed ashore to make us fast. They were still buoyed by the success on the Esk. All were eager to impress me again. I leapt lithely over the side. I had my shield across my back and I carried my helmet. I ran to the wooden palisade. It was new wood and had been recently placed there. I waved my arm and led my men along the wooden wall. There had to be a gate and we would use that. As we ran I noticed that, although the wooden wall was as high as a man, there was no fighting platform. That meant there had to be towers. I spied the first one just forty paces from us. It was wooden. Perhaps the sentries had been chatting or, worse, sleeping, for no one raised the alarm until we neared to within thirty paces and the sun was beginning to make the eastern sky lighter.

As soon as they shouted the warning that they were under attack I shouted, "Bergil break through the walls. The rest with me and we will take the gate."

The gate lay at the foot of the wooden tower. Arrows flew down at us. One hit my mail. It was a barbed arrow and just stuck there. I donned my helmet and drew my sword. Sámr Oakheart had an axe and, as we reached the gate, he began to smash his way through. Inside the town, I heard church bells. That would induce panic. As soon as more men added their axes to the gate it burst open and Ragnar the Resolute took three men up the tower to kill the sentries. We were inside the town. There were some stone buildings but most were made of wood. What they had not built was a citadel into which they could retreat. That cost them their town. We had to capture as much of the town as we could before the Franks, or the Bretons fled with what they had.

"Sven Blue Cheek secure the centre of the town. My crew, come with me, we find the other gate."

Such was the surprise that I did not need my shield. We ran through the dark, crashing into families trying to escape the wrath of the Northmen. I led and I had quick reactions. I slew those with weapons. There were few of them. Men turned and, seeing a giant, fell to their knees to pray to their White Christ to save them. Sámr Oakheart laughed as he slew one of them, "If he was any kind of god he would have stopped us before we got here!"

There was a danger we could become clogged and slowed by those fleeing, I waved men to the sides as we passed narrow roads. They would be able to get ahead of us. As the sky became lighter I saw the second gate. It was open and four mailed men were waving people through. They saw us and immediately brought around their shields. We did not pause. I was swinging my Long Sword even as the spear came towards me. I used my left hand to bat away the shaft. My sword smashed into the shield and was such a hard blow that the man stumbled. I grabbed a handful of mail and rammed his head into the wooden gatepost. The other three were slain by my men.

"Close the gates. Give the wounded a warrior's death and then take the mail from these men."

I saw that the dead warriors were Bretons. The King of Brittany had benefitted from the absence of my father and grandfather. He had increased Brittany at the expense of the Franks. I left a handful of men to watch the gate and I headed back with the bulk of my crew, to the centre of the town. The warriors who remained in the burgh were few in number and they surrendered. The burghers in the town expected slavery. We had learned, when in the Haugr, that it was better to take slaves from distant lands. Those were more settled and less inclined to flee.

"Ragnar take some men and bring the drekar closer to the gate. It will make loading easier."

As we neared the centre I saw that Bergil had done a good job with the walls. They were destroyed. We could have loaded the cargo from anywhere along the river. Sven had begun to organise the loot and booty. A disconsolate group of merchants stood with their families. These were the great and the good of Caen. I saw that they were Bretons too. I wandered over to them. Even the men shrank back when I approached. When I took off my helmet they relaxed a little.

"Who is the headman here?"

I saw that they were surprised for I spoke their language and spoke it well.

"I am Robert of Caen."

"You are Breton?" He nodded. "When last I lived here this land was that of the Frank. Did you have to fight hard to win it?"

I saw that Robert of Caen was uncomfortable. He shook his head. "The King of France gave this land and the Cotentin to King

Salomon of Brittany. My liege lord is Count Robert of Rennes. He will not be happy, Viking." The man was becoming bolder. "When you flee back to your land of snow and ice there will be your kind who follow you. The Clan of the Sword now follow, my lord. They have ships such as yours and they are fierce warriors!"

The knowledge that this was my brother stopped me from smiling. Instead, I nodded, "And if you see this warrior...?"

"Ragnvald Ragnvaldsson."

I nodded, "Ragnvald Ragnvaldsson." I said the name slowly as though tasting it. "Then when he comes here, tell him that Göngu-Hrólfr Rognvaldson looks forward to contesting this land with him. We will return! That is a promise."

It soon became obvious that the Bretons had only recently occupied the town. The new wood was a testament to that. They had relied on my brother's attestation that he would keep other pirates from the land. I began to fear for Folki. How could he have survived with his handful of men? We did, however, have a rich haul. They had harvested winter barley and oats. That would be welcome. We did not need wheat to make bread. They also had barrels of fermented apple juice. It was from the last year's crop and was ready to drink. There was a vast quantity of cheeses too. They had been made over the winter and were in perfect condition. The churches were stripped of all their finery. They were well endowed. Finally, we found many animals. They would begin to augment our flocks and herds. The surprise in their eyes was that they were not enslaved. As the tide turned in the afternoon and we left to take advantage of the current and the flood, I saw the looks of amazement on their faces. They had sent riders for help before we had closed the doors but I knew the land. To reach Rennes would have taken a rider most of the night and the day. Even as we left he might only just be arriving at the Count's citadel. We set the sail and used the wind to take us north. We would have to row but only once we had turned east.

I spoke with Sámr and Olaf Two Teeth as we headed north. "Well lord, that was as easy a raid as I can remember. They barely fought us!"

"I know, Sámr Oakheart, that is because it is my brother who is supposed to protect them. If nothing else our raid has hurt him."

Olaf shook his head, "What I cannot understand, lord is why the King of the Franks gave away the land!"

"Because of us. We had raided and enslaved so many of his people that he could no longer defend them. This way he has another King to protect his land while still owing fealty to him. The King of Brittany has to bow the knee to the King of the West Franks. Life is more complicated here than in the fjords. It is why we made just one raid. Our men need to learn and we need to strengthen. When I sent the knarr north it was not just for the information it was a call for more warriors. We need the crews of at least a hundred drekar if we are to control this land."

"You would be King?"

I shook my head, "I would do as my grandfather did, I would make a strong home for my people. My father lost his life because of treachery. I would begin to build slowly so that we have time to judge those who come to join us."

"And, of course, your brother will seek you out."

"He will indeed Sámr. He will not recognise the name but my description would sow seeds of doubt in his mind. Did I die? Am I a spirit come back for vengeance? What am I? Already we are winning the war for if he knew our small numbers and where we perch like hungry gulls he would attack from the sea and have the Bretons come by land. As it is he will try to sniff us out. He will send spies. He will send killers. We need to keep an even closer watch now."

Hrolf the Horseman was not interested in the loot we had brought back. He was more interested in what I had learned. Like me, he feared for Folki and the other, older jarls. We both thought that Ragnvald would have betrayed them. He sought power and he cared not who gave that power to him. He pointed to *'Dragon's Teeth'*. "She is almost seaworthy but, unless we get more men, we cannot crew four drekar."

"Nor would I wish to. I want a quarter of our men to defend here while we raid. You know my brother better than I do. It is a matter of time before he discovers where we perch."

Lord of Rouen

Over the next few days, I walked my land to see how we could make it harder for an enemy to take. The sea was the easiest place to defend. We would make a longphort so that no ship could get close to us. It was the landward side where the problem lay. I had my men dig a long ditch to augment the one we already had. It would stop a foe from bringing a ram.

The men who had come from Norway, and that was most of them, were used to clinging to the rocks of a fjord. Here the land was so full of things which grew that a man did not have far to travel to feed himself. They worked with a will to keep what we had.

When *'Kara'* returned she was the centre of everyone's attention. Harold had kept her away for some time. I had told him to gather as much information as he could. There were so many people who wished to hear his story that we had to hold a Thing so that everyone could attend.

My knarr captain knew how to tell a story. Some men have that skill. There are some men who can tell the story of the most mundane event yet it grips your attention while others try to tell a story of a mighty battle between two heroes and you wish for the end of it as soon as it is begun.

"We traded well. Thanks to the deeds of the clan and our lord we are now welcomed in the land of the Danes. We are not robbed and we receive fair prices for all that we trade. We went as far north as Eoforwic. There we saw the corpse of King Ælla of Northumbria. The sons of Ragnar Lodbrok extracted every morsel of revenge from his body for the death of their father. They gave him the blood eagle. Göngu-Hrólfr Rognvaldson was named as a friend of the brothers. They owe you a debt for finding the king for them. Their armies now sweep the length and the breadth of the country. The men of Wessex are forced to fight to cling on to their land. The mighty days of Egbert are long gone. Only the Land of the Wolf is safe."

I saw my grandfather smile and clutch his horse amulet. He owed Jarl Dragonheart's people much.

"When we were in Eoforwic we met Vikings from the land of the fjords. They told us that Haraldr Finehair is sweeping all opposition before him. Unlike the Danes, he has named Göngu-Hrólfr Rognvaldson as an enemy."

I saw Gefn frown. She knew the unfairness of the judgement. We could do nothing about his enmity. We had been in an impossible position. We could not fight for him for we needed to come to our home. If he chose to come to make a fight of it then we would have to fight him. I would not run away.

"That also brings benefits to the clan. Many of these warriors were in the land of the Saxons fighting for the sons of Ragnar Lodbrok but they wished to join Göngu-Hrólfr Rognvaldson here in the Land of the Horse. I told them that they would be welcome and that we sought hardy warriors who wished to fight alongside us."

I saw him look in my direction for confirmation. I nodded. He had said the right thing.

His face then became more serious. "However, not all Vikings have chosen that route. The seaways are now more dangerous places. There are some who are like the lake pike. They hunt their own. We heard of ships which left ports and never reached their destination. Some of these men without honour followed weakened drekar out to sea and afterwards all that was found was a pile of floating wreckage and bodies. Next time I sail I would have an escort of a drekar. I am not afraid to die but you cannot fight those without honour."

I stood, "Thank you. We will do so. Does anyone else wish to speak about the trade?"

None did.

"Then I ask the clan, are we happy with our home here for the winter? I have no doubt that the Bretons will come this summer. They will try to wreak vengeance upon us. We will have to fight for our home."

Sámr Oakheart shouted, "This land is worth fighting for. I care not if Haraldr Finehair or the King of France comes to take it from us he will find that Vikings do not let go of what they have without a fight."

The cheers and acclamation which greeted his words showed me that the clan was of one mind. The Thing ended with a feast of fresh-brewed ale and cheese. We had wheat and the fine bread we had with it made many of the older ones wonder if they had died and woken in Valhalla. I sat with my grandfather, Harold and my chief warriors.

"We could raid again. You lost not a man, lord."

I nodded, "I know Magnús Magnússon. It is tempting but we do not need the food yet and we do not need the land. At the moment we are hidden. I know that word will reach our enemies of our place here but I hope that these warriors whom Harold spoke of will have been able to join us. We have room here to build another stad. The citadel we have built gives us a good position above the river. We could, if we had more men, build a second that would make any attack by an enemy doomed to failure. When it is Gói we unleash our ships on the enemy."

Ragnar said, "Gói? Is that not early?"

"It might be in the land of snow and ice. Even in the land of the Saxons, it might be too early but here there will be buds on the trees and the earth will be warm. Then we begin to claw a home on the Issicauna. We clear away the Bretons who are there and move our people to land which is even more fertile than this. The King of the Franks has done us a favour by allowing the Bretons here. Our sea dragons have destroyed their defences and I do not think that the Bretons have yet built anything which might stop us."

My grandfather had been silent. I had thought it was the fine bread, new cheese and dark ale which had distracted him but it was not. "We need horses." The others looked at him as though he had lost his mind. He smiled, "My grandson will tell you that the key to holding on to this land is the horse. You have young men who could be trained to be horsemen. A drekar attacking up the river and horsemen raiding across the land are an irresistible force."

"You are right. If you feel that you are up to an expedition we could venture inland and see what we can discover within half a day's march of this place."

Sámr Oakheart said, "You will not raid, lord, yet you will risk walking abroad just to get horses?"

Harold laughed, "What I did not tell you was how the Danes conquered so much of England. They did not use their drekar.

They took horses. They found thousands of them and they rode up the Roman roads to reach every corner of the land. Guthrum told the brothers how to do that and he learned it from Göngu-Hrólfr Rognvaldson."

Sámr clapped me on my back, "We are lucky to have such a lord as you!"

Bergil laughed, "Aye when my uncle fished you from the sea he did not know what he caught! Perhaps we should have used a bigger net. Who knows what we might have found!"

My grandfather clutched his amulet, "When you leave your home you know not what the Norns have in store for you!"

Lord of Rouen

Chapter 5

We did not leave to search for the horses straight away. Another drekar limped into our port. There were twenty warriors and their families who had fled the wrath of Finehair. Even as they were being housed and the drekar beached for repairs two more arrived. They brought another forty warriors. We would not just leave. The families needed land and we had to spend time speaking with them. We made them understand that Djupr was just a temporary home and we would find somewhere stronger. I impressed upon them that we would have to fight for it. I wondered if some had had enough fighting. In the event, all were happy to stay under those conditions. My tribe was growing.

It was Heyannir when we left. There were just twenty of us. We did not wear mail. With shields slung over our backs and our swords hung from our scabbards, we travelled lightly. My grandfather and I took our bows. I knew that my huge frame gave me an advantage over most men but my grandfather was also a good archer. The others took bows but they had not begun using them early enough to be as skilful as we were. We headed towards Rouen. It was only thirty miles from where we had built our home and I was anxious to see what lay before it. I also knew that the land would suit horses and, it seemed to me, that we might kill two birds with one stone.

Gone were the days when I could scout. I was simply too big. We had found two young warriors who appeared to have skills. Arne Pétrsson and Bjorn Eriksson seemed to be able to blend in to the undergrowth. Of course, all of this was new to them for they both came from the fjord but they had learned quickly. They loped off ahead of us. We had explored the land within five miles of our new citadel and found neither danger nor enemies. The local farmers had hidden when my men had neared them. As we passed the five-mile mark we all became wary. We kept below the skyline and used natural cover. The fields which had been cleared of crops were approached carefully. We bellied up and peered across them. We found orchards and we found fields sown with new crops. We found neither horses nor ponies. We saw no sign that horses had been in the fields recently. It was disappointing.

We planned on walking for ten miles and then heading back. We had just stopped to make water in the shelter of a hedgerow when Arne came hurtling back. He pointed excitedly behind him. "There are men on horses, lord. There is a battle!"

As I could not hear much I doubted that it was a battle but I was intrigued at who would be fighting. Perhaps two local lords had a dispute. I turned to my grandfather, "What do you think, grandfather?"

"It is interesting. I cannot see Breton fighting Breton with us so close. Let us approach a little closer. I would have your men string their bows."

My bow was almost as tall as me. Few men were strong enough to string it. I did not nock the arrow I had chosen but I carried it next to the bow.

Arne pointed, "Bjorn waits close by." As we hurried we began to hear the sounds of sword on sword and sword on wood. It was painful to run doubled over and I know that I must have looked comical. We saw Bjorn huddled beneath a gnarled old apple tree. We bellied up and peered over. In the field, there were twenty horsemen fighting. I recognised four of them. They wore the familiar blue cloaks with the white sword. They had served my father and my grandfather. The cloaks were now faded and the helmets dented but they were still our men.

"The men in blue are friends. Kill the rest!"

They looked at me in surprise but did not argue. We stood and I nocked and drew in one movement. The twenty men were closely involved with each other but I trusted my men and their accuracy. We were just forty paces away. I released my arrow and the missile slammed into the back of one of the two men fighting

Stephen of Andecavis. The warrior was thrown from his saddle and my second arrow was nocked before the others realised they had more than four enemies. My second arrow took the other horseman fighting Stephen of Andecavis. It smashed through his cheek and into his skull. My bow was powerful. There was a temptation to draw swords and race into the action but that would have been a mistake. My companion's arrows were not quite as effective as mine. Their arrows did not kill. The Bretons wore leather and it afforded protection.

"Aim for their legs or their heads!" As if to make my point I sent an arrow into the face of a Breton who turned to see where the new danger lay. My grandfather's arrows were equally effective.

Four of the Bretons turned their horses to charge at us. Hidden by the hedge they could not know our numbers. I nocked and released. At thirty paces my arrow knocked the first Breton over the back of his saddle. My grandfather's arrow hit a second in the face. My next arrow was sent towards the Breton who was just twenty paces from me. I saw the look of horror as my arrow headed towards him. He could not avoid it and he too was thrown from the saddle. The last was hit by three arrows at the same time. With more than half of their numbers slain I heard the leader order them to retreat. The four horsemen who had once served the Haugr now took advantage of the levelling of the odds. As my next arrow hit the leader square in the back Stephen of Andecavis and the others used their swords to slay another four. One man escaped us.

I shouted, "Gather the horses! Search and then strip the dead! Arne and Bjorn go and make sure that we are not surprised!"

Even as we spoke Michel of Liger slumped from his saddle. He had been wounded. The other three dismounted. Grandfather strode over towards Stephen of Andecavis with his arm outstretched, "I am pleased that you live still!"

The horseman looked greyer and leaner but I still recognised him. "We were in Burgundy when we heard of a giant raiding Caen and there were rumours that Hrolf the Horseman had returned. When we left there were eight of us. We are the last four of Alain of Auxerre's horsemen."

"How is Michel?"

The horseman sat up, "I am alive Rollo! Your arrows are fearsome! We heard rumours of a warrior like you returning from the north with Hrolf the Horseman. I can see that you have become a giant! Now we see that it is true."

I nodded and saw that my men were returning. "Whence did these men come?"

"Heading to where we had heard that Vikings dwelt, we passed a Frankish castle ten miles east of here. They followed us. Our horses were weary. They are old. We could not outrun them."

"Use some of those we captured. Grandfather, you ride. Lead the men to our home. We will load the other horses with the armour and the helmets." He frowned, "Go! My men and I are young! It is not far from home. We will be behind you."

As the five of them rode off, leading the tired horses they had ridden, we began to load the other horses. "What did you learn, Sámr Oakheart?"

"These are not ordinary warriors. They had jewelled rings on their fingers and their boots were well made."

"Nobles?"

"That would be my guess. We have coins too. The swords are of high quality and the shields are well made. They have laminated wood beneath the leather."

"Then as soon as we can train up some scouts to ride the horses we can find out more about our neighbours. Lead off Ragnar; Bergil, Sámr and I will walk at the rear with our scouts."

As we walked Sámr said, "Those are the horseman of whom you spoke?"

I nodded, "At one time there were more than twenty-five of them. They were a potent force on the battlefield. It is sad to see them diminished. My brother has destroyed the clan!"

Bergil said, quietly, "And you would act sooner rather than later to remedy the situation?"

I shook my head, "That would be a waste of men. What little of the clan remains will still be there this time next year and our numbers are growing. These four horsemen could be worth as much as half a drekar crew! No, I was worrying more that if Stephen of Andecavis heard of us in Burgundy then it is likely that my brother will know where I am. The warrior who escaped cannot help but report the giant who led the Vikings in an ambush. We keep to the plan!"

When we reached our home Gefn and Bergljót had had the four warriors' hurts tended to. My father had put the horses in the new stables. We had built them when we had built the hall. Now they served a purpose. I saw that work was going on to build a new hall for the recent additions. Across the river, Olaf Two Teeth and his men toiled on the defences at the north side of the anchorage.

That evening my grandfather's four horsemen ate with us. They were hard warriors. Swords for hire they had left the Land of the Horse to continue to ply their trade and yet they had a gentle quality which impressed Gefn and Bergljót.

"What can you tell us of the Land of the Horse? What of Gilles' sons? What happened to you after Hrolf the Horseman left?"

"We had gone before then. Ragnvald made it quite clear that there was no place for us in his land. Even then he had begun to give parts of the land back to the Bretons in return for more power."

Michel shook his head, "He even began to take his ships to wage war for his Breton masters. It was sad to see. We stayed with Folki for a while. Folki grew old quickly. It seemed that without Hrolf the Horseman and his son he lost his direction. He led his clan on a raid towards Rouen. We guarded his flank. Ragnvald Ragnvaldsson and his men fell upon their rear. They died defending their jarl. It was a glorious end but it cost their families dear. We saved those that we could but many were taken as slaves. The ones we rescued we took to those families who still survived south of Carentan and the small isolated farms there close to Benni's Ville. We decided to hire our swords elsewhere."

Stephen looked sadly at Hrolf. "By then you had left to seek your grandson. We did not think you would succeed. We saw it as a glorious end to your life. We should have trusted you more. We heard that the Count of Burgundy needed horsemen. We made coin there but each campaign cost us more men. Even had we not heard that you had returned we would not have stayed longer. We are here to serve you now. We will ride your borders as we did in the Land of the Horse."

I nodded, "I need more than that from you. I need you to do as Alain of Auxerre did. We need men training to become horsemen. We have few horses. Train up ten warriors or so and then take them on horse raids."

"When do you go to war?"

"This time next year we will begin to take the Issicauna from the Bretons and within three years we will reclaim the Land of the Horse!"

Now that we knew that there were enemies close we kept men watching the south and east. We had small groups of men hunting in the forests six miles from our citadel as we had at Streanæshalc. We had five such daily hunts so that we would not be surprised and we also ate well.

Another drekar arrived at the start of Tvímánuður. This time it was a big ship with sixteen oars on each side. Each was crewed. They had their families with them. Olaf Two Teeth knew them. His wife came from their clan. It seemed that Haraldr Finehair would be the King of Norway by the next year. This drekar was among those who would not serve the voracious Finehair. It meant we now had a good fleet. We had eight drekar and we had repaired the damage to all of them. We had a stronghold to protect the anchorage to the north. With a winter to learn how to fight together, we would raid when spring came. Life was good.

With ten young warriors learning how to become riders I was happier about our ability to see further afield. Grandfather had found that one of them, Erik, was particularly keen to learn and he took it upon himself to take him under his wing. My grandfather had missed riding a horse. Stephen of Andecavis was happy that young Erik could keep an eye on my grandfather. He was still a fine rider but, at his age, a fall could be disastrous.

It was fortunate that we had found our horsemen and gained horses for, at the end of Tvímánuður, my grandfather and Erik, now called The Horseman, galloped in to the citadel. "Rollo! There is a force of Bretons heading here. They have some of our people with them! I sent back our hunter scouts. They will be back with us soon."

We had expected this. I was not surprised. We had made preparations. They could not know how many men we had ready to meet them. I sent for my leaders. "Grandfather, I put you in command of the citadel. Keep the horsemen within the walls. I would not have them know our numbers. It is too soon to use them in war. With the horses and the two small drekar crews, you have enough to defend the walls." He smiled as he nodded. "Olaf Two Teeth, keep one crew in the new stronghold in the northern defence. That will leave me with five drekar crew! Sven Blue Cheek, have the men readied. We will march to meet these Bretons and traitors!"

We had scouted out the approaches from the south and east. Two miles away was a slope with a wood and a hedge at the top. I intended to use the rise to hide my numbers. I would show them three drekar crew while the other two would be armed with bows and waiting in reserve. They would try to use their horses on the flanks. We had done so when we had had more horses. My men carried sacks of caltrops: twisted metal spikes, they were deadly to horses. In addition, we took stakes and hammers. With a dozen scouts a mile ahead of us to warn us of the enemy, we prepared our position. I had stakes laid along both sides of our position and then the caltrops seeded our flanks and our front. I wanted them to make a frontal attack. I had mailed men in my front rank. There were forty of us with mail. Most were men who had served with me in Norway.

As we stood there, waiting Bergil asked, "Why do we not use all of our men here? We have horsemen we could use! We could win today!"

"We will win today but the men who come here are not their best nor are they an attempt to rid the land of us. They are an attempt to see who we are and what sort of a problem we pose. They will be hoping to drive us hence but if they do not then they will not worry. My father told me that there were just over fifty horsemen. That is not a huge number. He said the horsemen did not wear mail. That means they are not leudes. These are local

70

farmers and the sons of lords. They wish to hurt us and to stop us from attacking them. I have expected this since we raided Caen. We make them think we are weaker than we are so that when we attack, with our full force, it will come as a shock to them."

Our scouts ran in. "Lord they are behind us. There are fifty horses, a hundred men on foot and a large drekar crew of Vikings. The men on foot look to be poorly armed."

Sven asked, "Will your brother be with them?"

I shook my head. "He will wait until he knows where I am. When he comes it will be as a murderer in the night. He will avoid fighting me if he can. To bring him within reach of my sword I will need cunning. It will be a trusted lieutenant. It may be Arne the Breton Slayer or this Ailmær the Cruel. They will not commit their Vikings unless they have to. They will use their levy first."

Sven Blue Cheek nodded, "And while they hold us then their horsemen will attack our flanks."

"And our archers will hold them. We have a good man in command of the archers?"

"Aye lord, Petr Jorgenson. They will not let you down."

I saw as the Bretons formed up, that these were like the horsemen we had fought a few days earlier. They would be the young sons of lords who had the coin to be horsemen. They would seek glory. If my brother thought that I was there then he would have warned his men to beware hidden horsemen. They would be seeking the horses which were not there. We had not enough. It was another reason I had hidden the few that we had.

A Breton lord on a tall horse rode before the assembled men. He had with him a priest on foot and a man with a standard. His words did not carry to me but I knew what he would be saying. He would exhort his men to drive the unbelievers and pagans back into the sea. He would be telling them that their god was on their side and they could not lose. Then he would retire behind their shields and watch them bleed on our swords. They began banging their shields on their spears and, as the lord removed himself and his priest and standard, they started the ascent.

We had chosen a place with an energy-sapping slope. They were desperate to get close to us for they had horsemen and

Vikings with them. We just stood in silence. That too was deliberate. It would raise questions in their minds. The horsemen advanced in two groups up the flanks. The Vikings marched behind the levy. They had more purpose about them. Their shields were well made. All had mail and they each carried a long ash spear. With fine helmets, they would be the best warriors that we would face that day. The horsemen reached a place from which they could charge first. The two groups chose a flat piece of ground two hundred paces from our left and right flanks. Perhaps they should have investigated the hedge and the trees which barred their progress. The line of vegetation was filled with archers.

They must have planned this attack with thought and care for the horsemen waited. Some of the ones who thought themselves better horsemen made their horses rear and flail their hooves. It did not worry us. The Vikings kept their line straight but the Breton line was ragged. It had begun as a three-line front. Now it was a ragged two-line front as some had lagged from the front ranks and the third had pushed up. They could now see the stakes. They were large enough to avoid. Their purpose was to break up the enemy line. The seeded caltrops lay within twenty paces of us. That was close but I wanted them distracted as they neared us for that would be when I would order my hidden archers to attack.

Three warriors were eager. They raced ahead of the main line. I heard an older warrior order them back but they ignored him. They were the three who discovered the caltrops. The first one managed to impale his foot and he fell writhing to the ground. The other two were stuck but knew not what they were. They became enraged and hurled themselves at Sven Blue Cheek, Sámr Oakheart and me. Their spears were aimed at me. That was not a surprise I was the biggest target. I held my shield before me and both spears cracked into the metal studs and the heads shattered. I lifted my sword. They both seemed to stare at it and did not see the two spears of Sven and Sámr which darted out to disembowel them.

My raised sword seemed to halt the Bretons or perhaps the leader, who had tried to order his two young men back into line, was making certain that there was some semblance of order when they hit us. I knew that my archers would be watching for my sword to descend. That would be the order for them to unleash stones and arrows.

"Forward for Count Robert!"

They all stepped forward at the same time. They had regained their breath and they had a solid line of shields. They reached the writhing man whose foot was still pumping blood on the greensward. As the caltrops began to take effect and men looked down to see where the deadly metal lay I dropped my sword.

"Lock shields!"

My archers sent their arrows to plunge vertically. Some Bretons had no helmets. Few had anything other than a leather jerkin. Sometimes that held the arrow but more than a few arrows insinuated themselves into flesh. The shower of missiles was relentless. My archers would keep sending arrows until they had none left. I glanced to my left. The horses there had discovered the caltrops. They were intended for horses and terrified animals threw their riders and plunged off down the hill. The hidden archers and slingers completed the rout. The scene to the right was the same.

Inevitably some Bretons managed to avoid the caltrops and the arrows. They closed with us and tried to take us man for man. This time I was not the sole target. The bodies before the three of us were an effective barrier and I was able to watch some of my warriors as they showed their skills. A man wearing mail knows that he can be struck and survive. That confidence often gives him the edge. I saw the leader reach Bergil. The Breton leader had metal discs sewn on to his leather. He had an open helmet and he had a sword. Bergil now had a helmet with a nasal and a mail byrnie over a padded undergarment. More importantly, Bergil had a solid platform for he was on dry ground. The Breton slipped and slid on men's blood. Bergil easily blocked the blow from the Breton sword and he surprised the Breton when he lunged at his unprotected middle. His tip was not particularly sharp but Bergil was strong. He had rowed aboard a drekar. His sword took the wind from the older warrior. Bergil punched with his shield boss. The open helmet afforded no protection to such a blow and blood-spattered as his nose was broken. His unsteady feet, the two blows and the falling arrows meant he was distracted. Bergil's killing blow came from on high. He struck diagonally across the unprotected neck. The blow was so hard it almost severed the Breton's head.

When the surviving horsemen fled down the slope it was the signal for flight. Their leader was dead. More than a third of those who had made the attack now lay dead or wounded and our line was intact. The Vikings were close enough for me to see them. It was not Arne the Breton Slayer who led them. I had not seen his shield before. He had a red boar painted upon the shield. The mouth was the boss. I did not recognise the man. He had a greybeard. It was not Arne The Breton Slayer's brother. I saw his eyes. He was analysing us so that he could report back to his leader. The Vikings had yet to be hurt. Arrows grew like headless flowers from their shields and there were even a couple with arrows stuck in their mail but the formation was intact. As the Bretons fled past them I saw the leader shout a command. Holding their shields above their heads they made their way down the slope. The battle was over.

Sven and I had fought in enough battles to be wary of a feigned retreat. When they finally quit the field Sven shouted, "Strip the bodies. Recover arrows!" He turned to me. "You were right, lord. That was never a serious attack."

"And they learned little. They know that we have more than three drekar crew. I would expect them to investigate us by sea. My brother and Arne the Breton Slayer might be treacherous but they are no fools. The Breton leader, this Count Robert, might be less than clever when it comes to war but they will now try to discover our true numbers."

Bergil said, "And come for you."

I nodded, "And come for me. We will now need even more vigilance around our citadel. The Viking I saw watched me. He will describe me to my brother. He will now know that his little brother did not drown. He has returned from the depths and come to haunt him."

"And your grandfather?"

I nodded, "He, too, is in danger. I am pleased that my horsemen have returned. They will be Hrolf the Horsemen's bodyguards and I will sleep easier."

When we returned to the citadel I told my grandfather of the battle. I told him of the Viking and his shield. "I do not recall such a shield but then at my age…"

"You are as sharp as any man. It is more likely that this is someone who has joined him since you left. I think they will do two things. They will scout out our drekar and they may try to send killers into our camp. Stephen of Andecavis, you and your men will watch my grandfather."

"None will get close."

We looked to the south and east as smoke began to rise from the pyres of enemy dead. We had also captured another eight horses while three dead ones would provide us with a victory feast. The war had begun.

For the next month, we had two drekar a day sailing out to sea. I wanted my crews to be as well practised as they could be and I wanted a deterrent against observation. If my brother sent his own ships to investigate our anchorage he would need to send large numbers. We also needed to practice our battle tactics. If we were just raiding Bretons and Franks it would be much simpler. Our ships would sail up the river and land our men. We would fight a battle and sail home with our plunder. If there were drekar there then we had to know how to use our strengths against theirs. I was aboard one of the two drekar each day. It was no hardship for I got to see how my new men performed and how each ship sailed. Every drekar was unique. Even more important was that I got to know the waters offshore as well as any man. I knew every shoal and ledge. I could identify, by the end of the month, every eddy and current within ten miles of the mouth of our anchorage.

When they came we spied the enemy early but it was from a distance. We saw the sails on the horizon. Unlike those who plied the seas for trade these did not keep well out to sea, these turned their dragons to draw close and when they saw two predators waiting for them they turned and disappeared over the horizon. As soon as I spied the two ships then I changed our procedures. I had another two drekar standing by just half a mile out to sea. If my brother sent more ships then he was in for a surprise.

I think the men were beginning to tire of the patrols. I was still young and some of the older warriors, especially from crews who did not know me well, began to grumble as they each took their turn to patrol off the mouth of the river. Their chiefs and jarls did not complain. They understood that there was a reason for it. I did not respond to the complaints. The complainers would either learn or leave. I wanted men with me who trusted me and my judgement. Together we would do great things. The reason became clear at the start of Haustmánuður. We saw four sails on the horizon.

My grandfather had told me how my brother had had bigger and, in my brother's view, better drekar built to replace those in which I had sailed as a young warrior. The four ships we saw approaching, under full sail, were big ones. They looked to have between thirty and forty oars. I doubted that they would be double crewed. They were there to squash two insignificant threttanessa.

That day I was in my own drekar, *'Hermóðr'*. We rowed without mail but we were all armed. With us was one of the drekar which had recently joined us. *'Wolf's Snout'* had thirty oars but she was not fully crewed.

Olaf Two Teeth said, "Do we lead them back to the river, lord?"

I shook my head, "There is no need. The wind brings them to us. Let us see if we can manage to capture or wreck one of them."

He grinned. The loss of a drekar would be a disaster. It would make a further attack from the sea highly unlikely. The crews of our ships were rowing. We continued out to sea to meet them. Our actions would confuse them. The ship's boys were already sitting on the mast ready to let the sail fly when we turned. I wanted to get a measure of these sailors who served my brother. He would not be with them. I walked to the prow to get a better look at them. I saw that they all had a dragon painted upon their sail. Each one was a different colour. It was a statement from my brother. He was telling his enemies that he controlled a fleet. The drekar moved well across the water but the true test would come when we began tight manoeuvres. Olaf Two Teeth had made adjustments to the ballast after each voyage and our hull was kept immaculately clean. The more Olaf sailed her, the faster she became. In fact, it was he who had recommended we continue our patrols. He gave advice to the other captains and soon their ships became as fast as ours. I was confident that we could outrun the four larger, heavier drekar which drew closer to us with each breath of wind.

It would have been useful to see their oars in action for that would have given us a good insight into the crew. All we could judge them on was the efficiency of their ships' boys and their steersmen. The four ships were giving each other plenty of sea room. They were not risking a collision if we made some mad dash to close to with them. When they were ten lengths from us I shouted, "Steerboard, Olaf, and loose the sail! Let us see her fly!"

'Wolf's Snout' was following and she would be able to turn inside us. Our turn allowed them to close to within four lengths. If they had had archers they might have hurt us. Either they did not or they were taken unawares by our rapid turn. The sail cracked as the wind caught her. I had to hold on to the sheerstrake such was the power of the turn. Olaf had given her wings and we gradually began to extend our lead. Anticipating my order, he had the boys reef the sail so that we moved at the same pace as our pursuers. They could see little beyond our sails. Already I saw the coast as a smudge on the horizon. Soon I would see *'Fafnir'* and *'Dellingr'* which were waiting in case we needed them. Our watchtower on the headland would have already seen the four drekar and signalled. My ships would be ready. The crews would be running out their oars and giving the two drekar momentum so that when we neared them they could race out.

I walked the length of the drekar to join Sven and Olaf at the steering board. Sven and I stared at the four dragons which were racing towards us. "Will they take the bait do you think?"

"I hope so. It would be good to damage or capture at least one." I glanced towards the shore. I could now see the entrance to the river. The tower over the water was also visible. I was trying to see Djupr the way that the four drekar captains would see it. The rest of our ships were hidden. They were tied up to the quays which now ran on both sides of the river. The citadel was hidden. Soon it would rise and become a feature but the only defence appeared to be the tower. I then glanced astern. Olaf was keeping them just four lengths behind us. The two sails would mask the river. It would be their boys on the mast who would report the tower. I saw our two drekar as they pulled from the shore. It was an efficient stroke. There was no rush. Once we closed then they could increase speed.

We had practised our turns. I saw that one of the boys on *'Wolf's Snout'* was staring at us and watching for the instruction to turn. One wrong move could see both drekar dismasted. We must have appeared to be highly vulnerable for they kept coming. From behind, I heard a shout and I guessed that my two drekar had been spotted. Would they turn and break off the attack or was I a prize which was worth the risk? Soon they would have to face the possibility of a fight with four on four or break and run.

"Olaf, whenever you are ready!"

He nodded, "Cnut, signal the other drekar to turn."

What we were going to do was dangerous and risky. We were going to turn across the bows of the four drekar which were chasing us. We hoped to cause confusion and make them collide. *'Fafnir'* and *'Dellingr'* would be able to pounce on the stern of at least one of them if they turned the wrong way. We would then continue our turn and join them.

I gripped the backstay as we fought the wind. Olaf and his boys were using all of their experience to stop us broaching. *'Wolf's Snout'*, being smaller, had an easier task. Two of those following us made a good attempt to follow us but the other two were slower to react. Even better, from our point of view, was the fact that their two captains did not do the same thing. As the leading ship of the two took in sail and tried to turn, the other just tried to turn. She fouled her consort. Olaf had seen it and he put us on the opposite tack. For a moment we were stationary as we hit the wind. Slowly our stern came around. The two ships which were following were drawing closer but they were also having to adjust their sails. They had not expected the second turn and they both sped by.

The two fouled ships were busy lowering their sails and cutting away fouled lines. *'Fafnir'* and *'Dellingr'* closed with them.

'Wolf's Snout' leapt ahead of us to join our other two ships. As soon as Olaf had the wind we headed for the two entangled drekar. The captain of one of them shouted something and I saw the forestay of the second ship severed. It snaked into the air and the mast, still rigged, began to slowly fall. The pressure of the wind and the collision had done the rest. Three of my brother's ships fled. The last was abandoned. That told me much about the men we were fighting. Had they fought us, ship to ship, then the odds were that they would have won for only my drekar matched their size.

"Prepare to board them. Ship's boys keep an eye on the other three."

I saw *'Fafnir'* and *'Dellingr'* close with the ship's prow. Both captains had the experience. Arnbolt on *'Wolf's Snout'* was less experienced and it showed. He went for her stern but he did not get his sail down fast enough. He hit so hard that I saw warriors from the enemy ship fall into the sea. Already damaged by the collision with their own ship she began to take on water. Olaf, in contrast, slid majestically alongside the drekar. I swung myself up to the sheerstrake and drew my sword. A pitching deck was no place for a shield. My men were pouring over the prow and the stern. I launched myself at the three men close by the broken mast. As I landed I drew my second sword. I was not worried by my isolation. My men would be close behind me. I swung my long sword before me. They moved back and tried to spread out. Fear was in their faces. They were intimidated by my size.

"Surrender and you will live! Lay down your swords!" Amazingly they did so. I saw then that they were young. Without a shred of mail between them, they were bareheaded with poorly made swords. I turned, "Olaf, have these three prisoners taken." My men were now behind me and they unceremoniously passed the three prisoners back over their shoulders.

Sven joined me, "If all the rest do the same we might even save this drekar!"

Arnbolt was attacking the steering board. I saw the captain was there and they were fighting for their lives. "Our young comrade needs our help first!"

Lord of Rouen

As soon as we moved towards them half-turned to face this new threat. I swung my Long Sword in a wide sweep. The crew had left their shields on the side and my sword bit deeply into the warrior's side. Such was the force of the blow that his dying body knocked over the man next to him who was skewered by Sven. We began to carve our way through the crew to the stern. Now that there were five ships tied together we had a more stable platform. For a man my size that made life much easier. It was almost as easy as fighting on land. Sven and I slew two men wearing mail. It was not the best of mail but it took a couple of mighty swings to defeat it.

As they fell I shouted, "Captain, yield. I promise you justice. You cannot win!"

The bloodied captain was surrounded by dead yet he shouted back, defiantly, "I swore to your brother, the Prince, that I would bring back your head. I would not be foresworn!"

I took in the title he had given my brother and nodded, "No quarter! Let us end this!" Now joined by two crews who had cleared the bow we were like farmers using scythes to harvest wheat. The last twenty men were surrounded and they gradually fell. The captain was the last to die. Sámr Oakheart ended his life. The captain was weakened by wounds and when he swung at Sámr's head, Sámr ducked beneath the swashing blow and gutted the Viking. As I stepped close I saw that Arnbolt had paid for his mistake with his life.

"Lord, this ship is taking on water. If we wish to save her then we need to get her beached as soon as we can."

"Aye. Everyone back to their ships. I will steer this one." I sheathed my swords and went to the steering board. The withies remained undamaged. The crew had cut away the wreckage and that would make life easier. Water lapped around my feet but I was unworried. We were less than a mile from one of the many beaches which lay close to my new home. My four ships attached ropes and soon we were speeding through the water. I had little to do but steer and I was able to examine the bodies of the men around me. I did not recognise them. Then I noticed that they were neither Norse nor Dane. They were Rus. I had detected a different accent in the ship's captain. This was unusual. The Rus normally sailed the rivers which led to Miklagård. How had they come to my brother's service? The three prisoners would be invaluable.

The water was almost at my knees when the four drekar cast off their tows. The ship bobbed up and down in the shallows. There was so much water in her hold that it was unlikely that she would broach but my men took no chances. Warriors leapt from the drekar and hauled us up above the high-water mark. We had managed to land her just two hundred paces from Olaf Two Teeth's northern stad. Once stakes had been driven in to hold her we returned to our drekar to sail home. We could strip the dead and salvage the weapons later. She was going nowhere. I nodded with satisfaction as I saw the water pouring from her hull. By the time we started work on her, she would be dry at least.

The three prisoners were huddled by the steering board. Olaf had used Magnus No Nose and Oleg the Claw to watch them. Both were terrifying-looking warriors. The crew were rowing and so I stood with Olaf. "They are Rus."

He nodded, "I thought the drekar had slightly different lines. What is a Rus doing here? There is a tale, lord."

"Aye and we were lucky. Had they chosen to stand and fight it might have been a hard-fought battle and we might have lost men we would ill afford to lose."

"Arnbolt lost his head, lord. He has paid the price but it is sad. He was a captain with potential."

"Perhaps that is my fault. I did not give them enough practice."

"But you did, lord. His crew were the ones who complained the most about the tedium of rowing, changing course and following other ships. This may serve as a lesson."

Maybe he was right.

Chapter 6

We had men who had hurts and they were dealt with first. The three prisoners looked fearfully around them. They expected a painful death. They had surrendered because they had seen the overwhelming numbers but I could see, on their faces, that they were regretting their decision. They were now alone. I had examined them on the way back in to the anchorage. They were little more than ship's boys. Their bodies were underdeveloped. Their lack of armour, helmets and weapons showed that they had only recently been promoted to take an oar. The excitement of being an oar brother must have suddenly soured when four ships had descended upon them.

My grandfather, Gefn and Bergljót brought in some ale, bread and cheese. The two women saw not warriors. They saw three frightened boys. My grandfather was still a grandfather. His eyes pleaded clemency. I waited until the three of them had eaten and had drunk their fill before I spoke.

"Answer me fairly and honestly and you shall live. Do you understand?" I spoke slowly. They nodded but they still looked terrified.

Gefn said, quietly, "Son, if you sit down you will frighten them less. All that they see is a giant."

"You are right." I sat. "You are from the land of the Rus?" I made certain that my voice was gentle.

I looked at the nearest one, willing him to answer. "Yes, lord. We came through the Skagerrak two years since. We were ship's boys then. Our captain heard that there was great treasure to be had in the land of the Franks and they had no snow. Our crew was young. We thought to make our fortune and then return home after a few years as rich men."

"What is the name of your ship?"

A second one plucked up the courage to speak, "*'Grim's Worm'*, lord."

"And you served this … Prince?"

"Prince Ragnvald the Great, lord."

I saw my grandfather's eyes widen. "And where does this Prince live?"

"Ċiriċeburh. It is a mighty stone fortress. Our jarl was most impressed by it."

"How did he get the title, Prince?"

They looked at each other in confusion. "He is a Prince, lord. He dresses like one and he has servants. Everyone calls him Prince. He is married to the daughter of the ruler of the land, Count Robert."

My brother had delusions of grandeur. "Now what was your purpose today? Give me an honest answer."

They had gained in confidence while we had spoken. Their ale horns had been kept filled and they had not stopped eating. The one who had spoken first paused with his horn halfway to his mouth. "You might not like our answer, lord."

I laughed, "Whether I like or not I gave you my word and Göngu-Hrólfr Rognvaldson is never foresworn. Answer honestly."

"We were sent to capture two drekar and take them back to Ċiriċeburh. The Prince wished prisoners."

"How many drekar does he have?"

"There were eight. Now ours is taken then he has seven."

"And you are the only Rus?"

"Yes lord."

My grandfather had been listening, "They have told you all, Rollo."

I nodded, "I know and I will keep my word." I turned back to them. "What are your names?"

"Næstr Dargsson."

"Habor Nokkesson."

"Thiok Clawusson."

"If you would swear allegiance to me then you can join my crew. What say you?"

Habor asked, "And if we refuse to join you?" The other two glared at him.

I shook my head, "A fair question. We have a knarr which trades with the land of the East Angles. Next time she sails you would be taken to that land. There are Danes there who seek crews."

Næstr shook his head, "Ignore my cousin, lord. Habor has taken too many blows to the head. We would be honoured to join you."

And so, we took on three new crew members. Inevitably they were all given the same nickname, 'the Rus'. They did not seem to mind. It was, perhaps a reminder of who they were. The three proved very loyal.

'Grim's Worm' was not badly damaged but it took a month to make her seaworthy. We saw no more drekar as we toiled on her but we did catch Breton scouts. Our own scouts were more efficient. One was always left alive. They lost their right hand but were sent on their way. They would take the message back that the new Vikings were vigilant. After three such raids, the Bretons ceased risking our wrath. Our halls grew. Each drekar crew had their own. Mine was the only one within the walls of the stronghold. My men had seen that our defences would give us warning of an attack. The other halls each had its own ditch but if a major attack came then they would take shelter in my citadel. The farms of my men were dotted around the halls. After the rocks of Norway, the fertile rolling land of the Franks seemed like a paradise.

As winter descended we sat to plan the next phase of raids. Before we took the Issicauna valley I intended to make the land around Caen mine. We had enough men to take and to hold at least one of the Breton strongholds. Caen, Bayeux and Lisieux were all close enough for us to hold. When we attacked the Issicauna then my brother would come. I intended to have a line of defences to the east of the Issicauna. He would be coming from the Coutances.

Our knarr continued to trade. Guthrum and the sons of Ragnar Lodbrok had been true to their word. My ships were welcomed.

Our goods brought good prices. Families returned with the knarr for there were still Norse who fled Haraldr Finehair. I was seen as a haven for Vikings who wished to live free from the rule of a King. Vikings do not like the concept of kings. The drekar had dried up for the jarls who had remained had sworn allegiance to the would-be King of Norway. There were still families who fled. The journey to the land of the Saxons often proved too much for their tiny ships. We took them all. Gefn made certain that they were welcomed.

My grandfather and my horsemen rode further afield. We had twenty horsemen. Only the ones who wore the blue cloaks could be called horse warriors. The others were warriors who rode horses but Stephen of Andecavis and my grandfather were both pleased with their progress. My grandfather was philosophical about it all. "You were reborn and so was I yet my life seems to be a chance for me to remedy mistakes I made in my first life. We will seek horses to breed. I allowed Gilles to do that last time. That should have been my task. We will end up with horsemen, grandson do not worry."

We kept up our patrols. Men now saw their purpose. We re-launched *'Grim's Worm'* at Mörsugur. Sven Blue Cheek chose the captain for that ship. Olaf Far Seeing was a young warrior but he had proved to be a good steersman. Arnbolt's younger brother, Gandálfr, became captain of *'Wolf's Snout'*. His crew elected him and I was pleased. He had come to me to tell me that his brother had known he had made mistakes and that he would learn from them. We now had nine drekar and almost all of them were fully crewed. I decided to raid Bayeux when the new grass grew. It only lay five miles from the sea. The channel of the river was not as wide as we would have liked but my grandfather remembered that it only narrowed a mile or so from the town. We would be able to land there and our captains turn the ships around while we raided. As far as he was aware none had ever raided there before. Caen was easier to approach from the sea.

Five warriors arrived in a knarr at Þorri. Our patrols saw the knarr being chased by two of my brother's drekar. We had not seen them since the battle but we recognised them immediately.

Lord of Rouen

The five warriors looked half-drowned as they were helped from the knarr. None wore mail yet all had the marks of the warrior about them. They dropped to their knees.

"Lord I am pleased that we have found you. We came from Eoforwic seeking to serve you. A wind took us to Bárekr's Haven. We might have been taken by the Prince of Ćiriċeburh had not an old Viking warned us that you lived north of the Issicauna. We fled and were pursued."

"You wish to serve me?"

They nodded, eagerly. "Aye lord, we have swords, helmets and shields. We have travelled from the land of ice and snow to join you. Haraldr Finehair took our land."

"Then you are welcome." I turned to Bergil. "Have them put in Gandálfr's hall. He has room."

The leader looked disappointed, "We would serve you, lord."

"And you shall but my hall is full."

My grandfather and Sven joined me as we discussed the event. "There may well be old warriors who remember your father, Ragnvald Hrolfsson, fondly. I hope that they did not pay for their kindness with their death!"

That set me to thinking and I sent for my three Rus. They lived in the warrior hall of Sámr Oakheart and Ragnar the Resolute. As we waited for them my grandfather said, "I wonder at their lack of mail. Those five were lean and hard warriors. I wonder why they did not come here first. All men know that Djupr is where the Vikings who fight the Bretons live."

I shrugged, the thought had crossed my mind, "Perhaps they thought I had gone to the Land of the Horse. I will ask them when I speak with them again. We need warriors with their experience!"

As if to prove the point the three young Rus appeared. They were almost emaciated in comparison with the five men who had just left us. Habor said, "Yes lord, is there something we can do for you?"

I nodded, "In the land of … the Prince, do all support him?"

They looked at each other and then Habor shook his head. "He has spies in all of the stad. Men are often taken in the night and never seen again. He has men who are like oathsworn but they do not spend all of their time at Ċiriċeburh. In fact, they were rarely there for that is his stronghold. All are loyal to him."

"And yet you were based there."

"No lord, we were at Angia, the island off the coast. We were sent for. The Prince needed us for this raid. The four ships he sent are amongst the biggest he has. He has three more which have forty oars each but they rarely leave his stronghold."

"Thank you, Habor."

They had smiles on their faces, "We will visit your smith. We have enough coin to buy a better sword. Each. All of us are embarrassed at our poor blades." I liked the three young warriors. They would make a good addition to the clan.

After they had gone Sven said, "We should have asked them the first time about the size of the ships. Three drekar that size would pose a problem."

"I am not sure that the three would have known too much more. They thought he only had seven. There may be many more. He may have many smaller drekar dotted about the coast. We did not see the one which was based at the Haugr nor the ones at Bárekr's Haven. We are still not in a position to attack him."

"We are much better prepared now, lord."

"Come Sven, we will walk our defences." We left my hall and crossed the bridge which led to the path. The path divided so that one side went down to the quay and the other to the watchtower. We had built an identical watchtower to the one we had used in the fjord. It could be used for defence but its main purpose was as a warning. It rose ten paces above the walls of the stronghold and was closer to the sea. It gave warning for any ships. I saw now, as we walked along the headland my two drekar as they tacked back and forth closer to the horizon. I did not bother climbing the tower. We turned and walked back towards the river.

Olaf's stronghold on the other side of the river was basic. There was a warrior hall for the crews and families of the knarr and a wall with a fighting platform. Protected by a sheer cliff on one side and a river on the other it meant that we could protect drekar and knarr on both sides of the river. We descended to the river. The drekar were all tied up facing the sea. If danger came then we could send them to sea in an instant. On the sides of the valley, towards the top, lay our halls. Each one had a ditch and a palisade. I saw the three Rus as they headed back to their own hall. It was the last one in the line. Between us lay Gandálfr's hall.

"Come we will go and speak further with our five new warriors." I spied the five warriors. They were standing on the walkway above the gatehouse. They looked like they were assessing our defences and the walls. It showed that they were good warriors. They were looking to defend their home. Seeing us approach they waved and disappeared.

Sven chuckled, "I dare say they will be coming to ask us if they can join our crew."

The three Rus joined us. They were talking animatedly. I smiled at them, "Did you see the smith?"

Habor nodded, "Aye lord and he gave us a good price. He will not rob us."

Thiok pointed to the five new men who had just emerged from their hall. "Lord, I know those men." Had he not pointed at them then events may have turned out differently but he did point and the five men saw him do so.

A chill went down my spine, "Where from?"

"They served the Prince. We often saw them at Ċiriċeburh. Have they joined us too?"

These three were simple and innocent. They were not lying. Sven and I looked at the five of them. These were my brother's hired killers. Now I understood why they had wanted to stay in my hall.

"The three of you stay behind us. If there is trouble then run for the men from my hall. Those five are our enemies." We began to move up the slope to the hall.

It was too late. The five knew that the game was up. They turned and they ran. Sven began to hurry after them. "Sven, stop!"

"But they are getting away!"

"And we have horses. Habor, go to your hall and tell the guards to watch where these five go."

We turned and ran to my hall. The men on the gate saw us run and sounded the horn. By the time we reached it men were armed and ready. "Stephen of Andecavis, I need a horse and your men."

He cocked his head to one side and shook it, "I am not certain we have one big enough."

"I care not about the figure I cut. I need to move as fast as you. There are five killers loose and I would have them dead."

"Aye lord."

The horse they brought me was the biggest we had but my feet still almost trailed along the ground. Even with the stiraps as long as they would go I had to ride with bent legs. I mounted. I had not been on a horse since I had sunk to the bottom of the sea! We headed inland.

As we passed the last hall a sentry shouted, "They headed down into the valley lord."

We had eighteen men. Stephen of Andecavis and his men were experienced warriors. The others were young men. It would be me and grandfather's four horsemen who would have to deal with the five killers and I was under no illusions, they would be hard men to kill. As we rode, following the clear trail on the muddy hillside I thought back to the meeting. It was obvious now that they did not look like men fallen on hard times. I had almost been taken in. Had it not been for the three Rus boys I had spared then we might have had wolves loose in the sheepfold.

"Lord, they do not know the land. This path leads to the stream. They cannot turn off it easily."

I nodded. I had recognised the path. It was well worn for it led to good areas for hunting. They had not had the opportunity to scout out their escape route. I suspect that had been what they had been doing on the walls of the hall. I caught a glimpse of movement ahead. It was human and not animal. My horse was struggling with my weight and I feared that I might end up lagging behind. Some of my younger warriors were trying to impress me. They were galloping alongside Stephen of Andecavis. He snapped, "Stay in position!"

We had been riding for an hour. I knew that the warriors we were chasing were in good condition but the ground was yielding after winter rains and would sap energy. I was just five men behind Stephen of Andecavis when the killers turned to try to hurt us. My four experienced horsemen were too wily to be caught by such a simple ambush. They jerked their reins and moved their horses left and right when they saw the swords. Leif Leifsson was too eager. The warrior stepped out and hacked through his leg and into his horse. The animal screamed as it tumbled away down the slope. Leif's death saved the others for they reined in. I did not. Drawing my sword over my back I rode directly at Leif's killer. He took a two-handed stance. He expected me to ride at his right. I did the opposite. I jerked my horse's reins to the side and he struck fresh air. I brought my sword over the top of my head to my left side and split his skull.

Stephen of Andecavis shouted, "Stop them getting away but do not close with them. This is man's work."

I slipped my feet out of my stiraps and placed them on the earth again. The four warriors formed a small circle. If they could then they would kill us and take our horses. Young Fámr could not resist the chance for glory. Faster than any of the older warriors he hurled himself at the four of them. Even before we could shout a warning or command him to cease he had run in and swung his sword to deliver a mighty hit on one of the enemy shields. The shield shivered but held. Fámr was slain by a backhand hack at his middle. He lay writhing. This had to stop. I had lost two young warriors needlessly. The four before us were simply not worth it. I slipped my other sword from my scabbard and I approached Fámr's killer. I swung my short sword at his sword side. He was expecting the blow and his sword came easily to protect it. What he had not realised was that in my right hand I held my Long Sword. I brought that all the way over at the same time as my short sword swung. He was not expecting two blows at once. His shield shook and, while he managed to hold, he was in no position to gut me. I stepped forward as he reeled back and I punched my short sword at his face. It was a blow I often used with my shield. It was an easy practised move. Still reeling he was using his right hand for balance and he tried to move his shield across. He was too slow and my pommel tore into his eye. He fell backwards. I raised my Long Sword and pinned him to the ground.

I heard a cry of, "No!"

I turned and saw Michel of Liger fall as the last warrior stabbed him. Stephen of Andecavis was just finishing off his opponent. I changed my short sword to my right hand and threw it. The blade arced end over end and embedded itself in the back of Michel's killer. The last of my brother's secret murderers had been killed but I had lost three men and one was irreplaceable.

"Take their heads and place them on spears here. Let the Bretons know their fate! It has cost us three good men but we will not fall for this trick again! Fetch their war gear."

Stephen and I rode together. He looked at the other two men who wore the faded blue cloaks. "There are just three of us now, lord and soon we three will succumb. We are no longer young men. It will be the end of an era. Under Alain, we built something fine. Your brother destroyed that."

"No Stephen. He only destroys it if we allow him to. This was my fault. I should have left you to guard my grandfather. I was not thinking. From now on you have two tasks and two tasks only. You guard my grandfather and you make certain that young warriors become horse warriors. You remind them of Leif and Fámr. I would not have others follow their fate. The era will not end because you will teach them all that you know. Generations from now men from this clan will talk of the first horsemen. You are my grandfather's creation and the young men you train will be his legacy."

Men were awaiting us as we approached the halls. They saw the three bodies draped over the horses and knew we had lost men. Sven approached. I saw the three Rus boys behind him with Bergil and Sámr. "Well, lord?"

"They are dead but it cost us dear. They were sworn killers. We must be on our guard." I pointed to the three Rus boys. "But for those three it could have been worse." I pointed to the laden horse. "You three have earned the war gear from the dead killers. Go and take their armour, helmets, shields and swords. Your vigilance deserves them." They eagerly ran to the horses.

Lord of Rouen

As we continued towards my hall Bergil said, "Will there be other such killers?"

I nodded, "There could be but it will take some time for him to learn that his first attempt has failed. His men will fail to return and then his Breton masters will tell him of the five heads found on their borders. All that we have done is to buy time. We now prepare for an attack on Bayeux. This year we begin to hurt the Bretons. I would lay waste to the lands by the coast and then we will begin, this time next year, our attack on their river. When I am Lord of Rouen then will be the time to take on my brother and his Breton masters."

Lord of Rouen

Chapter 7

The young horse warriors who had survived were chastened by the loss of the three warriors. Michel had been seen as a warrior at the height of his powers. There was a change that day and they dedicated themselves to becoming as good as Michel had been. When we went to war, they would watch my grandfather and my hall. To augment my horsemen, we found others to watch our walls in our absence. We also had older men who had been warriors. Many had fought with me in Hibernia but now were getting too old to go to war. The knarr crews would also leave some of their men to watch my walls so that we were able to take eight drekar for our raid on Bayeux.

In recent years the town had grown in importance. The Breton Count, Robert was known to favour the town. There was an abbey and he kept a hall there. Perhaps he thought that we might fear to challenge him there. It had never been raided before. When we had lived in the Haugr it had been too far to reach by land and the river had not been as deep in those days. Our knarr captains had told us that the channel was wider. Harold remembered the old river and had seen the difference. "Lord, I am certain we could get a drekar further up the river unseen."

It would be a risk but sometimes a warrior has to be bold and to do something which was unexpected. To me, this seemed such a moment. My brother would only wait a short time for his men to succeed and then he would come to finish the task. He knew that he could not afford for me to grow in power.

We left at Gói. It was both strange and, at the same time, comforting to see my grandfather flanked by Gefn and Bergljót waving to us from the gate of my stronghold as we sailed into the early afternoon sun. My new family and my old family were a symbol of our clan. The horseman and the people of the Norse. My drekar led. Olaf Two Teeth could make good decisions. Harold Haraldsson also steered the second drekar. He had the most experience of these waters and that was what we would need. We had a hundred miles to go. We rowed for the first miles for the winds were not perfect. It also allowed us to make our crews as one. They chanted as they rowed.

Behind us Harold had them sing my grandfather's song. It seemed right and so I began the chant too. It did not take them long to learn it and soon all eight drekar chanted his song. I wondered if the dead beneath the waves could hear it too.

The horseman came through darkest night
He rode towards the dawning light
With fiery steed and thrusting spear
Hrolf the Horseman brought great fear

Slaughtering all he breached their line
Of warriors slain there were nine
Hrolf the Horseman with gleaming blade
Hrolf the Horseman all enemies slayed

With mighty axe Black Teeth stood
Angry and filled with hot blood
Hrolf the Horseman with gleaming blade
Hrolf the Horseman all enemies slayed
Ice cold Hrolf with Heart of Ice
Swung his arm and made it slice
Hrolf the Horseman with gleaming blade
Hrolf the Horseman all enemies slayed

In two strokes the Jarl was felled
Hrolf's sword nobly held
Hrolf the Horseman with gleaming blade
Hrolf the Horseman all enemies slayed

By the time we turned and were able to take in the oars, it was as though the whole fleet was as one. I smiled as I heard young warriors asking who was this Hrolf the Horseman. My grandfather was grey but he was still the same warrior. I was immensely proud of what he had created.

The sun set behind us and the sea and land blended into one. We had two of **'Kara's'** ship's boys with us. They knew the waters well. They whistled when they saw the gap and Olaf took in a reef or two. It would not do to breach in this narrow river. It soon became clear that the wind would be a hindrance as the river twisted and turned. Olaf ordered the sail furled and the oars run out. It made it easier for him to see and we moved more efficiently. The ship's boys kept a good watch and they signalled when the river banks were getting too close to the oars. We stopped. We were the largest drekar and if we could turn then so could the rest. Using the oars Olaf turned us to face the sea. The ship's boys leapt ashore and tethered us.

We knew that our target lay to the south and east of us. We landed on the eastern bank and I led my eight drekar crews towards the distant town. We had no measurement of distance. The fact that we walked over fields rather than paths or trails told me that this was not a thoroughfare. Arne Pétrsson and Bjorn Eriksson scouted just four hundred paces ahead of us. I had deliberately not sent scouts in daylight. The last thing I wanted was for the Bretons to be warned of our interest. We had shown no interest in the place before and I wanted their vigilance to be relaxed. We would overcome whatever defences they had.

We had walked, perhaps two thousand paces when Arne returned. "We have spied the town, lord. It is not far ahead."

I nodded and we continued forward. I smelled the town before I saw it. It was the smell of wood smoke mixed with dung and sweat. I knew that my home smelled the same but each clan, every tribe has a slightly different smell. I had noticed that when I had first gone to the land of the Norse. Over time it became familiar. Another thousand paces took us to the walls of Bayeux. Just five hundred paces from us they had a wooden palisade and they had a gatehouse. It was still dark and so I sent Arne Pétrsson and Bjorn

Eriksson around the town to find the other gates. It allowed us the time to don helmets and swing shields around to our front. We did so in total silence. I had already formulated a plan with my leaders. Had they had a stone wall then we would have concentrated upon the gates. A wooden wall meant that a drekar crew would attack each gate while the rest would assault the walls around their whole perimeter. I would trust the skills of my men. Each crew would fight for their oar brother and their leader.

It did not take long for my scouts to return. They spoke quietly, "There are two gates lord, one is there." Arne pointed at the one I could see, "the other is on the opposite side."

"Sámr Oakheart, take your men with Arne. The rest of you take a section of the wall. May the Allfather be with you!"

That was as complicated as it got. I led my men to the gate I could see. I did not hurry for Sámr needed time for his men to get in position. Sven and Bergil flanked me. In many ways, I had the easiest task. I was tall enough for Bergil to be able to stand upon my shoulders and gain entry into the gate. I was a human ladder. I saw that they had a ditch. There was a bridge across it. As we neared the walls I saw two of the town watch leaning over the palisade. I waved forward my four men who had brought bows. Their arrows hit the men. One fell in the ditch but the other landed heavily in the town. I was not sure if any had heard the sound but it added urgency to our actions. I ran to the gate and braced my back against it. I held my hands out and Bergil stepped onto them and then my shoulders. Even as he sprang up Sven followed. I heard a cry from inside. They had either seen the body or Bergil. It was important not to panic. Ragnar followed Sven and I turned and picked up my shield. All along the wall men were using shields to boost my men up and over the palisade.

The gate swung open. My three men stood there and I saw that Bergil had a bloody blade. I turned to the warrior behind me. "Cnut Leifsson stay here with four men and stop any leaving." Although we did not need slaves I wanted no word of our attack to reach other Bretons close by.

It was a well laid out town. The streets were straight. First, we had to secure the hall. If they could defend the hall then we would be delayed and we could not afford that. The well-laid lines helped us for they led us to the centre, the square and there lay the church, the abbey and the hall. The Breton lord had not done as I would have done. He had not locked and barred his door. He and his men had emerged to see what danger there was. I slung my shield around my back and held my Long Sword in two hands. I charged towards them. They had no shield wall nor did they appear to know what they faced. I brought my sword down and hacked through the shoulder of a surprised Breton who suddenly saw the giant towering over him.

I heard the Breton lord belatedly shout, "Shield wall!"

It was too late a cry. As men, ill-prepared and badly trained tried to lock shields our swords hacked and chopped into them. My sword shattered a Breton shield. The man's arm was broken. I used my pommel to smash into his face and knock him unconscious. The Breton lord swung his sword in my direction. I blocked it and I saw his sword bend a little with the force of my hit. As he reeled I headbutted him. My height meant that my helmet hit the top of his. He staggered back and I swung my sword sideways. His head flew from his shoulders.

The death of their lord sucked the last breath of defiance from the Breton's bodies. More than half their number lay dead. They fought back but it was to no effect. More of my men had joined my crew and soon the last warriors lay dead.

I pointed to the church, "Search the church! Sven, take men to the abbey. Bergil, bring ten men with me and we will search the hall."

I sheathed my Long Sword and drew my short one. If there was danger in the hall then a short weapon would be of more use. I could hear screams and shouts from within. We opened the door. The inside was bathed with light. A brave servant stood behind the door brandishing a sword. He was a greybeard. There would be no honour in his death. I knocked the sword from his hand and said, "You have done your duty old one. Live."

He was still defiant, "Count Robert will have your head if you harm one hair of his daughter!"

The Count's daughter was here? That was a prize. At the very least she could be ransomed! "Where is she?" He realised he had said too much and he stood in silence. "Ulf, watch the door and guard this man. The rest of you we seek prisoners. Harm no one. If this old man is the measure then there is little danger within this hall."

It was a single-story building. The Count, however, had built well. He had had chambers built to afford privacy. I opened the first door and there were two young girls. They screamed and clutched at each other. "Are you the daughters of the Count?" They looked terrified. "Oleg guard the girls. Put them with the old man in the hall." The next two chambers were empty. Bergil found two older men in the next chambers on the right. From their age and the clothes, they had hurriedly donned they were officials. They too would bring ransom.

I opened the next door and saw a young woman with a younger girl behind her. The young woman held a dagger. She said, defiantly, "I am not afraid to use this, Viking. You will have no pleasure from me."

The younger girl, obviously a servant said, "Do not anger the monster, Lady Poppa, he may eat you!"

I smiled. I had found the daughter of the Count. Her words, her posture her actions all identified her. The dagger she held was ornamental it could not hurt me. I held out my hand for her to give it to me.

In answer, she lunged at my face. She would have needed a step ladder to reach it. I grabbed her wrist and took her dagger. "This girl has courage. Bergil, secure these two but do them no harm. We have the daughter of the Count! No matter what we find in the abbey or the church nothing is more valuable than the Lady Poppa!"

I went back outside to see, as dawn broke, what we had gained. Already my men were piling chests and sacks in the main square. Sámr Oakheart shouted, "We have found some horses and some carts. I am having them brought. This was even easier than Caen."

I nodded for I was distracted. I would have expected a strong warrior presence. This was the Count's daughter. The lack of guards was worrying. It implied she was of little value. That would remain to be seen. I had no time to worry about such details. I was not sure if we had left the drekar at high tide or low tide. The difference might be crucial. Olaf Two Teeth would know and the sooner we returned to him the better.

The prisoners, other than Poppa and her servant, were petrified. That was in direct contrast to Poppa who still looked defiant. By the sixth hour of the day, we were ready. "Sven, I want you and my crew as rear guard. Bergil and I will guard our hostage. She might choose to run."

He laughed, "With your long legs lord, you could easily catch her."

With the scouts out Bergil and I marched at the head of the heavily laden column. It was the richest prize we had taken. I knew it would invite retribution. The last raid had left them in doubt as to our position. Now they knew where we were. They would come. With the Count's daughter in my hands, I had guaranteed a confrontation.

The lady and her servant obviously thought we were barbarians who did not understand their words. I did. I kept a deadpan expression as they plotted. "When we get the chance, I want you to run. These giants will not be as quick as us."

"Run lady?"

"You know how to run, Sprota. Pull up your skirts and open your legs. Believe me, if we stay with these monsters we will have no life at all. Better we die trying to escape than submit to their advances."

I said, quietly to Bergil, "Keep a straight face but these two are planning to run. You watch the servant and I will deal with the lady."

"We could hobble them, lord."

"No, let us have some amusement with them. If they try to escape and fail it may well deter them from future efforts."

My captains had raised their masts and the sails lay furled, ready to be lowered. It was when she spied the masts that the Lady Poppa shouted, "Now, Sprota!" She plunged down a steep slope, wriggling between two wild crab apple trees. She was fast and almost took me by surprise.

Bergil easily grasped Sprota who squealed and then shouted, "Run my lady! Run!"

I was wearing mail and I just slid down the slope. I travelled faster for I was heavier. The mail protected my back. We reached the bottom together. She rose first and tried to flee. I grabbed her ankle. She found a broken branch and began to beat me with it. My men howled and cheered. This was better sport than they had thought! I had had enough and I picked her up and slung her over my shoulder. I tore the branch from her hand and hurled it away. She kicked and struggled as I clambered up the bank. I said, in Breton, "I have been kind thus far but any more nonsense and I will spank you! Be still!"

Amazingly my use of her language worked and she burst into tears. Ragnar the Resolute laughed, "Lord, you are a monster. You have reduced the maiden to tears!"

"Her value will go down!"

"You should have kept your helmet on!"

Ignoring the comments, I kept her over my shoulder and strode towards our ships. Her sobs subsided. "You speak our language!"

"I was born less than twenty leagues from here. Just because I am a Viking does not make me a barbarian. I can speak Frank and Saxon. I can even read a little. Do not judge, Lady Poppa, just with your eyes!"

When I reached the drekar I handed her to the ship's boys who hauled her aboard. "Watch her, she is slippery!"

When Bergil put Sprota next to her I heard the servant say, "You are brave, my lady, but foolish! There were too many of them."

"When my father hears then he will come and this barbarian will bleed!" She said it loud enough for me to hear. She had spirit.

I turned to Olaf, "When does the tide turn?"

"By the time you have loaded us, we will be ready to go. The wind will be with us and we will quickly make the sea. It was a good raid?"

"Judge for yourself from the carts and wagons which follow. This is the daughter of the Count of Bayeux and Rennes. There may be profit or more in her."

I took off my shield and my helmet. I undid my scabbards and laid them by my chest at the steering board. "Erik, help me take off my mail!"

"Aye lord."

I felt much better once the mail was removed. I placed it in my chest. Sprota giggled and said, "What if he takes off more clothes, my lady? What then?"

She shook her head, "Sprota, you are an empty-headed wine vessel; he can speak our language. He knows what you are saying."

She put her hand to her mouth, "Oh!" She began to blush.

We were loaded first. *'Fafnir'* was the last ship in the line. I shouted, "Ragnar the Resolute, we will wait for you at the mouth of the river!" He waved his acknowledgement and I said, "Let us fly Olaf Two Teeth!"

The wind soon bit as the sail was lowered. Slowly, at first, we built up speed. We were lower in the water but not dangerously so. The deck was littered with chests and sacks. The Count of Bayeux liked to live well. We found much wheat, spices and even some of the fortified wine that made in Lusitania. Much of what we had taken I had yet to see but the raid had gone well.

I turned to Poppa. "The Count is your father then?"

I saw her debating with herself. If she answered would that be seen as giving in? Could she use it to her advantage? Eventually, she nodded but she did not look me in the eye. Was she hiding something?

"How old are you?" She dressed as though she was a woman but when I had grabbed her body she felt like a girl.

"I have seen fourteen summers." I saw Sprota look at her. "Well, almost. I have definitely seen thirteen."

Perhaps that was why she had not been guarded. There had been no need. I changed my questions. I did not need to have a direct answer. "You were not guarded well. Does your father not value you?" She coloured again. "Ah, perhaps you have a temper and you are willful. You were not guarded well as a punishment."

She almost spat her words at me, "That is not true. He loves me as much as the daughters of his Countess!"

I had my answer. She was not a legitimate daughter, "Of course and your mother will miss you."

"She will. She will make certain that the Count pays whatever ransom you ask."

"And what should that be?" I was enjoying this game.

"I know not." She hesitated, "What is the rate for the daughter of a Count?"

"Well, that depends. The eldest daughter, she is likely to be given a good dowry. She would need her weight in gold. But you are not the eldest nor the daughter of the Countess. Perhaps he might not want you returned."

I saw fear on her face, "He will! He may even bring his Vikings to take me from you! I should like to see that!"

I tired of the game, "So should I for the leader of those Vikings is my brother and the next time I see him I shall kill him." I looked astern, "You had better rest. We have many hours of sailing ahead of us." I handed her my cloak, "Cover yourself with this. The sea can be cold, even at this time of year and I would not wish you damaged by the elements."

I walked down the centre of the drekar to speak to my men. From what the girl had said my brother was little more than the King's guard dog. That did not seem like my brother. I needed to know more about the land of the Bretons. Perhaps I would hang on to the girl for a little longer to see what else I might discover. It took some time for all the ships to navigate the river. Olaf and Harald were the best two captains. Others did not find it so easy. We loosed the sails and sailed north in a v-shaped formation. We flew. Once we turned around the headland we would have to row but the first part was almost a dream. I saw that Sprota had curled up under the cloak with the Lady Poppa. The Breton stared at me; she would not sleep. She did, however, use the cloak to keep herself warm.

Lord of Rouen

Perhaps it was nostalgia or maybe the thought that my brother had almost destroyed the clan that made me choose the chant I did for the last thirty or so miles.

Fótr and Folki were brothers free
Seeking fortune they sailed the sea
The Norns brought them to the land of the horse
They sailed they thought a charmed course.
Clan of the Horseman
Warriors strong
Clan of the Horseman
Our reach is long
Clan of the Horseman
Fight as one
Clan of the Horseman
Death will come
Lying Frank and treacherous Dane
Proved to be Fótr's bane
They fought as men all shield brothers
None fled, none left the others
Clan of the Horseman
Warriors strong
Clan of the Horseman
Our reach is long
Clan of the Horseman
Fight as one
Clan of the Horseman
Death will come
And now Folki is the last of his line
Revenge is sweet like aged wine
The Franks have paid a fearful price
Their slain by Heart of Ice
Clan of the Horseman
Warriors strong
Clan of the Horseman
Our reach is long
Clan of the Horseman
Fight as one

Lord of Rouen

Clan of the Horseman
Death will come

The men enjoyed the song. Olaf Two Teeth asked, "Will we ever find the rest of this Clan of the Horse, lord?"

"There will be many who will still be alive. I hope that they hear of me and that that they know I will come. It pains me that I can do nothing yet to hurt my brother. Our drekar are enough to raid. We can hit and run but when we face the Bretons and my brother then we shall need a much bigger army. This raid may spread the word. Another few drekar and their crew will make our task easier."

We reached our home in the middle of the night. Men were watching for us so that, as we tied up, our families came down to greet us. Gefn and Bergljót looked relieved as Bergil and I stepped ashore. Grandfather just said, "It went well?"

"It went better than well, Hrolf the Horseman. It is hard to see how we could have bettered it. We have two captives." I waved an arm as Poppa and Sprota stepped ashore.

Gefn's hand went to her mouth, "They are children! You have not harmed them, have you? They must be terrified!"

I saw my grandfather hide a smile. I shook my head, "Of course not. One is Lady Poppa, the daughter of the Count and the other is her servant. They do not speak our words."

Grandfather said as Gefn put her arms around Poppa, "I will teach you their words, Gefn." Gefn glared at me as though I had somehow defiled the girl on the way back.

Bergil said, "Our mothers did not see much of the slaves we took in the land of snow and ice. My uncle sold them before we reached home. Do not take her harshness to heart."

"But they were not harmed!"

He laughed, "You can never win where women are concerned."

The treasure took until dawn to be carried up the hill. Each hall received its fair share of the food and animals. Each ship shared in the weapons and mail. All that I retained, to be sold, were the items from the church and the abbey. We would have to work out where they might make the most profit. The coins we had collected were divided equally between all of the crews. Even the ships' boys were rich after the raid on Bayeux. Once the last of the chests had been shared I felt much better. Other crews would hear of our success and of the clan's generosity. It would encourage more to join us.

Chapter 8

Of our captives, there was no sign. I guessed Gefn and Bergljót had taken them somewhere. My grandfather awaited me and my crew at the table. He had a barrel of ale upon it. "Come Rollo, Göngu-Hrólfr Rognvaldson, you must celebrate for none has ever achieved what you have achieved. King Salomon has to have been hurt by your two attacks. The King of the Franks gave him those towns to protect his people from Vikings and you have taken them both with eight drekar. They will sing songs of this."

I nodded and took the proffered horn. The ale tasted good. I sat between him and Sven Blue Cheek. Sven said, "When first I saw him I thought him young but I saw in him something I had never seen before. He is a leader. There is nothing we cannot do together!"

I had my horn filled and then pointed to the women's quarters, "But what do we do about the Lady Poppa?"

Sven said, "Nothing."

"Nothing?"

"Let the Bretons come to demand her return. That way we hold the reins. We took great chests of treasure. We do not need the coin."

Grandfather nodded and supped his ale, "Sven is right. Besides we need to send the religious items for sale. Now that the Danes hold Eoforwic that is a good market. The Danes, so Harald tells me, have decided to allow the churches to continue to function. They tax them. They do the same with the Saxons. They tax them in return for peace. They call it Danegeld. They have realised that instead of destroying the churches of the White Christ they can make gold from them. It is easier than raiding and more profitable.

They do not have to leave port. Send our knarr, escorted by a drekar to Eoforwic. Their churches will buy that which we took."

It seemed like a good idea and I agreed. Sven shook his head and refilled his horn, "I like not this taxing of men rather than fighting them. The Danes might have an easy life but I would want my warriors lean and hungry. It does no good to allow a warrior to become fat and enjoy comfort. What if the Saxons rise?"

My grandfather shook his head, "When the Jarl Dragonheart was alive and fought the Saxons he did so with just four drekar and yet he defeated them every time. Until they get a strong leader who knows how to fight they will be no threat. Egbert was the best that they had. The one they have now is weak."

For once I drank too much. My grandfather and Sven carried me to bed. I must have had some bad fish too for I found myself vomiting for most of the night. In the small hours before dawn, I went down to the beach and stripped off. I dived into the sea. Most men feared the sea. I had been to the bottom and I had returned alive. To me, it was a friend. My brother was the enemy who had tried to kill me. I dived to the bottom and chased a surprised lobster. When I broke surface, I was a hundred paces from the shore. I turned and kicked. I had long legs and arms. I moved through the sea like a drekar. I swam up and down the shore. By the time dawn broke, I felt better. I stood and walked from the water. The tide had gone out and my clothes were further from the sea than they had been. I saw the men in the watchtower. They were waving at me. I waved back. As I looked up at the cliff path I saw Gefn and Bergljót. They were with Bergil and the two captives. I suddenly realised that I was naked. I ran to pick up my clothes. When I looked up they were gone.

As I walked into the hall Sprota giggled and Lady Poppa coloured. Bergil could barely contain his mirth and Gefn just shook her head, "An ill-advised swim, my son."

I tried to muster as much dignity as I could. "And how are our guests?"

"They are guests?"

"Until her father decides how much he would pay for them then yes, we will treat them as guests."

I saw that Poppa was confused by our interchange. I spoke in Breton, "I was just telling my mother that until I hear from your father, you are our guests."

"Guests?" There was scorn in her voice.

"Have you been badly treated? Starved? Kept chained?"

"Well no but …"

"Believe me I know the difference."

My grandfather had been silent. He said, quietly, "My wife was a Frank. Our clan killed her father and warriors. She was enslaved along with many others from her land. She was kept as a slave yet she was treated well. You, my lady, are not a slave. You can wander where you will. There will be men to watch over you but that is for your own safety as much as anything. All we await is word from your father. When he decides he wishes you returned then we will send you back. We are not barbarians."

She still looked confused. I might be a terrifying monster but my grandfather and Gefn were not.

The mail and weapons we collected were most useful but what I missed was Bagsecg my smith from the Haugr. He and his father, who lived in the Land of the Wolf, were gifted workers of iron. I had been tempted to slip ashore and to fetch him and his family to my new home but I knew that his children had all married. I could not bring some and leave others to suffer the wrath of my brother. The smiths we had were good but they did not have the feel for metal which produced the finest armour, helmets and sword. Even so, we were now in a better position. The clan had fought twice and defeated our enemies both times. We had fought a sea battle and we had won. My men now had better weapons and better mail. We continued our daily patrols. My horsemen rode the borders. Often my grandfather would ride with them. Now with only three experienced men, Stephen needed Hrolf the Horseman. It did not stop me worrying.

It was at this time that I sent my smaller drekar to explore the coast around our headland down towards the Issicauna and beyond. The Franks had retreated inland after our earlier raids when my grandfather had been younger. The Bretons had just fortified their new towns which lay inland. Neither the Franks nor the Bretons used the seas well. There were people who remained; they were the poor or the fisherfolk who could not leave their livelihood. It meant we could explore the narrow rivers which fed into the bay. The captains of the small drekar enjoyed it as they were able to raid the small settlements while they did so. Sheep and goats were captured in this way. Our flocks and herds were growing.

Our ships returned at the start of Harpa. They had seen no defences being built and they had raided without hindrance. What was worrying was that the Bretons had made neither an effort to rescue the girls or to open negotiations for them. I put that from my mind as we heard the news which my captains brought. The first news was that there was a new King of Wessex, Alfred. He was, apparently, very pious and had promised to drive the Danes from his land. That seemed unlikely. Guthrum was now seen as King and one of the leaders of the Danes. He had done well for himself.

My brother's position amongst the elite of the Bretons was confirmed. He had helped King Salomon defeat and kill, in battle, Robert the Strong. The Frank had been a serious rival to Charles the Bald. The success had increased further the land of the Bretons. Other sea captains had told Harold Haraldsson that the Count of Bayeux was fond of Poppa but he could not afford to ransom her. The rumour was that the Countess was happy for the young girl to be a prisoner. She did not like the illegitimate daughter of her husband. Politically it suited their family as they could appeal to their neighbours to help them drive the Vikings from their land.

Financially we were never better off than then. We could have afforded to build our walls from stone but I wanted a stronghold closer to the Issicauna. Two drekar returned with my knarr. They were heavily laden for they had their families. They wished a home in the land of the free Vikings. The land of the Saxons was ruled by the Danes and the land of Norway by Haraldr Finehair. The effect of the war in Norway continued to send ripples across the sea. We benefitted. I knew that we could take Caen in the spring and then begin our attack up the Issicauna. I should have been ecstatic but my mind still worried about Lady Poppa.

In the time she had been with us she had changed. Gefn and Bergljót found her a delight. She could sing and she could sew. She was funny. I often found Gefn and Bergljót laughing at something she had done. She appeared to embrace her position as some sort of penance to make her stronger. With no priest in the stronghold, she spent hours each day praying to her god to aid her. One evening I waited until Lady Poppa and her servant had retired for prayers before I revealed the news I had discovered. I told the others that it seemed unlikely that we would receive ransom for the girls.

Gefn became most upset, "The poor girl! How could any father leave his child a prisoner of another man? He does not know we are looking after her."

My grandfather shook his head, "It is a game Frankish lords play. She is not his legal child. He needs to do nothing and yet he will still gain sympathy. This way we look like barbaric monsters. Perhaps we should just send her back."

Gefn shook her head, "No, Hrolf, I would not do that. She would be ruined for life. It seems to me that this Countess would make up stories about what we had done to the daughter of this Count. Her life would be ruined. We know that she is unharmed but the Bretons..." She shook her head. "We have room enough. We keep her here. We will give her a home. It seems to me she has not had one up to now." She looked at me, "And you should speak to her! Not as a prisoner but as a clever young woman. All you speak with are hairy warriors and old women such as us. One day you will need a bride. Practise with Poppa. She is a clever and beautiful young woman. We cannot speak her words. Only you and your grandfather can do that."

I was relieved. I thought I had just brought a problem back with me. I did not know the solution was so simple. Then I realised what Gefn had said. She was right. Poppa lived in a world of foreign tongues. She lived in a world of old women and warriors. My hall had few families. I resolved to do as I had been told. As part of that, I had Petr trim my beard and my moustache before I spoke with her. Both were wild and made me look even more frightening.

We began to plan our next raid. This time it would be at Lisieux. We would raid when they were gathering in their crops and storing them. Our knarr had discovered a river which was navigable up to three miles from the town. Our experience at Bayeux had shown us that we could turn our ships around easily. The town was the closest to us. If we could destroy its defences then when we took Caen we would be the masters of the Orne Valley.

We had just finished speaking of the raid and I was alone adding details to the map we had made when Poppa and Sprota came in. "I am sorry, lord, I thought that all had left." She turned to go.

"No, come and sit with me. I would speak with you."

They came over and sat opposite me. Now that they were there I was unsure how to begin. I began to roll up the map to give me thinking time. Poppa smiled, "And what would you say to us lord, that you would let us go home?"

I shook my head, "No, I cannot offer that for… Your lives are not unpleasant here in my home, are they?"

She shook her head, "Not unpleasant but not the life I would have chosen. Your mother and Bergljót are kind. They cannot speak my language but they try and your grandfather is a gentleman. He reminds me of my mother's uncle."

I smiled, "Good, for we would not wish you unhappy. What can we do to make your stay here happier?"

"You could teach us your language. It seems to me that you Vikings are here to stay. When I am returned to my father I might make myself useful if I could speak with his barbarians."

The last barb was a reminder of the first Poppa but I did not mind for in her eyes it was true. We were barbarians. "Then I will be your teacher." I tucked the rolled map under my arm and rose, "Come, it is a pleasant day. We will walk and I will tell you the words for that which you see around you and we might try a conversation with some of my people."

The area enclosed by the palisade was a hive of activity. The smiths' forges rang as the metal was beaten. Girls and women husked wheat. Women churned butter while others made cheese. As Poppa and Sprota rarely left the hall we were a source of interest. Poppa's fine clothes attracted smiles and I saw that the Breton girl grew in confidence as we walked. The time flew and when the sun began to set we headed indoors. Gefn and Bergljót greeted us at the door to the hall. I had taught the girls the names of my family and how to greet them. Her accent made the words sound strange but the look of joy on Gefn's face, when she used them, was worth it.

"Good afternoon, Gefn, mother of Göngu-Hrólfr Rognvaldson. I have begun to learn your..." She looked at me.

I said, quietly, "Words."

"Words."

Gefn hugged her and said, slowly, "And they are good, Poppa." She then reached up and pulled me down by the beard so that she could kiss me. She said, quietly, "So you do listen! I wondered!"

In the days leading up to the raid, I spent many hours with the two of them. Sprota learned less quickly but both picked up enough words to be able to speak with the servants and slaves. I took them down to the quay where they saw the fish wives gutting and salting fish. We walked along the beach where the children scrambled in the rocks collecting shellfish. All of the children spoke with the two girls and that seemed to help.

By the time I was ready to leave I knew I would miss the walks and the talks. I asked my grandfather to spend the day of the raid continuing my work.

We took just eight drekar. We now had enough to leave a couple of drekar to patrol our river mouth. To our enemies, if they returned, it would appear as though we were still behaving as normal. This would be our last raid. Many of the crops had been harvested. What we took would keep us over the winter. We now had many mouths to feed.

We left in the afternoon. We crossed the Issicauna estuary at dusk. The mouth of the river was like a wasteland. Even those who fished had fled. When we took the river, I would build two strongholds, one on each side of the river. The Haugr had taught us that a strong home deterred attack. It was as we rowed towards the mouth of the river that Sven Blue Cheek said, "Women, lord, we need women." I looked at him in surprise. Sven was almost a greybeard. He laughed and shook his head, "We have far more men than women. There have been few fights but this winter when we do not go to war and men become bored there will be. Besides warriors like Samra, Bergil and Ragnar, they need to father children."

I added his unspoken words, "And Göngu-Hrólfr Rognvaldson needs to sire sons!"

Sven nodded, "I did not say that but others have."

"We have avoided taking women as captives for they might try to flee home."

He shrugged, "The Lady Poppa and the girl have not and even if they do, what of it? So long as our young men have spilt their seed then they have served us."

"That sounds a little harsh Sven but I can see that you may be right. Perhaps we could raid Hibernia too."

"That is a long way to go for women, lord. Wessex is closer and the women less wild."

"We will see what the Allfather lays before us. Tell the men that if there are women they wish to take as wives then I do not object."

As we approached the coast we took down the sail and stepped the mast. Darkness had fallen and we would be invisible. This time we were not the first in the river. *'Wolf's Snout'* had scouted it out and she led. The entrance to the river was wide. It was an illusion for soon it narrowed. It was still wide enough for a drekar even with oars out. I doubt that many other ships could have passed up the river but our ships were cunningly crafted. With a shallow draught, they could sail up rivers which would ground many smaller vessels. Progress would only be barred if the river narrowed too much.

The ship's boy at the stern of *'Wolf's Snout'* waved us to the north shore and we ran in the oars. With my shield on my back and my helmet in my hand, I stepped ashore. Our scouts followed the river valley. This was a well-used trail. As we padded down it I saw that it was a local thoroughfare. We estimated that we had three miles to run. Our scouts had gained in confidence and we had two new ones with them. The four ranged well ahead of us. Leif returned first. My leaders gathered to hear his words.

"Lord, the town is a thousand paces from here. They have wooden walls and they have two gates. They also have men watching the walls."

"One or two at the gates?"

"Five on each gate and another six patrolling the walls."

I turned to Sven. "They are expecting us."

"We should not be surprised but it makes little difference. We still attack in the same way. Last time we were lucky. This will be a better test of our warriors. If we always fight weak foes then that will make us weaker."

I nodded, "Magnús Magnússon take your crew and that of Cnut Sámrsson. Go to the far gate and, when you hear my horn then you attack. Leif, take them so that they are not observed." As the two crews were led off I said to the other captains, "This changes our plans. We will have half of our men use their bows. I will assault the gate. Olaf Strong Arm take half of the men and assault the walls to the east. Ragnar the Resolute take the other half and attack the walls to the west. Sven Blue Cheek, Sámr Oakheart and Bergil, bring your men with me. We will not spread out our attack. When we make the walls, I want all of our men together. If they have men on the walls then they are prepared. Men will sleep with weapons close to hand."

"How did they discover our plans?"

I turned, "Erik Yellow Hair is this really the time to speak of that? The Allfather has set us a problem or perhaps the Norns spun. We deal with it and discover why later."

We moved off silently. I had not asked Leif about the height of the wall but I guessed it would be the same as Bayeux. They had not had enough time to increase the height by much. It made little difference. We were committed. If we turned back then the confidence of the clan would plummet. If more men died than in previous battles it would just delay our next wave of attacks.

Perhaps Sven was right. Maybe we did need Vikings to make more Vikings. This might be a long war.

We found some cover just a hundred paces from the walls. The Bretons had been careless. They had not cleared it far enough back. It allowed us to observe them and, more importantly, it was well within the range of my archers. As they strung their bows and nocked arrows I studied the walls. They were the same height. I tapped the four men who would come with me. They would use a shield to boost one of our jumpers and they would join the ones who climbed Göngu-Hrólfr Rognvaldson, the human ladder. I donned my helmet and said, "Now!"

The arrows flew and we ran. I had a young warrior, Petr, with me. He had the horn. "Keep behind me, Petr!"

Most of the men on the walls died silently but inevitably two cried out and others fell noisily. I heard the alarm given. Fortunately, we reached the gate unscathed and I said, "Petr, now!" He blew the cow horn three times and then three times more. I had my back to the wall and my hands cupped. Bergil had this practised now and he ran at me, trusting that he would plant his foot. As his seal skin boot came into my hands I boosted him high.

Petr said, "Lord, he flies!"

Gámr was less confident but even he was propelled up to the walls. The last man was Ulf and he made the walls easily. I could hear the sound of metal on metal beyond the gate. All along the wall, my men were pouring over. I slipped my shield from my back and drew my sword. Sven and Ragnar flanked me. The door came open. I saw that Arne and Gámr lay dead. My other men faced the town. I saw that the Bretons were ready. My men had slain six sent to repel us but there was a shield wall being formed. It used two buildings to protect its flanks. This would be bloody. Magnús Magnússon and his two crews were the surprise the Bretons might not expect.

"Boar's snout!" It was a good formation for it allowed us to bring two points of attack at the Breton line.

We stepped forward. Sven and I were the two tips of the boar's head. Behind us the men formed up and, as I felt each shield add pressure I stepped forward. By the time we were ready, the Breton line was just thirty paces from us. I banged my shield with my sword. As I did I moved my legs up and down. It helped us to get the rhythm.

Clan of the Horseman
Warriors strong
Clan of the Horseman
Our reach is long
Clan of the Horseman
Fight as one
Clan of the Horseman
Death will come
Clan of the Horseman
Warriors strong
Clan of the Horseman
Our reach is long
Clan of the Horseman
Fight as one
Clan of the Horseman
Death will come

When the noise became a crescendo I raised my sword and shouted, "For the Clan!" We stepped forward as one. I knew that behind me I had sixty warriors. The Breton line was five deep at most. Sven Blue Cheek and I would be subject to the spears of five or six men each but once we broke through their first rank they would feel the full force of a Viking wedge. I was in a better position than Sven. He was shorter. The spears which came for my shield and my head were rammed upwards. Had they had more wit they would have stabbed at my legs but they fought the way they had been taught. I took most of the blows on my shield. Two came for my eyes but I had a good helmet and the spearheads grazed and scraped along the side. I lunged down and my Long Sword stabbed a Breton in the eye for he wore an open helmet. As he slid to the ground the weight of men behind me forced my body into the gap vacated by his falling corpse. I felt his chest crunch beneath the weight of my mail and my body as I stepped on him. I lifted my sword and raised it above my head as more spears stabbed at me. Behind me, I heard the shouts of my men as they tried to get to grips with the Bretons. I brought the sword blindly down. It smashed into the helmet of one man in the third rank and continued down to bite into the shoulder of the man before me. It was a double hit and the pressure from before me evaporated. The force of men behind me propelled me forward and I saw that there was just one line of Bretons left to face me.

My shield was now stuck with four spears. I used the Breton spears against the Bretons. I pulled back my arm and rammed the spear shafts into the faces of the men to my left. I was lucky. One ash shaft entered the eye of a Breton. A spear slid into my right side. I heard it tear the mail and felt the blood. I had been wounded. The look of joy on the Breton's face as his spear came back bloody was replaced by horror as Long Sword split his helmet and head. We had breached their line. I shouted, "Break wedge!" I turned to my left knowing that Sven Blue Cheek, if he still lived would turn to the right. We would have two shield walls.

The Bretons were breaking. It was one thing to face an enemy with your flanks protected but quite another to be surrounded by them. Suddenly the walls of their hall seemed an attractive prospect. It was a mistake. They would have been better to make us bleed and give the rest of their people a chance. As they tried to pass us swords and axes hacked into unprotected backs. I even saw Petr, boy that he was, laying about him with his short sword.

When the numbers dwindled I shouted, "To the citadel!"

We ran towards the centre of the town. We caught up with those men who had been wounded and fled. They died as we passed them. I saw their hall. It had a stone base and men were pouring through its doors. Just then Magnús Magnússon and his men appeared. They had not been seen and they managed to take the gate and to disappear into the hall. There would be no escape for those who sought sanctuary in the hall. I waved Sámr Oakheart and Bergil forward to join them.

"Sven, find the church and secure the treasure."

"Aye, lord!"

I turned to Petr, "You stand by me."

He saw the blood seeping from my mail, "Lord, you are wounded."

"Aye and as soon as we can I will take off my mail and have it seen to. A warrior endures such pain."

Wounded men were brought to where I stood. It was our way. Those with lesser wounds tended those more seriously hurt. I saw that the sun had risen while we had been fighting. There was a thin grey light now. We had the advantage this time of a shorter journey back to our ships and a better-used trail. However, the fact that we had been expected had me concerned. Were Bretons or even Vikings on their way to attack us?

The noise of battle subsided. My men began to drive the girls and young women towards us. Bergil pointed behind him, "Einar the Bold has found carts and a few horses. He and his men are bringing them." He saw my bloody leg where my wound had seeped. "You are wounded."

"I can be hurt, you know. My size does not make me immune from blows. It is a minor inconvenience and it will not slow me down." I turned to Petr, "Sound the horn four times. Then repeat it." Some men would have pursued enemies beyond the walls. This was their command to return. I heard the creak of wagons and the neigh of horses. My men might not be the best of riders yet but they knew how to attach them to wagons. "Einar, when you have done have your men put kindling in the buildings and close to the wall. I would destroy Lisieux."

"Aye lord. And the people?"

"They will soon realise what we intend."

Sven, Sámr, Ragnar and my other leaders arrived with their treasure. "Load the treasure. Send the captives back first and then each wagon as they are loaded. I am loath to linger."

"And our dead?"

"Put them in the hall. Einar the Bold is firing the buildings. It will be a funeral pyre fit for a hero and it will tell the Bretons that Göngu-Hrólfr Rognvaldson is an enemy who bears a grudge." I hoped that my brother would risk a battle with me over the winter. A winter war suited us for we had a good citadel. However, if he waited until summer then I would be stronger and he would be weaker. Either way, I was confident I could now defeat my brother.

The thirty or so girls and young women we took were frightened but the presence of so many fierce-looking warriors ensured that they were compliant. I left when the first flames flickered up the wattle walls of the hall. When the thatch caught the flames leapt higher and black smoke filled the sky.

Sven said, wryly, "They know we are here then!"

"If they can reach us before we are at our ships then it means that this was a trap. However, save the guards on the walls, I have seen little evidence of that. I think they spotted *'Wolf's Snout'* when she scouted. They knew of the fate of Bayeux and Caen. They thought to see our approach and defeat us at their walls. Soon we will be able to use horsemen to scout out our targets. Once Caen is ours we can begin the march to Rouen!"

We reached our ships in the mid-morning. We had to wait for the tide to rise. It allowed us to load everything. This time we were even able to bring back six horses. They would add to the herd we were building. Sven insisted upon stitching my wound while we loaded the drekar. It was a long cut and I had bled. He used vinegar which we had taken from the Bretons to cleanse the wound and then he applied honey before stitching it. With more honey covering the stitches I was bandaged.

As we sailed north I mentioned something which had been bothering me. "We know that we will be fighting Vikings for my brother's men are Norse and Dane. We know that there are other warbands who have sold their swords to other lords like Robert the Strong. We need to know who our enemies are when we fight them."

He looked at me, "You wish us to have a sign?" I nodded, "That is hard. Men will not take kindly to losing the sign on their shield. Many believe that they will bring them luck."

"I do not intend that. Stephen of Andecavis and his men use a blue cloak with a silver sword. I thought to have all of my men paint a long silver sword on their shields. It is my sign. Any who do not wear the sword is an enemy."

He nodded, "I cannot see that they would object to that. I will seek the counsel of those on this ship. It does not do to fight against luck."

Chapter 9

I was not surprised that Gefn was upset by my wound, Bergil could not keep quiet about the hurt, but Lady Poppa appeared distraught. When we resumed our lessons, she took me to task, "Lord you have a people to lead. My father, the Count, he does not lead his men into battle. He has others who do that."

"And that may explain why we defeated them so easily. Do you think that when your father comes for you he will find it easy to take this hall?"

She looked sadly out to sea, "He will not come for me. It has been too long that I have been here. I am now a summer older. Soon I will be a woman. It shows me that I am of no importance. To whom could he marry me? My brother has the chance of a title and he may marry the daughter of a minor lord. As for me? If there is a fat old man whose wife has died and wishes to sire children with some Breton royal blood in their veins then I may marry. But I have been with barbarians. My value has diminished. He is happy that I am here. He can gain sympathy of other leaders and the Pope. This just brings more grief upon you and your people."

"And that makes you unhappy?"

She looked uncomfortable and studied the backs of her hands. "You all look rough, wild and uncouth but you are kind. Even warriors like Sven Blue Cheek who is the most frightening looking man I have ever seen is kind and he is respectful. He treats even empty-headed Sprota like a lady. I do not understand you. Why did you leave your land?"

I waved over a servant and had him pour us some wine, "The fact is that Sven, Gefn, Bergil, they all followed me here but my grandfather was born a slave not far from where we live. Had he

121

not been rescued by the Jarl Dragonheart he might have ended his days as a slave. My grandmother was a Frank so, as you can see, I am from this land. I have returned."

"But this is the land of the Frank."

I sipped my wine. "That is because of the man you call Charlemagne. He conquered the land from the people who lived here first. Some of those came from the land of the Britons. It is why it is called Brittany. Before that there were Romans."

"So it is like a melting pot?"

I nodded, "Where Gefn was born has never been invaded and never conquered. It is a land of snow and ice. I am humbled that she and her people followed me here to help me realise my dream."

"She sees you as the son she lost and the husband who was killed. Those are mighty boots to fill."

I laughed, "The gods made me this size for a reason. Perhaps it was to fill those boots!"

She laughed too. I saw Gefn and Bergljót peer into the hall and smile at our laughter. They left and Poppa and I chatted easily.

We sent the knarr and two drekar to Lundenwic. The Danes now ruled the land from there. I sent Sven Blue Cheek to ask Guthrum if he objected to our raiding the land of Wessex. It would not do to offend the Danish army which had conquered almost all of the island. Guthrum might be king of that island one day. The new mail and weapons had made us even stronger. True we had lost warriors; we had lost more than on the earlier raid but there was a feeling of hope amongst my warriors. We had fought four times and were yet to suffer a defeat. Sven, Stephen of Andecavis and my grandfather spent many hours planning how to remain that successful.

"Ragnvald will come, Rollo. I am surprised he has not done so already. When he does he will know how to take our walls. He will not come ill-prepared."

I nodded, "And I intend to meet him at sea if I can. We have more skill, better ships and better warriors. Even if he outnumbers us we can hurt him. Then, when he lands to attack us, he is defeated already."

"That is a fine trick if you can manage it."

"When we sailed to Lisieux I saw that the old ports which lay at the mouth of the river have been long abandoned. I would fortify one and base a drekar there. We are full here in the river. One more drekar's arrival would be too much. We build a tower and we keep watch. We use fire so that we are warned of their arrival and we meet them at sea. His alternative is to march a long way and he has no more strongholds left to defend. Of course, if he obliges us by waiting until after we have taken Caen then we need not build a tower and a port!"

"If he waited then it would mean something of great moment had occurred."

A few days after our return Bergil, Sámr and Ragnar were among the young warriors who took a Breton woman to their beds. I saw Gefn looking wistfully at me. The three girls chosen by my three closest warriors were actually happy to be picked. My three young lords wore fine mail and had embroidered tunics. None had tattoos and all of them had clean hair and bodies. Lady Poppa had told me that was important. The weddings, if you could call them weddings, were simple affairs. The three of them each spent a week building his small hall. Each of them carried his bride within and the deed was done. They left the communal hall to begin their own families.

Later Lady Poppa asked me about the practice. She was not shocked, merely interested. "My father took my mother to his bed. She was not noble-born. She was... well she had humble beginnings. That is why I have few rights. What of the children from these marriages? Will they be inferiors?"

I shook my head, "I do not think so. The opposite was true of my grandfather, he married high born. My grandmother was a follower of the White Christ. We cannot have marriages such as you have for we have no priests. The women will be protected. The children will be brought up as Vikings." I spread my hands. "That is all that I can say on the matter."

She nodded, seemingly satisfied, "Thank you Göngu-Hrólfr Rognvaldson you have ever been honest with me." She smiled and hesitated, "Lord, do you mind if I do not call you Göngu-Hrólfr

Rognvaldson? Your grandfather calls you Rollo. I like the sound of it."

I smiled, "Call me what you will. Gefn's husband and the clan gave me the long name. I am not that grand!"

For some reason, the ease of using Rollo rather than of Göngu-Hrólfr Rognvaldson changed everything. She smiled when she spoke my name and she laughed more. Our lessons improved and soon she could hold conversations with Gefn.

When our knarr returned it was with momentous news. The Danes had defeated a large Saxon army. The new king, King Alfred had been forced to pay reparations for the Danes to leave Wessex. Sven Blue Cheek told us that the Danes did not mind us raiding Wessex. They would not be breaking their word. They had only agreed to leave Wessex. They did not say that there would be no more raids. More momentous was the news that King Salomon of Brittany had been murdered. It was rumoured that Ragnvald had done the deed. That was a theory I believed but it may have been a story made up by his enemies. People liked to believe that Vikings were treacherous! The result was a civil war in the land of the Bretons. This changed everything. We need not build a haven at the mouth of the Issicauna. We could take Caen and use that as a second stronghold.

We held a council of war. Two more drekar had followed our knarr to join us and we needed a second anchorage. The Norns were spinning and they had decided that Caen would be our second stronghold. I would not leave Djupr undefended. We had our families there. I left three drekar and my grandfather to watch over our families. All the other ships I would take to Caen. Instead of waiting for the following spring, we decided to attack at Haustmánuður. That would give us winter to make it strong. Our attack on the Issicauna would take place in spring. That evening I sat with my grandfather and Sven.

"Do you think that this change in fortune is a good thing? Are the Norns toying with us?"

Grandfather shook his head, "No, Rollo. This is just the result of others making bad decisions." He gave me a gentle smile, "Perhaps the Lady Poppa has softened you and brought you good fortune. Since you began to teach her she is happier as are you. You should take her as a wife."

"She is a girl!"

"Many younger than she are mothers already."

"And many are marred by such marriages. She would not have me."

Sven laughed, "I confess, lord that I know little of the world of women but I know this, the Lady Poppa would take you as her husband without a second glance. I have seen the looks which she gives you. But you may be right. Give her a couple more years. She is a little skinny at the moment!"

"She is not! She is perfect!"

Both of them laughed and I felt foolish. I threw myself into the preparations for the attack. We knew they had few defences. For that reason, I intended to attack during the day. In a perfect world, they would flee. The River Orne was straight and our approach would be seen. It would warn them of our approach. The Breton civil war meant that it was hard to see to whom they could appeal for help. Poppa's father was one of the men vying for power. This was the first battle in which we all fought with the white sword on our shields. Some had one painted on their helmets. For those who had a nasal, it was quite effective. Any Viking without a sword on their shield was an enemy- even if they smiled and feigned friendship.

We left before dawn and all the crews were in high spirits. Once we had Caen we would control both sides of the mouth of the Issicauna. It would be our river. As dawn broke we were at the now deserted village of Ouistreham. The handful of fishermen who made a living there hid as our mighty ships of war sailed down the Orne. We rowed and we chanted. Once again it was the song in honour of my grandfather which sounded across the water as, with sails furled, we beat against the current.

The horseman came through darkest night
He rode towards the dawning light
With fiery steed and thrusting spear
Hrolf the Horseman brought great fear

125

Lord of Rouen

Slaughtering all he breached their line
Of warriors slain there were nine
Hrolf the Horseman with gleaming blade
Hrolf the Horseman all enemies slayed

With mighty axe Black Teeth stood
Angry and filled with hot blood
Hrolf the Horseman with gleaming blade
Hrolf the Horseman all enemies slayed
Ice cold Hrolf with Heart of Ice
Swung his arm and made it slice
Hrolf the Horseman with gleaming blade
Hrolf the Horseman all enemies slayed

In two strokes the Jarl was felled
Hrolf's sword nobly held
Hrolf the Horseman with gleaming blade
Hrolf the Horseman all enemies slayed

We were able to row in pairs of drekar and that made us even
more intimidating. We spied Caen in the distance and saw that it
remained in a state of disrepair. The gates remained torn down and
the palisade had not been repaired. It made no matter for the
Bretons and the Franks fled as our dragon ships approached. The
attack in daylight had had the desired effect. By the time we
reached Caen, it was deserted. The taking of captives from Lisieux
had had an effect. They had left so quickly that their bread was
still baking in the ovens and we ate well.

Defence was the key and I set the men to building good gates. I
sent the strongest of men out to find as much stone as we could.
We used the stone from the church and the abbey. Stones were
taken from the sea. All would make us a citadel. I had seen a good
builder's work. All I did was to copy him. Other men went to hew
down any trees which lay close to the walls. It increased our range
and it gave us wood for the gate and the walls. We worked
tirelessly. We had plenty of men! Twenty warriors stood watch as
the rest of my crews toiled on the walls or the citadel. Olaf and the

126

knarr kept us supplied with food and with news. Men hurt during the construction were replaced and, as Gormánuður approached the base of the square citadel rose above the ground.

Bergil stated the obvious, "Lord we will not have enough stone for many more courses."

I nodded. "That is why when the walls are complete I want you and Sven to take most of the men raiding the land for stone. Find their churches and bring me their stone. At the same time scour the land for food. We can eat well and we can starve the Bretons. I want them to beg me to be their lord and to serve me in return for food."

He nodded, "And when do we raid Wessex for slaves? Many men are envious of the women we took in Lisieux."

"When you have all of the stone then you can raid. I will not leave here until I have a tower which is twice the height of me. When my brother comes he will see that we are not to be shifted."

With the walls and gate of the town completed my men began to ravage the land for miles around. Lisieux was still a burned-out husk but the stone remained and the blackened stone of Lisieux formed part of my tower. My men were amazed as the tower grew. I remembered the priest had used buttresses to give extra strength to the walls and I made sure that we had them. The gate had to be reached up a winding ramp. They would not be able to use a ram. The ground floor I made into a stable. We would live above it. The warmth from the horses would be a gift from the gods. The river formed one boundary to the tower and the winding ramp the other. It was not perfect but it was stronger than the Haugr and that had never fallen.

Once we had all the stone that there was to be had we sent five drekar under Sven's guidance to raid Wessex for slaves and treasure. Thanks to Ragnar Lodbrok's sons Wessex was broken. The days of Egbert were a distant memory.

I continued to work as hard as any of my men. The physical labour seemed to make me even stronger. I even remembered how to make a treadmill crane. We needed the machine once the walls were higher than a ladder. Those who had come from Norway with me thought that I was some sort of magician that I knew how to make such things. The larger stones were placed on the outer and inner walls and the gap between the outer and inner wall filled in with the beach cobbles and smaller stones. I was pleased for the tower had strength.

When our drekar returned it was three weeks after they had left me. "We left the women at Djupr, lord. That is an incentive for the men to finish the work here."

"How many did you find?"

"Almost forty and we took great quantities of swords. The churches had already been raided and there was little there. The Saxons are as weak as I have ever seen them. When the brothers choose they can walk into Wessex and simply take it! We also took many sacks of grain. We brought some here. We can make our own beer and bread. I take it we winter here?"

I nodded, "Those who took wives can go home for the winter solstice. It will make Djupr strong and make my married men less restless. I will stay here with the single men. I would have this as strong as any citadel in the whole of the Empire."

Thanks to their efforts the tower exterior was finished by the start of Mörsugur. Half of my men sailed home. Sven and I did not. We had the living quarters to finish and the fighting platform to complete. I planned for a time when Gefn and my grandfather might live with me. I had chambers constructed so that they had their own small halls within my walls. I took the whole of the floor below the fighting platform. I had a family who would have comfort. The wind was blowing sleet and rain into the town as we completed the last of the walkways upon which we would fight. The four corners of the tower had small wooden towers and archers could rain death upon our foes. We had put slits in the walls so that we could use them for arrows. Even the chambers intended for Gefn and Hrolf the Horsemen would be used for defence. The only aspect which did not please me was the kitchen. It lay outside the tower but within the walls. I did not wish to risk a fire. If we lost the walls we would have to endure cold rations.

The land rarely endured snow but one morning, before the bulk of my men had returned, we had a harsh frost. It made walking easier for the wet winter weather had made the paths we walked into muddy morasses. I took ten of my men for a walk to the west. Later Sven Blue Cheek would say that the Norns directed my feet but the reality was that I was just restless. I needed to walk. If truth were told I missed my daily talks with Lady Poppa and I envied Sámr Oakheart, Bergil and the others.

We went without armour but we were armed with bows. We walked a good five miles before we saw our first Breton or perhaps he was a Frank. He had a farm on a piece of rising ground. He was outside his farm chopping wood. We did not tarry. We spied other deserted buildings and villages. There was room to grow here. The local populace had become terrified by our presence and finally fled. Perhaps the process had begun while I still lived in the land of snow and ice. The land was empty.

Then I heard the neigh of a horse. A horse meant Bretons. We strung bows and nocked arrows. Without a command being given, we went into a defensive formation. I dropped to one knee. We waited. We heard the murmur of voices. It was a large number of people who were approaching. I waved my right hand and Ulf Beornsson crawled away to flank whoever it was on that side. I waved Einar Ketilson to the left. Both were smaller warriors and could crawl and hide. We were not on a Roman road. This was a Frankish trail. It twisted and turned through hedges designed to stop the wind from scouring the crops from the field. It prevented us from having a good view of whoever approached. Patience was needed. I frowned when I heard a child's laugh. What was a family doing heading towards Viking land?

Then I saw the horse and riding it was a grey-haired woman. I recognised her though she had aged, it was Anya, Bagsecg Beornsson's wife. I stood and as I did so I saw that it was a party of Vikings. It was Bagsecg Beornsson, my grandfather's old blacksmith and he was with his family. I counted more than sixty people accompanying him. When he saw me, the old smith ran to me to embrace me, "The rumours are true, Rollo grandson of Hrolf the Horseman lives still! The Allfather has guided us well!"

I looked around and saw familiar faces. I saw his sons, Beorn, Siggi and Bagsecg. They each had a wife and children. There was another horse and upon it sat Bagsecg's daughter Baugheiðr. Her horse was led by Gilles' son Erik. A woman and two children walked behind the horse. Then there were Viking warriors and their families. I recognised some, Sigtrygg Rolfsson and Nagli Naglisson. Others looked familiar.

I grasped Bagsecg's arm, "Come this is too cold a morning to stand around. Ulf and Ketil head down the trail and make certain that no enemies follow. The rest of you guard the rear. These are honoured guests.

"Aye Göngu-Hrólfr Rognvaldson."

As we began to walk Bagsecg looked up at his wife. "It is the name we heard and did not understand."

I nodded, "It is a long story but we have solid walls and a fine fire before which it will make better telling. Grandfather will be pleased to see you."

The smith looked relieved, "He lives still?"

I nodded, "We found each other on the edge of the world. He is well and lives in Djupr, to the north of the Issicauna."

"Much now makes sense. Life was hard when he left. Your brother was cursed. We all knew that. What we did not know was that the curse was on the Haugr. After your mother died and your brother moved to his new home people died. Some were old and others seemed to lose the will to live. I would have said it was the plague or the pestilence but there was no reason to any of it. Then we heard rumours that you were alive. The men who brought the news were killed by your brother's men. He said that any who uttered your name or that of Hrolf the Horseman would be driven from the land and exiled. We knew not if the stories were true."

Erik Gillesson said, "Few visit the Haugr now. Even Bárekr's Haven sees little trade. My brother Rollo, led some men to seek you out. He and his men's bodies were found. They had been ambushed. The Land of the Horse is filled with death and suspicion."

The old smith nodded, "Aye, we might have withered and died ourselves but for this war between the lords of Coutances and Rennes. A ship put in for repairs at the Haugr and the captain, a Dane, spoke of the conquest of the land of the Saxons by the Danes and the arrival of a giant who had taken hold of part of the land of the Bretons. He said the giant had been to the bottom of the sea where he had spoken with the gods and had been sent back to make the land of the Breton, Norse. He said that this Göngu-Hrólfr Rognvaldson was revered by the sons of Ragnar Lodbrok and was a mighty warrior." He smiled, his rheumy eyes filling with moisture, "We decided to leave with what we could carry. We put our trust in the Allfather and you have found us. I am afraid that we bring nothing save mouths to feed. We have but eight horses. Our forges and most of our tools lie in the Haugr for we sneaked out after dark. When your brother discovers we are gone he will seek us."

I pointed to the tower of Caen which could now be seen, "Old friend I care not if you come naked and barefoot. We have a town. There are forges and workshops which the Bretons abandoned and as for my brother seeking us out? Nothing would give me greater pleasure. He killed my father and tried to kill me. There is a blood feud and until he is dead then my father and the men who fell with him will remain unavenged."

His hand went to the hammer of Thor around his neck. "He killed his father? Your grandfather suspected as much. The curse is stronger than we thought!"

"And I am the warrior to break it! We have much to say and there are stories to tell. You have new warriors you will get to know. This is not the Clan of the Horse, my brother destroyed that. This is something new. I know not what to call it but we have warriors from the far north, west and now the south. It is like a sword you might make which blends the iron from many places to forge steel which is stronger than any other."

Chapter 10

That first night they all stayed in my tower with my men. It was crowded but no one objected. Sven was most impressed that they had managed to bring the old and the young seventy miles in the depths of winter. "These are strong folk, lord."

I nodded, "Some were with my grandfather on Raven Wing Island. This will be the third time they have had to begin again. It has filled my heart with joy."

We had sent a small drekar back to Djupr with the news. I knew that my grandfather would wish to come and see his oldest friends. Erik One Hand, Rurik One Ear, they were dead and gone but Bagsecg was a link to the Land of the Wolf. He was my grandfather's smith. He was a symbol of the clan. More than that his daughter had married Gilles who had been a Frank. Erik, his son was the union of two peoples, much as was I. The Norns had been spinning. When my brother had begun his search for power he had begun to be trapped by the Norns' web. When he had killed King Salomon he had ignored the Norns. You ignored the sisters at your peril.

That evening as we ate well and sat before a roaring fire in my new hall and tower I heard of the men who had died at the hands of Ragnvald. It made me both sad and angry. Some jarls had simply taken their men away. Einar Asbjornson and Einar Bear Killer had taken their crews to sail to the Blue Sea and seek their fortune at the court of the Roman Emperor. They had heard he was hiring warriors from the land of snow and ice. I was glad that they had not shared the fate of those who had been killed or sent into futile and suicidal attacks to gain my brother power. There were other, more sinister deaths and disappearances. The brothers

132

Einarsson and their families had been among many who had questioned my brother's version of events. Their hall had mysteriously burned down with all within. Some said the door had been barred. The list of men I had to avenge grew.

"So, Bagsecg, what do you know of this civil war? How can we profit from it?"

"It is a war which your brother can never win for he does not have enough men. He has just over two hundred and fifty warriors but the Breton army numbers more than two thousand. I know that because Count Robert had me make helmets for some of his men. Your brother will throw in his lot with whoever looks like winning and he will seek a title and power."

"Then we have time."

"Time?"

"I intend to make the Issicauna mine. While the war rages the Bretons and the Franks will be distracted. You have brought us more warriors already. I believe I outnumber my brother. I would draw him here and fight him on the ground of my choosing."

"And what of the Haugr?"

I looked into the flames of the fire as they licked around the log. "When my grandfather and the clan settled on Raven Wing Island, they thought it their home forever."

"And then evil sprang up and divided the clan."

I nodded, "And you found the Haugr. There you carved out your home and it was good. You were happy."

"Until the curse."

"Until my brother was born and the land was cursed. I believe that my grandfather was meant to become the lord of this land. It was where he grew up. You made two good homes." I pointed to the stone walls of my tower, "This, I believe, will be stronger than both of those homes! We have the river to protect us. We can raid where we will. I believe that I had to sink beneath the waves and be rescued by the men from the land of snow and ice, the Norse, to be reborn. We are the future and this land will be our home."

"And I think you are right. The long winter journey was worth it!"

Lord of Rouen

Some of the older women and younger children had suffered
during the four-day march to Caen. My men ensured that they
soon recovered. Bagsecg and his sons took over the forges and
were soon hard at work. I noticed that Bagsecg supervised more
than he worked these days. Brigid the alewife was still alive. She
had three daughters. None had married and they found somewhere
in the town to brew their ale. She had pointed to the river, "This is
good water and will make fine ale. You do not want us to burn
down your hall. We will happily brew in the town. It is well laid
out and your walls are strong. "Brigid nodded towards my
warriors. "And your warriors are young lusty men. They will enjoy
my ale and they will keep us safe. Besides I have found a building
they used as a tavern. It will make a change from selling my ale in
the open."

In the end, there were few who chose to stay in the tower. Erik
and his family did so. They took advantage of my stables and I
broached the question of a large horse to Erik. I would ride but I
have yet to see a beast that could bear me.

He laughed, "Lord, you are a large man and there is no getting
away from that but we had begun to breed horses to pull ploughs."
He patted two horses which looked bigger than the others. "If we
can find a couple of larger horses then within a few years we could
have a horse for you."

My grandfather arrived a few days later. He came with Sámr
Oakheart and the others. Some had brought their wives. Harold
brought him and the two became quite emotional as they greeted
those they thought they had lost. I left them to it and spoke with
Sámr. "Events have turned out better than we could have hoped.
We have those who will make Caen live. You do right to bring
your wives. There is room within the walls for fine halls."

"Gefn and Bergljót are keen to join you. They miss you." I
nodded, "And of course the Lady Poppa pines for you." I looked to
see if he was teasing but he was serious. "She does, lord. Everyone
says so."

I did not know what to say. Instead, I told him and the others of
the news our people had brought. "Eventually the civil war will

end but by then I would have the river as far as Rouen in our hands."

Bergil said, "That will make the King of the West Franks nervous. It will also make the Bretons worry about us."

"Be under no illusions. Our raids will bring a battle. It is what I wish. We fight one battle. It will be winner takes all. I am confident in our shields, our swords and our men's hearts. I take comfort from the success of the Danes. The Saxons are finished. They did so by staying in the land and raiding over land. That is what we will do."

Ragnar asked, "Can we win? Will not the Franks and the Bretons join forces against us?"

"They have shown how they view us by hiring Viking swords. You do not hire a sword if you have better men in your own army. They fear us. We use the Danish style. We make them pay to cease raiding." I smiled, "When we have land enough."

"And how much land is enough?"

In answer, I took a piece of sheepskin which had been used to carry sword blanks from the ships. I took a piece of burned wood from the fire. I drew the coast and the river. I put one cross at Djupr, one at Caen and one at Rouen. "When we have this piece of land in our hands that will be enough. The rest will be for my son."

Sven laughed, "And you have not even lain with a woman. That is some time in the future, lord!"

That evening I walked the fighting platform with Sven Blue Cheek and my grandfather. "This is solid. I will fetch Gefn and Bergljót. This is a better home. There are those who are happy to stay at Djupr. I know that Olaf Two Teeth likes the anchorage."

My grandfather nodded, "He would be a good jarl for that land."

I shook my head, "Not a jarl but a Count. That is a title they use here and it is not open to abuse."

Sven nodded, "Aye, your uncle showed that. And who would he answer to?"

"Why me, of course."

"And what is your title, grandson?"

"I have none yet. I am happy to be Göngu-Hrólfr Rognvaldson. That is a mouthful in itself." I suddenly doubted myself. These two men were the ones I trusted most in all of the world. "Will that work, do you think?"

"Olaf will not ask for a title but he will happily take it. I have never had a title. I am a warlord. So long as men do as I say then I am happy. The same is true of you, lord. We all afford you the title lord."

Grandfather nodded sagely, "Sven is right. I was jarl but men followed me before I had the title. This is good. You will have to ask Olaf to move into the hall and the stronghold. I know he likes his home by the river but we need the high ground defending."

"Then I will speak with him next time he comes here. We can begin to plan the raids." It was a fine day and we had a good view of the river valley we would be raiding. "I thought to send drekar down the river at the same time as we sent men across the land. To help us I am going to have Erik scour the land for horses. We do not need to fight on horses but, like the Danes, we can use them to travel greater distances."

Erik had sons and they were true horsemen. They had been trained by their grandfather and Gilles, along with Lord Bertrand and Alain of Auxerre had been the finest of horsemen. They rode out each day. It resulted in a couple of horses each day for the first week but as they travelled further afield so they gathered more. They also brought back, one day, the last remnants of Folki's band. They had been hiding in the forests close to Falaise. Their leader, Fótr Folkisson had kept just twenty warriors and their families alive. They had had to eke out a living after they had been betrayed by my brother. They were in an even worse way than those who had been in the Haugr but they had a burning desire for revenge and we welcomed them with open arms. We put them in my hall for they needed much love and care. When Gefn, Bergljót and Lady Poppa arrived it involved a great deal of effort to accommodate all in my tower.

My adopted mother nodded at the solid walls but was less happy about the chambers I had built. Gefn shook her head, "Typical Göngu-Hrólfr Rognvaldson, you are like all men. You think of war and not of comfort. This is not yet a home. Bergljót and I have our work cut out. Lady Poppa can help us."

As more of Fótr's folk recovered so they moved out and the tower became less crowded. The overcrowded hall pleased me for it meant I bumped into Lady Poppa more frequently than when the hall emptied. I had more opportunities to speak to her. However, she could now speak our language fluently and I had no excuse for my lessons.

One day I found her and Sprota on the fighting platform. She was looking towards Bayeux. "Are you sad, lady, that I took you away from your home? I confess that I do feel guilty about that."

She smiled, "No, lord, for that was not my home. We were sent there so that the Countess was not embarrassed at our presence. No, I was thinking that you have wrought a change on this land yet you have been here such a short time. It is remarkable."

"I am lucky. I have good people."

"That is not luck. They follow you because you are a good leader. Why a whole clan marched seventy miles just to be with you. I cannot see any of my father's people marching seventy paces to be close to him."

"You do not show your father much respect."

"He does not deserve it. I have been with you for almost a year and he has made no effort to ransom me. You and your people have shown me more respect than I ever saw at court."

"You would stay here, freely?"

"Of course!" She laughed, "Sometimes lord you miss that which is before your eyes. It adds to your charm. Come Sprota I promised Gefn I would teach her to read a little more."

I was left to reflect on the words she had said. What did they mean?

I had little time for such indulgences. It would soon be time for our raid. Leaving just one large drekar crew at Djupr we gathered our other drekar and our men at Caen. Stephen and his horsemen still guarded my grandfather but we now had Erik's sons and they rode long patrols each day. They sought horses and they sought signs that the Bretons and my brother were coming to teach us a lesson. I left one drekar crew to guard my tower. It now had all of my jewels inside and I would have those precious people kept safe.

Lord of Rouen

I used four of my drekar to sail down the River Issicauna. We headed east and went parallel to the water. It was an old hunting technique. The drekar would startle those who lived by the river and they would flee south. We would trap them. The Danes had told us that there were keen to buy slaves who were Franks. We would empty the valley and make a profit at the same time. We moved in warbands made up of a single drekar crew. It was easier that way. We each had a horn and if an enemy came in numbers then we could summon help. Our first camp was at Pont-l'Évêque. We camped there because we found our first opposition. They had a wall and they had horsemen. Until then we had captured farms and small villages. We had collected four horses as well as cows and pigs. The boys we had brought with us as slingers were sent back to Caen with them.

It was as we approached the river that we saw we were expected. I had with me, sixty men. A few miles either side of me were another two warbands of sixty men each. I could have summoned them but Sven Blue Cheek and I were confident that we could deal with the Bretons who blocked the bridge. They had twenty horsemen on one side of the bridge. I think they thought to threaten us. We were unworried. The fifty men who were on the bridge were without mail. They were locked together and I saw a leudes in armour. He was in the third rank. We formed up into a wedge with three men in the centre. Sven and Bergil flanked me. As we formed up I said, "Those horsemen on the right will charge in as soon as we move forward. Einar the Bold, you command the right. Present spears and hold them off. They wear no mail."

"Aye, lord. We will keep them from you."

My men were among the few who were not intimidated by horsemen. They had learned that if they kept tight shields and weapons presented to the horses then they would be safe enough.

I began banging my shield as we moved.

Men of Caen with leader tall
Fight the Frank and his walls do fall
Men of Caen fear no pain
They will fight and a land will gain
Men of Caen we come for you

Men of Caen bring your doom!

I raised my sword and we headed towards those on the bridge. The horsemen readied their spears. As we moved forward I saw that the town walls were lined with boys and old men. They did not trust to their walls or perhaps that had spoken to the men of Lisieux and discovered that such walls were no obstacles to Vikings.

Suddenly the horsemen charged. My men did not miss a beat. We headed towards the bridge. Einar the Bold and his men merely swung their spears and their shields to face the threat. The Bretons had expected us to either halt or to turn. Their horses galloped close but would not approach the hedgehog of spears. Some of the horsemen tried to throw their spears. Einar's men were mailed and the spears which did not hit shields caught up in cloaks and mail. The horsemen could not engineer enough force to penetrate mail. Worse more than half had lost their best weapon. When Einar and his men rammed their spears at horses only a few spears jousted with them.

We continued to move towards the men on the bridge. Their fear-filled faces reflected the fact that they had expected us to be whittled down by their horsemen. We had yet to endure a wound! When we were just five paces from the bridge I shouted, "Charge!" The bridge was only wide enough for five men and Einar kept his men facing the horsemen. I led the other forty at the shield wall. A spear raked along my mail hood. It caught on the rings but my helmet had good straps and it held. More importantly, I was able to ram my sword into the shoulder of the man who held the spear. As it bit through his leather and into his flesh I twisted and then pulled. There was bone on the blade and the man sank to his knees. My knee caught him under the chin.

Sven and Bergil had both been hit by spears but they had not been hurt. Sven brought his sword over to half sever the Breton's neck. Bergil was able to ram his sword up under the hauberk of the Breton and gut him. The weight of the men behind us pushed us into the Bretons. I swung my sword blindly and was rewarded by a cry as I hit something. The weight of our men made it impossible to stop. The Bretons fell beneath our feet. We were tramping not on the wood of the bridge but the flesh of the men who had fallen. Those behind us ended the suffering of those who had been crushed by our boots. As we neared the leudes I saw him turn and shout, "Back to the town!"

That was a mistake. His men knocked each other over as they ran. Sven Blue Cheek, Bergil and I followed the lord. His three oathsworn remained with him. We ignored all of those around us. Gradually we caught up with them. One looked over his shoulder to see where we were. He tripped and fell. Sven contemptuously slew him as we passed. They should have closed the gates but their lord was outside and they waited for him to enter. As the doors began to shut I hurled my giant frame at the gates. They burst asunder and Sven and Bergil hacked and killed those who were trying to close them. When my sword split the skull of the Breton lord all resistance ended. We had the bridge and we had the town. More importantly, we had somewhere safe to sleep and ten horses we had captured. Our first day had been successful!

We ate well and our prisoners were well guarded. "I wonder how the others fared?"

I threw the duck bone into the fire, "Today would have been an easy day. They were not expecting us. Tomorrow will give us something to judge them by. Our ships will be further upstream and those who fled will have spread the word of our approach."

In the event, we found little opposition. The villages we found had been abandoned. We heard no horns summoning us to the aid of our comrades. It was though we had pushed the door ajar and the house was empty. We met no refugees fleeing south. I wondered if our ships had suffered instead of us. When we reached the Issicauna we met more of our warbands. They all reported similar success. There had been skirmishes. Sámr Oakheart had even met a band of horsemen but they had fled when Sámr had presented his shield wall.

We saw our drekar appear from upstream. Audun the Quiet pulled his drekar close to us. "We sailed as far as Rouen. That was too great a citadel for us to attack. We landed and raided the lands close by the river but there were few men to fight us. We have returned for our holds are full and we have more animals on our decks than is safe. You were right, lord. The civil war has emptied the land."

"Tell the other drekar to head home. We will sweep south and pick up the rest of our men."

There were almost two hundred of us who headed south towards the tributary of the Issicauna. From my grandfather's description, I guessed that we were close to where we had taken the stone to build the Haugr. We found a stone quarry. The workers had long fled. I decided to take advantage of their absence. I sent out runners to find the other warbands and set the men to hunting in the forests and hewing trees to make rafts. We would use the stone to make Caen even stronger. The lack of opposition had shown me that the Bretons were in disarray. I was almost tempted to march towards my brother and bring him to battle.

As we ate fresh game I mentioned my idea to Sven. He shook his head. "Lord for one so young you have shown great wisdom yet to attack your brother would be reckless and would lose us all that we have gained. This taking of the stone is an act of genius. We could have marched back to Caen and feasted well on that which we took but you have come up with an idea which will make us even stronger. Do not deviate from your plan."

"Sven is right," counselled Bergil, "the longer this brother of yours takes to bring you to battle then the stronger you become. His men will wonder why he does not squash you like a fly. They will think he fears you. I know that is the view of your grandfather. Ragnvald Ragnvaldsson hopes that you will fail and men will desert you. He is desperate for you to go away. It does not take a galdramenn to see that. Make our walls the envy of the Franks. The strength of the Breton and the Frank is in their horsemen. Horsemen cannot reduce stone walls!"

We spent twenty-eight days hewing logs and stone. With all of our men with us, we gathered great quantities. We only ceased when we had exhausted the quarry. I sent three crews across country to fetch our drekar and we began the long journey down the river towards the Issicauna. We had long poles but they were only needed to keep us from the banks. The current did all the hard work for us. Each raft had ten armed men on board but it was hard to see where the opposition would be. Once we reached the Issicauna we tied our rafts together. It made it easier to navigate. Half the men poled and half ate. It was a pleasant journey.

Our four drekar met us close to the mouth of the river. Each drekar towed three rafts and we sailed steadily along the coast to the Orne and our home. We were greeted like conquering heroes. The animals, slaves and treasure we had captured had already been sent back. The slaves were, even now, being sold in Lundenwic. My grandfather greeted me. He hugged me, "You are like a giant and younger version of me. With this rock, even the walls of the town can be stone-built."

I shook my head, "Some can be used for that but I would build a hall attached to the tower. Our families need protection!"

"Each day you grow wiser." He looked towards the gate where Gefn, Bergljót and Lady Poppa waited, "and yet in some matters you cannot see what is before you."

"Grandfather, she is too young. When she has seen sixteen summers I will take her... if she will have me. She may change her mind. You did not marry my grandmother straightaway did you?"

"That is because she was a slave and..." he laughed, "you are more like me than even I know. Set your own course, Rollo, you know your business."

Chapter 11

Our work on the walls and the new hall was halted when our patrol ships spied the enemy. Our drekar patrols, which now traversed the sea from the Haugr to Djupr spotted the fleet which put out from Ċiriċeburh. There were ten drekar and as many more stubby Breton ships. They were coming for war and they were coming for me. They sailed along the coast. As they were sailing at the speed of the slow-moving Breton ships we had time to put my plan into operation. Leaving the old men and the slingers in Caen we loaded every drekar. We sent for the drekar from Djupr. We had, in total, fourteen drekar. The enemy would outnumber us but there would be a sea battle and that was what I wanted. I knew that the Bretons would have another army coming by land. They would have the horses. If we could defeat the fleet then we had a better chance of routing the rest. The fleet contained the Vikings and they were the most potent force the enemy possessed.

As fortune would have it the wind came from the west. That meant we had to row out to sea. That, in itself, was not a bad thing for we would then have the wind when we turned to attack. The effort would come in putting us in a good position. The drekar which were ready and crewed rowed west first. We did not row hard. There was no need. We had to get every ship, no matter how small into position. We knew where the enemy was sailing to. We could sail further out to sea where they could not see us. The enemy fleet would try to land as close to Caen and Bayeux as possible. That meant they would land on the beaches between the two rivers. If they landed further west they would increase their journey to Caen. We waited five miles offshore. As each ship joined us it increased our chances of success. We knew these waters and we had the wind. Our captains aligned the ships so that we were parallel to the coast. We had our sails furled and we waited. The wind nudged us slightly closer but it saved us having to run out a sea anchor.

As the last of my ships arrived I signalled them into position. We would use *'Hermóðr'* as the tip of the arrow. With our bigger ships flanking us the smaller threttanessa, on the periphery, would be able to nip in like terriers and take out bigger and slower adversaries.

"Lord, Sails to the west!"

We all ran to the steerboard side and peered at the horizon. At first, we saw nothing, and then, gradually tiny dots appeared. Sven slapped the sheerstrake. "They are inshore of us! We have them! The wind is in our favour.

"Do not judge until they are closer but it bodes well." I too was satisfied. We had the weather gauge. To engage with us they would have to man the oars and row out to meet us. The Breton ships were not equipped for such manoeuvres.

"Olaf, turn the drekar!" Without using the sails Olaf turned the steerboard so that our prow faced the coast. The wind would move us, inexorably towards the shore but we had five miles of sea room. The enemy fleet was less than two miles from shore. They did not have that luxury. We let the wind take us. Had they turned and tried to land then we would have headed east of the river which flowed from Bayeux. We would have been able to hold them at the river. When it became obvious that they were going to land to the east of the river I gave the order for the sails to be lowered. *'Hermóðr'* was just waiting to be released and she leapt forward towards the shore. When the other ships in my fleet set their sails, it became obvious that we were going to attack. They did not know how many ships we had. They saw a fleet approaching them. We covered the ground between us rapidly. I saw the stubby Breton ships turn to shore. They were east of the river and they were going to land their men. That meant they would have a long journey to reach Caen. We surged towards the ten drekar. We outnumbered them. More importantly, they had their elite aboard their ten ships; they had the Vikings. Each Viking we slew made our task easier.

The Breton ships landed their men on the beach to the west of the river from Bayeux. Their captains had panicked. The Vikings had more strength of character about them and they turned to face us ship to ship. They had to take to their oars for the wind was not with them. We were flying. I trusted to Olaf to make the decision to furl the sail. I wore no mail. This would be a battle on the water. I recognised three of the larger drekar. We had fought them before. The Rus boys who had joined us had told us that they had been named after Ragnvald. *'Ragnvald's Sword'*, *'Ragnvald's Dragon'* and *'Ragnvald's Revenge'*. It did not do to name a ship after yourself. The gods did not like such arrogance. Nor did I think that Ragnvald was on board any of them.

Leif, one of the ship's boys who was at the masthead ready to furl the sail shouted down, "Lord, some of the ships at the rear are turning and heading to shore."

Then Olaf shouted, "Furl the sail! Prepare to strike."

The leading ships were our target and all had oars run out. Olaf intended to strike the nearest ship and crush the oars. I could now see that there were just six drekar. The captains saw their dilemma. Thanks to the desertion by their companion ships they would be outnumbered. They tried to turn. Their sails dropped and they spun around. The ships might be badly named but they were lithe. We would, however, catch one. Such was our speed that we caught one beam on. Our prow tore through oars and then rose across the mid-ships. I was holding the forestay else I might have lost my footing. As it was my helmet tumbled from my sword hilt.

As we ground down the side I leapt into the well of the stricken drekar. The shattering oars had speared men. Our hull had ground over a ship's boy and two oarsmen. I saw that there was water in the bottom. She had sprung her strakes. I drew my Long Sword and used it two handed. The first four men I killed were trying to stand when my blade took them. A mailed warrior, I guessed the leader, ran towards me with shield and sword ready to slay me. He sloshed through the water. He was so intent upon my death that he did not look where he was going. I stood braced against the thwarts. As he stumbled I swung my sword sideways. I hit his right side and my blade bit deep into his side.

From behind me, I heard, "Lord, she is finished and she is sinking! Back on board!"

It was Olaf. He was Captain and I obeyed. The men who had joined me slew their opponents and waded back to the side. Waiting ropes helped us walk up the side of our drekar and I saw that the enemy was well underwater. My other ships were chasing the enemy into the shallows. Their ragged flight meant that the Breton ships were on the far side of the estuary. The first few drekar to have landed were also close to the river but the last five, the ones we had pursued were more than a mile from help.

Sven Blue Cheek handed me my helmet, "There was no need to have boarded her, lord, she was sinking."

"We did not know that until we boarded. They might have saved her and we need this fleet destroying. Olaf, land us close to their bigger drekar."

Olaf Two Teeth said, "When we land we will need to check the hull. That was a mighty blow."

They had a mere five drekar and fourteen vengeful Viking ships were heading for them. I saw the warriors streaming ashore. They clambered up the dunes to make a shield wall at the top. As soon as we had landed I jumped ashore and I walked to within two hundred paces of the warriors standing on the dunes. We outnumbered them but we would have to clamber up sinking sand to reach them and it would be a bloodbath. I had a better plan. Over my shoulder, I shouted, "Burn their drekar! Shield wall and archers here!"

My men formed up. The ships' boys would gleefully set fire to the ships. I had almost six hundred men. I counted less than one hundred and fifty Vikings on the dunes. I began banging my shield as my archers strung their bows. We were three deep and they would be the fourth line.

Men of Caen with leader tall
Fight the Frank and his walls do fall
Men of Caen fear no pain
They will fight and a land will gain

Lord of Rouen

Men of Caen we come for you
Men of Caen bring your doom!

We began to move towards them. They locked shields and they began a chant of their own. When we reached the bottom of the dunes I held up my sword. I shouted, "I am Göngu-Hrólfr Rognvaldson. I am the lord of this land. Is Ragnvald Ragnvaldsson or Arne the Breton Slayer amongst you?" My words were greeted with silence. Sometimes you can win a battle without even bloodying your sword. "If they are here I will fight them both at the same time and save brave men their lives! Are they here?"

A voice answered, "Our Prince is with the main army! He will fight you, giant, when he takes your town!"

I nodded, "Then I will make the same offer when next I see him. I will see you in the otherworld! Archers! Release!"

One hundred and ten arrows soared in the sky followed by another one hundred and ten. The warriors raised their shields but some were too slow. Many bodies tumbled down the sand dunes. When the next arrows hit another fourteen men fell. I heard a command and a horn. The Vikings turned and fled. In the time it took to disappear another twenty men fell. We had rid ourselves of two drekar crews and not lost a single man.

"Do we follow them, lord?"

"No Ragnar the Resolute. We have hurt them. We will return to our ships and Caen. We need to meet them in battle and to end this."

Their wounded were despatched. The swords and mail were taken and we headed home leaving five smoking hulks on the beach. Our ships' boys had found the treasure in the chests of the rowers. They had escaped but just with their lives and their weapons. All that they had accrued we now had. That would add to the hurt of the men who had fled. We had humiliated them. Their captains had turned and fled. I had offered battle and been refused. They had lost comrades, their ships and now the treasure they had accumulated. When we fought them, they would either be eager for vengeance or their hearts would not be in the battle. I suspected it would be the latter.

147

Lord of Rouen

As we saw the Orne ahead I knew that we had given ourselves that most valuable of luxuries, time. It would take a day or more to gather their forces spread out over eight miles of beaches. They would have to make their way to meet their horsemen and my brother.

When we disembarked I had the drekar taken to the far side of the river. It would not do to risk them being cut out by our enemies. Olaf took my drekar back to Djupr. He needed to check her hull and he would command Djupr for me. My grandfather came to greet me, "Well?"

"Six drekar are destroyed and more than sixty Vikings are dead but they are coming. Ragnvald was not with them. He and the Breton horsemen must be coming over land."

He nodded, "And how do we fight them? We stand in the tower and let them bleed?"

I shook my head, "That would cost us the town. I would not have the people lose their livelihoods. I want the horsemen, all of them to ride to the small hamlet five miles west of here. The enemy do not know of our horsemen. There are only forty-two of them but they will come as a shock. I would have Stephen command them and when we sound the horn three times to attack the enemy flank."

"And the rest will be on the walls?"

I shook my head. "We have one hundred and twenty warriors who wear mail. They will be before the town gate. Every other warrior, every man and boy who dwells in Caen will be on the walls or within the tower with slingshots and with bows. We rain death upon them."

"How many do they have?"

"Judging by their ships I would say that it could be a thousand men."

I saw even Sven's eyes widen. He said, "Lord, you fight at odds of ten to one?"

"Perhaps," I laughed, "but they will not be the odds we fight. We have a night and a morning, at the very least. We dig pits. We use stakes. We sow caltrops. We make them come to us. All the time that they do so then our men on the walls will wreak havoc. Did you not wonder why they sent so many men in ships?"

"They thought to surprise us?"

"Perhaps Sven but it is more likely that the ones they sent by ship were the ones with mail. They would not wish to tramp for seventy miles carrying their mail with them. I think that the ones we slew were the mailed warriors. They have more mailed men but not as many as they would have liked."

Sven Blue Cheek nodded. "We recovered much mail from their dead and the chests of the drekar also yielded mail. I will get the defences begun." He nodded to Hrolf the Horseman, "Your grandson threw himself on to the deck of a dying drekar. I would, Hrolf the Horseman, have you counsel him to become a little wiser! We need him to lead the clan."

He went off and my grandfather looked at me sternly, "Is this true?"

I could not hold his gaze. I lowered my eyes and I nodded.

"You are more than a warrior, Rollo. If you fell then the hopes of all of us would be dashed. We have a tenuous grip on this land. If you fell then…Gefn's heart would break, as would Lady Poppa's. Promise me that when the battle comes you will stay within the shield wall."

I nodded, "I will but if my brother is there then I will have to challenge him."

"That is out of your hands. If the Norns have spun and it is ordained then that will be so. Now go and see Gefn and Poppa. They are worried."

I smiled when I greeted the two women for Poppa was not becoming a woman. "We lost no men and we slew Vikings!" I said that for the benefit of Poppa. She was Breton and I did not wish her to think me a Breton killer.

Gefn looked relieved, "The Allfather be praised. They still come?"

"They do but we have hurt them and when we fight them it will be here before our walls." I was trying to reassure Gefn. The world of war had evaded her until I took her from her home.

"You do not stay within the walls?" Lady Poppa was a clever woman. She had spoken to warriors. Her elder brother was a warrior. She knew more of war than Gefn.

I shook my head, "Lady Poppa, I know my brother. If we stayed within my walls then he would retake all the land around us. He would camp around our walls and starve us out. We must meet him beard to beard. When I have killed the snake then we can talk with your father."

"He is with those who come?"

I shook my head, "To speak truthfully I do not know but the civil war is over. He is either with the victors or he lies dead."

"Göngu-Hrólfr Rognvaldson!"

Lady Poppa smiled, "No Gefn, your son is right, to be honest. I spent many years hiding behind lies and falsehoods. Since I have met Rollo he has given me nothing but the truth. That is how it should be. Thank you, Rollo."

I suddenly saw in her a woman. She had grown in the time she had been with us. I turned to Gefn, "Could you leave us alone?"

She smiled, "Of course."

When she had gone I said, "Lady Poppa you have just said that I am truthful then know this; I would have you as my wife. If you say no then I will understand. I took you by force from your home. I would have us wed when you have seen sixteen summers."

Her eyes lit up and then she frowned, "But why wait? I am ready now!"

I suddenly realised that she was happy to marry me. I was almost bereft of words. I gave her another chance to back out, "You are still growing into womanhood. I can wait and if you change your mind then so be it!"

She stood on my boots and stretched up. She grabbed my beard and pulled my face down. She kissed me, "I will wait but I swear that I will not change my mind!"

Gefn and Bergljót had been listening and they burst into the gateway, "Grandchildren! I will have grandchildren!"

I shook my head, "She is barely fifteen!"

Gefn waved her hand, "It matters not. There will be children and I will be a grandmother! The Allfather has answered my prayers!" I rolled my eyes but I saw that Poppa was happy.

It was after dark when the horsemen rode away. I was not certain if the Bretons had sent scouts ahead of their army but I was taking no chances. My horsemen would disappear. They had a crucial role. So far, we had not used them. My brother would not know of them and in that surprise, lay hope. It was another reason why I wanted to be before the walls. My brother would see me and he would use all of his men to get at me. I was confident in the mailed men who would stand in the three-deep line alongside me. As for those who would face us? I had sown the seeds of doubt in his men's mind. I was not afraid of their leader. Would he face me? No man likes to follow a coward.

My men and I spent all night digging pits and planting stakes. My scouts were spread out in a ring four miles from our lines. We would have warning of their approach. We had just finished the pits and had covered them when our scouts arrived.

"Lord, the Bretons and your brother are camped three miles from here."

"How many men?"

"There are over a hundred campfires and there were many horses."

I nodded. I was not upset at the lack of precision. My brother was clever. By arriving after dark, he kept his true numbers from me. Then the thought struck me that, perhaps, my brother did not command. "Whose standard did the Bretons follow?"

"We caught one of their scouts. Before he died he told us that it was King Salomon's daughter's husband, Pascweten who was in command."

That made sense. My brother had thrown in his lot with someone related to the royal family. If I was this Pascweten I would be looking over my shoulder. My brother was a backstabber. We had made our preparations and we withdrew behind our walls. I saw that there were stacks of arrows on the fighting platform. The boys had collected bags of river stones and there were javelins ready to be hurled. My brother was in for a shock.

The table was full. We had all of my leaders as well as the wives of my leaders. I confess that I was distracted. I knew that we had made good plans. I trusted my men and I knew we had good defences but it remained a fact that the Norns could interfere and mistakes could occur.

I said, "Lord, you have decided to marry?"

I turned to Sven, "What?"

The tattooed warrior laughed and pointed to the three women whose heads were closeted together. "Lady Gefn could not wait to tell all that you had agreed to marry the Lady Poppa." He waved a hand at my grinning men. "Your warriors were teasing you about it yet you seemed distracted."

"I think about the battle tomorrow. Have I done all that I could?"

He nodded and became serious again, "I thought you worried that you have made the wrong decision about the Lady Poppa: you have not. As for the battle? Everything is in place. It is a good plan. No matter what the enemy does we are prepared. You need to drink the ale and eat well. Hewing enemy's heads needs strength."

"You are that confident and yet you have not faced my brother."

"From what Hrolf the Horseman has said and what I have seen then your brother is no war chief. He is a plotter. You are a war chief. We bloodied their nose at the beach and they will be praying to Thor and Odin for help this night."

He was right. We had hurt them. They would expect us to wait behind our walls and when we did not then that would put more doubts in their mind. Why were we standing with so few men to face them? They could not know our numbers. Even in the last few days another drekar full of warriors had arrived from Djupr. Olaf Two Teeth still had enough to defend the walls there. We would have a tower lined with archers. The height of the tower would increase the range of their bows. The walls could be packed with warriors, boys and old men. Each one would have a weapon. Even Bagsecg had insisted upon standing at the gatehouse. He would defend his new land. In his case, his weapon of choice was a war hammer. Any man who came within striking distance was a dead man!

Everyone was in high spirits and I slipped away. I knew that I would not be able to sleep but I needed to be away from the banter and drink-fuelled bravado of my hall. I went to the tower. The fighting platform was reassuringly solid. I nodded to the sentries. I did not know them by name. We had too many new men for that. They gave me space. I walked to the side where I could see the fires of the Bretons and my brother's men burning. There were many of them. That could be a trick. Often Vikings would light more fires than there were men to make their enemies fear them. They also liked to sneak up in the dark and slit throats. We had done so ourselves. It would not work with us. We had burning brands two hundred paces from the walls. I did not want to risk men sneaking up at night and discovering our traps. The sentries had bows at the ready but all seemed quiet. Perhaps they feared that we might have had Ulfheonar. My grandfather had told us tales of Jarl Dragonheart and his shapeshifters. That was enough to worry my brother. He would have sentries watching for the knife in the night.

"Something worries you, lord? People have asked where you have gone."

I turned and saw Lady Poppa with a cloak around her shoulders. She looked so small and frail. "No, there are no worries. We have a good plan. I came to reassure myself that nothing had changed."

"And tomorrow you and your best men will stand in harm's way?"

I nodded, "That is our way."

"Do you fear death?"

"I do not yearn for death. I am no berserker but if I should die tomorrow with a sword in my hand then I shall go to Valhalla. I will see my two fathers and I will see Folki, Erik Green Eye and the others who are waiting for me."

"It would pain me if you died, lord. Stay alive. I know that it would break Gefn's heart. She has lost a son and a husband. All of her hopes are in you."

"I know and I feel the weight upon my shoulders." She shivered, "Come I will take you back to the fire. I am the host. It is remiss of me to indulge myself like this."

I put my arm around her and she slipped her arm around my back. I know not why but at that moment then I knew that we would win.

Chapter 12

I slept better than I expected and Sven and I were up before false dawn. We took ale skins, warm bread and cheese to our positions. I wanted us there when the Breton scouts scurried out to spy our lines. I had Petr with me. He would not be fighting. He had one task, to summon our handful of horsemen and to try to convince the enemy that we had many more horses than we actually possessed! The warriors left the town walls with me. We had all fought together many times before. Shield brothers chose their places. I had Sven Blue Cheek, Bergil, Sámr Oakheart and Ragnar the Resolute flanking me. Much blood had flowed beneath our blades. We laid our shields and helmets on the ground. We would not need them for a while. Watching the sun peer in the east we ate the warm bread and fresh cheeses washed down by Brigid's famous ale. Even Sven was impressed with her brews.

As I finished the last of my first horn I said, "She comes from Hibernia but she developed her craft on Raven Wing Island. She has learned to use the best of the grain that we grow. She mixes it with secret ingredients. It is almost witchcraft."

Sven nodded, "It puts power into a man." He put the stopper in the top of his skin. "When I have hewn enough heads then I will have some more. It will be a reward!" Dawn fully broke and bathed our lines in a warm red light. Men walked forward to the edge of the stakes and made water. It was a small thing but the ground would be muddier as a result. Some dropped their breeks and emptied their bowels too. A man fought better with an empty bladder and bowels. The enemy would have to wade through our waste.

Behind us, the men on the gatehouse and the tower had a better view of the enemy. "Lord, they come!"

I nodded, "Stand to!"

I picked up my shield and helmet. I need not don them yet. The men shuffled into the three rough lines we would use. There was no hurry. The enemy would form up first. I also intended to speak with the enemy. Now that I knew the name of the leader of the enemy horsemen I would use it.

The first to appear were the horsemen. There were about two hundred of them. Some were mailed. They would be the young nobles. Others wore just leather armour. All were armed with a round shield and a long spear. Ragnar said, "Axes will make short work of those, lord. They are small horses and they do not use stiraps."

I nodded. Ragnar was right. These were not the larger horses used by the Franks. I saw that some of the Bretons had bows. I had yet to see bows used effectively from the backs of horses. Perhaps this would be the first time. Then then the banners of the lords appeared. The lords who led this host rode larger horses. They wore fine mail and they had plumed helmets. Along with them came the bulk of their army: the men on foot. They were a mixture of the levy and farmers who had enough coin for a good helmet, short mail shirt and a good sword. They also had about sixty boys with slings. They would be brave and they would be reckless. My own archers and slings had the protection of a palisade. The young Breton boys would die. Finally came the Vikings. I saw my brother and I saw Arne Breton Slayer. They rode horses. There were fewer Vikings than I had expected. I knew we had killed a large number but, from the number of drekar, there had to have been desertions. It took some time for them to arrive. The horsemen did not move to the flanks as I had expected and the Vikings formed a three-deep shield wall behind them. The Bretons were using their Vikings against us. That suited us. I would back my men against any warriors.

When they had formed their lines I turned to Sven Blue Cheek, "Come, let us give them a chance to surrender!"

He laughed, "And here we are all dressed for war!"

Lord of Rouen

I walked to the line of the stakes and looked beyond them. I placed my feet carefully to avoid the caltrops and the pits we had dug.

Looking up at the men on horses I said, "Lord Pascweten, I know not why you have come here save that I suspect you have been led astray by faithless father killers and Vikings who have no honour. If you leave now then I swear that you shall live. All I want is Arne the Breton Slayer and Ragnvald Ragnvaldsson to fight with me for they owe me weregeld. They are murderers!"

I saw that my words had the most effect on the Vikings. The Breton lord, flanked by three other nobles nudged their horses until they were just fifty paces from us. "You must be the one they call Göngu-Hrólfr Rognvaldson. I can see why." He pointed to my tower, "You have the daughter of Count Robert here as a hostage. We would have her returned."

I nodded, "I expected ransom more than two years ago. He has not once sent a communication to me. I have to tell you, Lord Pascweten, that it is too late now. The lady has agreed to be my bride. Count Robert, as a favour, I will give you a swift death!"

I saw that I had caused confusion. An older lord shouted, "You lie!"

I drew my sword, "I never lie and if you will bring your horse closer, Count Robert, then we will settle this before our gods." He backed off, as I had expected. All of this was for show. He had had no intention of ransoming an embarrassing illegitimate daughter. "So, do you leave or will we stain the ground with Breton blood?"

Lord Pascweten raised his sword, "You will die, giant barbarian, as will all your folk!"

I turned with Sven and we headed back to our lines. Suddenly there was a shout from my men and then a pair of arrows flew over our heads. I turned and saw that Count Robert had been riding at us to spear me. He had made ten paces before his horse was slain. He rose groggily. I laughed, "If that is all you have, Breton, then this will be a short but bloody battle!"

As we joined our men Bergil said, "That was cowardly!"

I smiled, "I had my shield beneath my cloak. There was no danger. I have learned, where my brother is concerned, to expect

157

treachery. I donned my helmet and swung my shield around, "They will try to use their horsemen to soften us up. They will charge and throw their javelins. Then my brother's men will attack. We stand firm and trust to our men on the walls. We are the bait, the tethered sheep but we have teeth!"

My men began banging their shields. We were next to my walls and the first line of our defences was just eighty paces before us. More importantly, the Bretons and the Vikings would be within the range of bows and slings as soon as they reached the stakes. The horsemen moved forward. We had sown caltrops before our first pits. Some of their horses found them. Two of their mailed warriors were unceremoniously dumped from the saddles. The two horses galloped off. Others ran back through the Vikings. The horsemen halted and the Bretons ordered some of the levy forward to clear the deadly spikes. I raised my sword and dropped it as the first of the levy came within range of my men on the walls. Without mail, it was a slaughter. When forty had fallen the rest fled. They took shelter behind my brother's Vikings. They had a dilemma. They needed the traps clearing and did not know whom to waste.

The leaders of the horsemen began a heated debate. We were annoyingly close but the caltrops and the stakes meant that a quick and direct approach was out of the question. A decision was made and they began to walk slowly through the stakes. With their shields above them, the horsemen peered at the ground and their horses picked their way through. They avoided the caltrops. Their horses were unprotected and they began to suffer wounds as stones and arrows hit them. Two died quickly as stones hit their heads. Others were maddened as arrows hit the rumps and necks of the horses. Some Bretons were thrown. When the first of the horses found the pits we had dug and were impaled on the spikes in the bottom the horsemen had had enough and they turned and fled. They had to run the gauntlet of arrows and stones. Horsemen were left dead and dying. The horsemen could be used again but only if they won and pursued us. That would not happen.

The enemy had to reform. Their first two attacks had failed and now they needed another plan. Some of my men ate bread and drank ale. It was a pleasant day out for them. A debate ensued between the Bretons and my brother and his lieutenants. I saw the Breton leader remonstrating with my brother. He was no fool. He had seen the pits and knew that there were more. His men were mailed but it was hard to carry a shield to protect your head while looking at the ground for traps. They compromised. My brother's men made two wedges and between then they filled it with the levy. The ones in the front rank of the levy were mailed.

They began to move towards us. Arrows and stones flew from behind us. We had plenty. The Vikings suffered the least from the missiles but they fell into the traps. The weakness of the traps was that once the first men had fallen into them they were no longer hidden. That did not matter overmuch for it slowed up their approach and it broke up their lines. The closer they came to us the more damage was done by our slingshots. At fifty paces a stone which struck a helmet would render the wearer unconscious. The Vikings moved slower than the levy. They were keeping their formations. The men of the levy were rushing. The sooner they reached us then the sooner the stones and arrows would stop hitting them. They outnumbered us. There was a kind of twisted logic to their thinking.

They struck us piecemeal. I brought my sword sideways to hack through the neck of one Breton as Sven used his spear to stab one in the face. Bergil and Sámr Oakheart used their swords to slice into the necks of their opponents. It was important to keep up the momentum. The Vikings would strike our flanks soon. I saw the cunning of my brother. The levy would face me and his men, the Vikings would fight the ones he thought were weaker on my flanks. They were not weaker! Magnús Magnússon commanded one flank and Ragnar the Resolute the other.

I had room to swing and I used the full length of my sword. I split the helmet and skull of one Breton. We had a wall of bodies before us. Their attack was slowing. As it did so then the archers and boys with slings struck more and more of their men. The attack on our centre slowed and finally stopped. When Sven Blue Cheek and I stepped over the bodies to slay three Bretons who had originally been in the fifth rank then the rest fled. We had broken their spirit. The Vikings gave ground and moved back more slowly. Weakened by swords and spears they began to die as our arrows and stones found gaps. Thirty Vikings lay dead along with more than a hundred and fifty Bretons.

I took off my helmet and handed it to Sven Blue Cheek, "Come with me. We can end this battle now!"

We strode through the bodies. Some men were still dying. We halted at the edge of the line. I pointed my sword at Ragnvald Ragnvaldsson. "You are a coward and a father killer. You do not even have the decency to lead your men into battle. I give you and Arne Breton Slayer the chance now. Let us save the lives of your Vikings. I will fight the two of you here before my men. It is your chance to rid this land of me. With me gone you have a chance to win. While I am alive then you will be haunted for I know what you did! What say you? Two to one?"

Sven growled, "Lord!"

I said quietly, "I know what I am doing. We have torn the heart from their horsemen and their levy. The Vikings are the last threat. I can neutralise them with one battle!" I looked at the Viking warriors. Their faces were eloquent. My request seemed eminently reasonable. I was giving them a chance. If my brother refused then the Vikings would simply walk away and the biggest threat to us would be gone.

I saw my brother and Arne put their heads together. They knew the stakes as well as I did. They would also be working out how to kill me quickly. There were two of them. They dismounted and hefted their shields. My brother drew his sword and I saw that it was our father's weapon. He pointed it at me, "We will fight you brother if only to prove the lie that I killed our father. It was the Danes as well you know."

I stared at him and said, quietly, "That is a dangerous thing to say. The gods watch and they know. The Norns have spun and they know." I smiled, "Most importantly, treacherous brother mine, I was there and I know."

I swung my shield around and drew my Long Sword. My brother's Vikings used their shields to make an arena. I could trust them. They wanted to see a fight to the death. They would not interfere. The more dangerous of the two was Arne Breton Slayer. He was a big man. He had a good sword. He came towards me and I was aware that my brother was sneaking around my back. He would attack once I was engaged with Arne. Many men think that because I am so tall and so big, I am slow. They are wrong. I did not wait for Arne to attack I ran at him covering the ground in two enormous strides. I punched at him hard in the face with the boss of my shield. He tried to block it with his own shield. My speed and my power were such that he was knocked to the ground. He covered his body with his shield. The only unprotected parts were his legs. I rammed my sword through his knee cap and I twisted. I felt it grate against bone. He screamed. It was the feral scream of a badly wounded animal. He rolled to the side as I drew the blade out.

I turned just as Ragnvald swung his sword at me. I blocked it easily with my own. I was helped by the action of pulling Long Sword from Arne's knee. When I looked at my brother I saw the fear on his face. Arne's blood still dripped from my sword and, behind me I heard him moaning. It was not a mortal wound but he would be crippled for life and I had bought time. I spun my Long Sword in my hand. I had waited a long time for this chance. I knew that I could beat him, "You thought when I was knocked into the sea that I was dead and that your guilty secret died with me. The Norns were spinning, brother."

He looked around to his men as though seeking support. He ran at me and brought his sword down again on my shield. All he succeeded in doing was blunting his blade. My shield was well made. He rained blows upon my shield. I held my sword behind me. I saw his eyes drawn to it. Sweat poured down his face. He was tiring. I feinted with my shield and when he recoiled I swung my sword sideways at him. Long Sword was powerful and tore through his mail, mail protector and into his side. I felt it grate along the bones of his ribs. He winced. He swung again at me and I blocked it with my shield. I barely felt it.

I stepped forward, "Brother you will die and you will die without a sword in your hand." He looked at his sword. My hand darted forward and I sliced off his hand at the wrist. His sword fell to the ground. Blood poured from the wound. He was already dying although he did not know it. "Hel awaits you." I rammed my sword into his middle and twisted so that when the sword came out his guts followed. He crumpled in a bleeding heap on the ground and I turned. Arne had risen to his feet. "You are a murderer, Arne Breton Slayer. You killed my father."

"You may have won, Rollo but I will die with a sword in my hand. Perhaps I can wound you badly enough so that my brother can end your life." He turned and shouted, "Ailmær, I charge you with killing this monster!"

A younger version of Arne with a red shield shouted, "Aye brother! I will give him the blood eagle!"

Arne the Breton Slayer suddenly hurled his shield at me and drew a seax. He limped towards me. I threw my own shield at his good knee. It hit him hard and he stopped. I drew my second sword. I could use my left hand as well as my right. I walked towards him spinning the two swords. He made the mistake of watching the two of them. I suddenly swung them both and took his two hands and then spinning them I brought the swords together to take his head.

I sheathed both weapons and picked up my shield. I faced the Vikings. "The blood feud is over. If you fight me again then you begin the feud again and I will not rest until this land is bathed in your blood. Ailmær the Cruel, run to the furthest corners of this land for I swear that I will kill you!"

I saw Viking leaders nodding and they simply turned and began to walk through the Breton lines. Sven Blue Cheek still had his sword drawn. I walked towards him. My men began banging their shields and chanting, "Göngu-Hrólfr Rognvaldson, Göngu-Hrólfr Rognvaldson, Göngu-Hrólfr Rognvaldson."

The battle was still not yet over but my father had been avenged. The Vikings would not fight us. We now had a chance. We joined our men and Bergil said, "What now?"

Sven answered, "Now they will attack with all that they have. Their horsemen will begin the attack. We must be strong!"

I nodded my agreement, "If they leave now they have lost this land forever."

The Bretons began to rearrange their men. They gathered all those with mail and packed the others behind them. They divided their horsemen into two groups. This was the time to trust that those on my walls would defend the ground on our flanks. The attacks by my brother's Vikings had cost us many dead and wounded in the flanks. In the centre we were solid but the flanks were vulnerable. With a great clamour of horns, they moved forward. The horses rode through the periphery of our defences. The Viking attack had removed the caltrops and their dead lay in the pits but they still had stakes to avoid. Stones and arrows from our walls began to thin them out.

Then we had to concentrate on the men to the fore. They too had merely to avoid the stakes. The ones at the front had good shields and our archers and slingers concentrated upon the men towards the rear of the mighty phalanx.

"Brace!" We placed our right legs behind us and held our shields supported by our shoulders and left arms. Most of our spears were shattered and so we faced them with swords. My bloody Long Sword stuck out from the rest. I had not had time to clean it and there were pieces of bone and guts clinging to it.

When they struck there was a clatter of metal on wood and metal on metal. Both of our front ranks were mailed. My sword took the first Breton. He was not in the front rank. That warrior had turned his head to the side to avoid my blade. The weight of the men behind drove the Breton on to my sword. I found myself facing a second Breton. His head came up to my chest. We were too close for a swing and so I raised my sword high in the air and brought the hilt down hard upon the top of his helmet. It stunned him. I could not move my shield. It was locked with his but I managed to bring my knee up hard. I felt the air knocked from him. I slammed my hilt down on his head once more. The double blow worked. He sank to the ground and I stepped into the void his body had left. Sven joined me and we stood on the Breton's body. Soon he would be dead for we were big men and our combined weight was crushing him to death.

As I stepped onto the body I saw that our flanks were holding. The men ahead of me were being thinned by our archers and slingers. I was able to swing my sword, as was Sven. I swung right and he swung left. Our swords hacked into the backs of the necks of the Bretons. Sámr and Bergil stepped forward and we began to eat our way through the mailed men. A sword clanged into my helmet. Had I been shorter it might have had an effect. As it was just the tip struck it and it merely discomfited me. I looked down at the man who had struck the blow then I stabbed down and into his neck. My sword drove down and we continued to push. It was only the weight of men behind me which forced the body from my sword.

It was time. "Petr, sound the horn!"

Petr was behind the last line of warriors and the horn sounded. The Bretons would not know what it meant. The archers on the walls did and they and the men in the tower began to rain death upon the horsemen to our left. Stephen of Andecavis would be bringing our meagre force of horsemen to slam into the flank of the Breton horses. I hoped that it would tip the balance in our favour.

We were now a wedge with Sven and I the tip. I saw that we had carved a path through the Bretons. Many more still awaited us but they wore no mail. Many had no helmets and they saw a fearsome giant leading bloody and vengeful Vikings. Most held their swords and shields as though they expected to die. They died. Ahead of us, I saw the Breton lords on their horses. They had oathsworn with them. They had mailed men who had yet to fight. If they joined the fray then we would struggle to cope.

It was at that moment that my horsemen struck. I did not see them but I heard the crack as their spears knocked Breton horsemen from their saddles. Then they hit the flank of the Breton foot and they crumbled. Attacked by Vikings on two sides they now had horsemen on the third. The right flank of the Breton attack disappeared in a heartbeat. Horns sounded and flags signalled. The nobles and their oathsworn moved away. They were heading back to their camp. It was not over for us as we still had a sea of Bretons to harvest. The more we hurt them then the safer we would be. I did not see it but I heard a roar from behind as my grandfather had the gates opened and fresh warriors joined us. I sheathed Long Sword for it was becoming blunted and drew my second sword. We were now a mass of warriors surging forward. When we reached my brother's body and Arne the Breton Slayer I stopped. The battle was over. My men would continue to hunt and to slay but my battle was done. I reached down and took my father's sword. It was a good sword and I would use it with Long Sword.

Petr found me and I said, "Sound the recall! I would not have men waste their lives."

Ragnar the Resolute was close by, "But the Breton nobles still live!"

I nodded, "And they have fresh men and horses." I pointed up at the sun. "It is gone noon. I know not about you Ragnar but my arms are weary and my weapons are blunt. If you could have been given this victory when we started would you have taken it?"

"Of course, lord. We have defeated many times our number. It is a great victory."

"And yet we are still outnumbered. Now is the time for talk."

Sven had rejoined us, along with Sámr, "Göngu-Hrólfr Rognvaldson is right, Ragnar. We have lost men; good men. This was not a cheap victory. Our lord is clever. He will negotiate us into a position of power."

Stephen of Andecavis rode up. He was grinning, "I have never seen so few horsemen have such an effect, lord!"

"Did we lose many?"

"Just six lord, and only three died. We captured twenty horses. I will take that trade."

"Then ride to the Bretons and say that I would talk with them."

"Aye lord."

He and my horsemen headed off towards the Breton camp. My men began to clear the battlefield. Our dead were reverently removed and taken back to Caen. The enemy dead were stripped. I walked to my brother and to Arne the Breton Slayer. I took an axe from a dead Viking and hacked off their heads. Taking two spears, I rammed the spears into the ground and, after taking the helmets from their heads, planted their heads on the spear shafts. The men they had led had left. This was a reminder to them of who had won.

My grandfather rode from the walls to join me. "You were brave, Rollo, although a little foolish. Why did you fight two of them?"

"Would my brother have fought me alone?"

My grandfather shook his head. "He always hid behind others but you took a risk."

"As did you when you first came to the Haugr. We are here to win a home." I pointed to the nobles who headed towards us. "Perhaps we have taken a giant step towards that goal."

My men stood behind my grandfather, Sven and me. A young Breton noble rode towards us, "We are here for talks and yet you have your men behind you!"

"And I have spoken. There will be no bloodshed here." I pointed to the two heads, "As you can see I know how to deal with treachery. I would speak with this Lord Pascweten. At the moment he is lord of this land and it is he I will deal with!"

The young noble nodded. He rode back to the others and three Bretons approached. They remained in their saddles. "You will dismount if we are to talk of peace!"

They did so reluctantly. Lord Pascweten said, somewhat ungraciously, "You said that you wished to speak; speak!"

"The battle has ended not because it is over but because I have decided that enough men have died. If I chose I could continue the battle and slaughter your army." I pointed behind me. "As you can see more of your men remain on the field than mine." I waited until he nodded. "Here are my terms, Caen, Bayeux and Lisieux are mine. Do not attempt to retake them or I will lay waste to the whole of the Coutances."

"And what of Djupr? That is not included?"

"Djupr was nothing until we came. It is mine and we do not negotiate for that citadel! And I have not finished. I will send my drekar to the Haugr, Bárekr's Haven, Valognes and Carentan. Any of my grandfather's people who live there will be allowed to leave and to join me here."

"They can go for we have had enough of dealings with barbarians! And what then? Do you bow the knee to me?"

"Of course not. It means that we will not attack the land that was the land of the Bretons."

He frowned, "This does not end the war?"

"You still have a civil war. Let us say that so long as my three towns remain at peace then the land to the west of the Issicauna will not be raided." I could see him working out if that was acceptable. "Lord Pascweten, I have many drekar. Your Viking mercenaries will not fight for you. Do you really wish my men to raid Angia, Sarnia, Rennes and Nantes?"

He shook his head, "Let it be recorded. I will have my clerks make up the document," he gave me a sly look, "if you can read!"

"Oh, I can read, and I will study it to make certain that you are not trying to cheat us!"

It took three days but we were granted permission to hold the three towns we had taken. I had my horsemen follow the Bretons until they had passed Bayeux. I sent my grandfather with the drekar to seek any of our people who remained in Coutances. Bagsecg assured me there were. He had only been able to contact and gather a few of the Clan of the Horse. They would lead a parlous existence now amongst the Bretons.

As we buried our dead and sorted through that which we had taken my sentries alerted me to the return of the Vikings who had fought us. I ordered the men to stand to. I was unworried when I reached the gate. There were just a hundred or so of them and they did not look to be well-nourished. Sven and I went from the gate to greet them. To have spoken from my walls would have suggested that I was afraid and I was not.

The leader, or the one who spoke with me, was a gnarled warrior. He looked to have seen forty or more summers. His battle scars bespoke experience. He took off his helmet and laid his sword at my feet. "Göngu-Hrólfr Rognvaldson, I am Rolf of Agder. I lead these men. Ailmær the Cruel went with the Bretons." I nodded. "We served your brother and fought against you." I said nothing. "Many of our brethren have left to serve other Breton and

Frankish lords. We have no drekar. You burned them. We would not serve Bretons again. They are faithless. We would serve you."

"And I can trust you?"

"We stood and let you fight our Prince for that was right and the Allfather showed us that you spoke the truth. We have seen that you are a mighty warrior and we would serve you. We know you can command ships and command men. We would have you as our lord."

"I would need an oath; it would be binding. I have many Vikings with me they would not rest if you were foresworn."

"Lord, we are Vikings. We came here to hire out our swords. We thought your brother was a true Viking. He was not. He sat atop his horse and never fought. We know that Göngu-Hrólfr Rognvaldson leads his men. We have heard from our brothers in the land of the Saxons that the sons of Ragnar Lodbrok speak well of you. We chose the wrong brother."

I looked at Sven. He nodded. My men would soon get to know if any of these were men without honour. If they were they would rue the day they tried to deceive us. "Very well then when you have sworn you can join us."

They were hungry. They had had three days without food and we fed them. While they ate I spoke with my chief warriors. "We have too many men for Caen and now we have two more towns we can fortify. Sámr, Bergil, I would have you become Counts of Bayeux and Lisieux. I would have you rule them for me. What say you?"

They both grinned. Bergil said, "When I first followed you I knew my life would change. I did not know by how much. Of course, I accept!"

"And I!"

"Sven, I wish you to spend the next few days choosing the best eighty men who have just joined us. Forty each can go to my new lords. I know we have the Breton's piece of parchment but walls defended by Vikings will be a better deterrent."

"Aye lord."

"And you, my most loyal of friends and warriors will be Count of Caen."

Lord of Rouen

"I am honoured but you give us titles and have none yourself."

"Fear not. I have a title in mind but that will wait until we are ready to take the river!"

Part Three
Lord of Rouen

Chapter 13

We sent drekar to raid Wessex again. We had exhausted the quarries which lay close to us and we would need to buy stone for our two new towns. It was easier to catch and sell slaves and then buy stone rather than steal the stone. While our ships hunted my grandfather returned with more than a hundred and twenty of our people who had remained in the land close to the Haugr and Valognes. I knew none of them but my grandfather remembered their fathers and, in some cases, grandfathers. We went from a small clan with less than three hundred folk to a tribe of almost a thousand in four strong towns. The incomers all spoke Breton. Some, mainly the women, were Christian. They stayed in the large groups in which they had lived in the Land of the Horse. More than any they wished strong walls. They had lost their homes once and they would not do so a second time. Our success drew men and their families to us. One such was Rolf of Agder who had come from the southern coast of Norway. His people had been defeated by Haraldr Finehair. The newly crowned King of Norway was ruthless. He killed the men and married the women to his warriors. One day we might have to fight his people. However, for the moment, we benefitted. We were a safe haven for the Vikings who fled.

Bergljót followed her son and his pregnant wife to Lisieux. It would have made Gefn sad if it was not for the fact that she spent every waking minute with Poppa. Poppa was no longer Breton.

Lord of Rouen

She had seen her father try to kill me and in that instant, she became one of our tribe. We were not Breton and we were not Norse. We had people from many lands. We were, simply, *'the people'*. That was how we called ourselves. We were the tribe. It was a tribe without a name. When my people spoke of the tribe they either called it Rollo's tribe or, if they had come from Norway, Göngu-Hrólfr Rognvaldson's tribe. We did not care what the Franks and the Bretons called us. Mainly they referred to us as barbarians or pagans. That was because most of us did not worship the White Christ. Along with the people who came with my grandfather came a white-haired priest; Æðelwald of Remisgat.

I frowned when I saw him for I knew that he had been the cause of the curse on Ragnvald. I knew that those who came would need a priest but I had hoped for another. He was a reminder of the curse. Poppa was delighted to see a priest and she and Sprota immediately took him off so that they could confess. They had not confessed since we had taken them.

I spoke with my grandfather, "I find it hard to understand why you brought the priest of the White Christ. He is the one that caused my father's death!"

Hrolf the Horsemen nodded. He was white-haired and people said that the whiter your hair then the wiser you were. He had to be the wisest man I knew. "Firstly, your brother is dead and the curse died with him. Your father and your mother paid for their mistake with their lives. The priest was not to blame. It was the Norns. We need a priest now. He came with us for many of the ones we brought are all followers of the White Christ. He came with, what he called his flock. You are to marry a Christian. She will need a priest."

"He will not marry us!" For the first time in my life, I raised my voice and I regretted it instantly for my grandfather recoiled.

He recovered and nodded, "And not even Poppa expects that. You will take her as a wife as all Vikings take their wives. You will carry her into your bedroom and that will be the marriage made but you are the lord of Christians as well as Vikings. Will you create division?"

171

I shook my head. That was not my way but I could not bring myself to speak with this Æðelwald of Remisgat. "And he will want a church?"

"The followers of the White Christ will build it and they will do so where it does not offend you. Do not drive away your father's people. I know you can never forgive the priest but you can put it from your mind and think of your people."

I smiled, "It is good that Hrolf the Horseman still leads this tribe for Göngu-Hrólfr Rognvaldson still has much to learn."

The rest of that year passed so quickly that I wondered if the sun was moving faster than it had in times past. My warriors' wives had babies and Gefn kept looking at Poppa hopefully. Our raids on Wessex afforded us great quantities of gold and we bought good stone. The walls of Bayeux and Lisieux grew. The Bretons fought amongst themselves and we heard that Pascweten had been defeated and they had a king. The King of Wessex, Alfred, was besieged in his swamp fortress of Athelney and Guthrum was now the leader, some said, King, of the Danes. For myself, I had no time to think. When I was not raiding I was helping my men build their towns. In that Æðelwald of Remisgat proved to be useful. Like Father Michel he understood how to build. The two towns we rebuilt were stronger as a result of his work.

I was sitting and reading the latest messages from Djupr when Poppa entered the empty hall. I also had the maps of my land laid out before me. My servants knew that I liked to be alone. She smiled, "Something of interest, my lord?"

"Olaf Two Teeth tells me that Charles the Bald has ordered the building of two bridges across the Issicauna although the Franks now call it the Seine. The King of the Franks thinks that will stop our raids."

"You have not raided Paris yet?"

"Not yet. We have much to consolidate here. I intend to take the land between here and Rouen for my own."

"And then what, lord? What would you do when you have Rouen?"

I sat back. I had not thought that far ahead. "I know not."

"Your grandfather began this dynasty. You are all that is left now. Sámr and Bergil are fathers yet you do not even have a wife."

"I told you that when you have seen sixteen…"

"That will be in the month you call Þorri."

I had not realised that so much time had passed, "That is just two months away."

She smiled, "Gefn and I have been counting the days. She thought you ought to know."

"You still wish to be my bride, my, what do you Franks call it, *more danico*?"

"I care not what it is called save that I am your partner and that we will have children together."

"I will not marry in the manner of the White Christ."

She laughed, "And each time we lie together I will confess to Father Æðelwald of my sin. I hope to keep him very busy!"

"You do not wish to return to your father?"

She shook her head, "He has left me here too long. I have spoken with Gefn. She is wise. The Countess thought it expedient that I was gone. I was used. I gained sympathy for my father and his cause." She cocked her head to one side, "You are sad that there will be no ransom?"

It was my turn to laugh and I stood and swept her into my arms. "You are worth more to me than any treasure but I have promised the Bretons I will not raid their lands and I will keep my word." I tapped the maps. "It is the Franks who live along the river who should fear us." I took her hand and led her to the maps. "You could be of some use." I waved my hand around the river basin. "I know who rules here and who rules in the land of the Angles and the Saxons but further afield I am unsure. What do you know?"

"Little more than you lord save that Charles' brother, Louis, is Emperor of the Germans and the Italians. I know that the Bretons almost defeated Charles the Bald but his brother's support prevented that. His brother is not well."

I looked at her askance, "How do you know that? You have lived with us for some years."

"When ships come to trade here I do as I did at Djupr, I speak with their captains. They know much of the world. It is in their interests to know who rules."

I realised that I had just spoken to my captains. They knew the politics of Wessex and Northumbria, Flanders and Denmark but further south was a mystery. "And how would the building of two bridges at Paris affect us?"

"You would not be able to get beyond Paris. It would add to their defences. I went to Paris as a child. It is a wondrous city. There are fine churches there and they are made of stone."

"One day I shall raid it." I took her hand and led her back to the room where Gefn and her ladies were sewing a tapestry. Poppa had given me much to think on. The King of the West Franks had seemed to me a powerful man yet if the Bretons had almost defeated him then that strength was an illusion. I took her to Gefn, "We shall be wed at Þorri." Gefn kissed my hand and then Poppa's. I had made two women happy.

When my drekar returned from a raid on Flanders I gathered my captains together so that we could plan. It was almost the heart of winter and our ships would be laid up for cleaning and repair. The season's raids were over and we were much richer. Those riches had gone into mail and men, swords and helmets. It seemed to me that the Franks and Bretons put their coin into clothes and furnishings. Since my talk with Poppa, I had also spoken with Æðelwald of Remisgat. I still found it hard to look at the man but he was a source of information. He confirmed all that Poppa had said and more.

"The man you defeated, lord, has power but he will not be king. That will be Alan, his cousin. He managed to avoid joining any of the factions in the civil war and his hands are untouched by blood."

"And from what you are not saying he will wish to drive us from this land."

He shook his head, "Not here, lord. There are many of your people still in the Coutances and around Avranches. They eke out a living there. They did not wish to come with your grandfather. He wants a land which is free from enemies of Brittany. He looks inward to the borders of the old Brittany. This land was ceded to King Salomon by Charles the Bald. It is not Brittany."

I appreciated the priest's knowledge. "Tell me, if I were to attack one of the main Frankish strongholds, one of their fortresses, how would I do it?"

He was a priest of the White Christ but he had a mind which was inquisitive. He was well-read. He had studied in Rome and Ravenna. He nodded, unperturbed by the underlying message in my question. "The Romans made wooden rams which can be used to break through a gate. They have wheels and are covered in hide. Manned by strong men they can break down gates and are hard to destroy. They also built mangonels and onagers which could hurl stones at walls. They wear down an enemy. I have heard that the Emperor in the east uses them with fire. Then there were the deadly bolt throwers."

I frowned, "Bolt throwers?"

"Imagine a bow which does not need a man to use it. The cord is wound back and when it is released the bolt, as long as a man's leg, can travel up to eight hundred paces and still kill. It punched holes in wooden walls. And, of course, most walls can be mined. Men can dig beneath the walls, support their workings with wood, light fires and burn the supports. Walls come down."

I nodded.

He studied my face as though trying to read my thoughts, "I have to warn you, lord, that such machines are hard to build and, in the cases of onagers and bolt throwers, prone to breaking down."

"Thank you. When we have need of such machines I would have you build them for me."

He looked shocked, "But, lord, I am a man of God."

"And if I allow you to live in my land and to minister to my followers of the White Christ then you are my man and you will do as I command. I suffer you, priest, I do not enjoy your presence."

He smiled, "After the Breton lords your honesty is refreshing lord. A man knows where he stands."

Lord of Rouen

After he had gone I realised that we could never have reclaimed the Haugr and the land around Valognes. It would have cost us too much in blood. The land in which we now lived was better for it had longer rivers which suited us and citadels we could defend. We had to strike quickly to take advantage of the weakness of the Franks. If the Bretons could defeat them in battle then so could we.

My drekar captains had also learned much in their raids. Only Wessex still remained free from Danish control and Guthrum, who now led the Danes, was confident that it would soon fall. The Kings of Frankia had supported the Saxon kings and the fact that the Danes had had so much success showed the weakness of the Franks.

"We will raid the river the Franks now call the Seine in Einmánuður. The last raid we made was slow. It was cautious and it was measured. This time I intend to use every drekar to take us to the land around Jumièges. I intend to capture a base quickly. We can build a defensive camp between the two bends in the river. We ransack and ravage the land and when the Franks come to fight us, defeat them in battle."

Only Sven and my grandfather were not surprised at such a bold move. Sámr said, "That is far upstream, lord. We would be close to Rouen and to Paris. They would not take kindly to the presence of so many raiders that close to their capital."

My grandfather spoke, "When Charles the Bald's father ruled we made our first raids up the river. We sacked the churches. Since then others have ventured up the river as far as Paris. My grandson has discovered that they have built two bridges across the river to prevent us from doing so again. They fear us Sámr Oakheart. If they thought that they could have defeated us then they would have brought an army here to evict us."

Bergil was not convinced, "We have a large army but surely the Franks will have a larger one."

"It could be as large as the Emperor's army and it would avail them little. I have been told that the Emperor of the Romans so fears and respects our warriors that his personal guard at Miklagård is now made up of Vikings. It is not numbers that win battles. It is the quality of the warrior. Bergil you lead your own

176

warband. They are mailed and trained by you. Would you fear to face in battle the same number of Franks?"

He laughed, "We would not lose a man."

"Twice that number?"

"They would need ten times that number and even then, we would win."

"And the Franks do not have that sort of army to bring against us. We raid and we ravage. We take from the land around the river. They will come to fight us and when they are defeated then we take Rouen. Once we have Rouen we control the river. They can put a dozen bridges across the river with Rouen as our citadel then we control the whole basin."

Sámr still looked worried, "And what of my home in Bayeux? With my men away, what is to stop the Bretons from retaking it?"

"The men you leave to defend its walls. You do not take all of the men from your town. We did not replace the walls we destroyed with wood. We built in stone. We put ditches and diverted water so that our homes were protected. The land you hold is Frankia. The Bretons will be scouring their homeland for Vikings. One day they may bring war here but not for some years. When we have raided then you can return to your home but you will be a much richer man. Your warriors will be richer and, more importantly, we will control the mighty river. We will have a land which we can defend!"

I seemed to have no rest. When I was not planning the raid, I was adjudicating over legal matters. I was the judge for Caen and disputes were settled by me. All the while Gefn and Poppa were planning not just a wedding but a hall in which we would live. Gefn had used her own coin to have a hall built next to my tower. I had no say in its position and its design. The two of them chivvied the builders. Æðelwald of Remisgat designed it and he made it strong. It had cellars for food and a door on the first floor. He built a chamber for guards to sleep close to the main door and a sleeping chamber as big as Gefn's hall back in Norway. I was dragged, each day to inspect the progress. I confess I was impressed with the hall.

"See, my son, you can have your privacy here and yet there is a door which takes you to your hall so that you can hear cases. The priest is a clever man. I can see why Poppa is a follower of the White Christ."

I had glared at Æðelwald of Remisgat who had understood my look, "I have not tried to convert any of your people lord. Those who wish to become followers of Christ I baptise but I do not try to persuade any."

"Good for the day that you do is the day that you are thrown from my lands."

I saw Poppa roll her eyes and Gefn tutted but I wanted all to know my views. We practised the old ways. The way of the White Christ was the way of weakness. I knew that many women had converted but so far, no warriors had dared to risk my anger.

We now had enough horses for two hundred of us to ride to war. We would not fight from the backs of the horses but we would be able to reach the river in one day from Lisieux. Erik had even managed to breed a horse for me to ride. Gilles was a young horse but I could ride him without my feet trailing along the ground. He was not the swiftest of horses but when on his back, I had a commanding view over the other riders. I was content.

The warriors who had come with me from Norway insisted upon throwing a party for me before I was wed. Most of them, Sven apart, were already married and had children. To them, it was a symbolic act. When I wed I would have children and then there would be others to lead the tribe. My grandfather attended too. He sat next to me and was in his cups. His rheumy eyes filled as he spoke of my father and the hopes he had had had for him. "My daughters were all taken early. I was not as upset as I should have been. I expected Mary or Anya to have had children but the Allfather did not. When your father became a father, I had hope." He leaned over, "Have many, many children!"

"Poppa is not a Viking, grandfather."

"Nor was your grandmother and yet she bore four children. We should have had more." He shook his head. "When you are old you have regrets. You see what you should have done when you had the chance. You are still young. Poppa is even younger. The

Norns spin and you know not what will bring harm to your young. Clothilde cut her hand on a bramble bush and it killed her." He shook his head. "Neither my wife nor I knew why. Have children. Keep Poppa with child! Our blood is now in you alone. If the witch I met in the cave all those years ago was right then it is my blood which will rule this land."

It was then that I knew what drove my grandfather. It was the prophecy. If it did not come true then that was his fault. I suddenly felt the burden of expectation fall upon my shoulders. Did Poppa know what she had taken on?

I was more nervous on the day of my wedding than my bride. I knew not what was expected of me save that I had to produce children. I had never been one to lay my seed about me. I had lain with one woman. Perhaps my early brush with death had made me different from other men. The ceremony was ridiculously simple. I picked up Poppa. She was no weight, I had worn heavier armour. I took her through the door to my new hall and up the stairs to our bed chamber and then I laid her upon it. All those who were gathered cheered as though that in itself was an achievement. Gefn had sent to Bruggas for some of the fine linen they made there. I had never felt anything as smooth. Poppa smiled and patted the bed. "Come lord, I have waited some time for this."

I sat next to her. She began to comb my hair and my beard. The only woman I had laid with before had been the Hibernian Princess, Kaolin. That seemed many years ago and I was nervous. Kaolin had been rough-hewn clay compared with this fine porcelain vessel I was about to enter. She laid down her combs and brushes and began to take off my kyrtle. I wore nothing beneath. I suddenly realised that I still had my boots on my feet. I knew that I would look foolish and I did not wish to dirty the fine linen. When they were removed I saw that Poppa had undressed and she lay on the bed. I had worried about knowing what to do. As I saw her lying there all such doubts went from my mind. The Allfather had given me the answer.

The next morning Gefn and my grandfather knocked on our door and brought us food and ale. It was a tradition going back to the land of snow and ice. They did not seem to notice our nakedness. What Gefn did notice was the stained sheet and it seemed to delight her. Hrolf the Horseman said, "Welcome to my family, Poppa, lady of the Bretons." He handed her a blue stone on a silver chain. I vaguely remembered my grandmother wearing it. "This is for you. It belonged to my wife Mary and she would be happy that you wore it."

Gefn took the ring from her ring finger and slipped it on to Poppa's. It fitted only loosely, "This was given to me by my husband. I give it to you that it will bind you to our family. Welcome, Poppa, daughter, mine."

And with that Poppa became part of my family. Sprota moved into one of the smaller rooms which adjoined mine and Sven appointed two young warriors to be chamberlains. Their task would be to sleep, each night, across the doorway. I was now a lord and a married man. I felt different. When I went to war, I would be fighting for the tribe and for my family.

Chapter 14

The army we gathered was the largest I had ever commanded.
Even my grandfather had not seen such a large gathering. We had
twenty drekar and each was double crewed. That gave us over
twelve hundred men on the river. I led two hundred horsemen
from the south and Ragnar the Resolute led two hundred men from
Djupr. Vikings came from Norway and from the land of the
Angles to join us. They saw the chance for land and treasure. The
best land in Northumbria and in the land of the East Angles and
Mercia had been taken. King Haraldr of Norway had rewarded his
own jarls. Serving Göngu-Hrólfr Rognvaldson offered land and a
chance to gain even more. We left good garrisons in our four
towns. The Bretons had begun to war amongst themselves and
were not a threat yet I would not leave my wife and family in
danger. My grandfather wished to come. He saw the prophecy
being fulfilled. I forbade it, "Your place is here to guide our tribe. I
promise that when Rouen is ours you shall be there to see the
victory."

"You can take that mighty rock?"

I smiled, "Sven and I have worked out how to do so. We beat
their armies piecemeal. We make a camp in the bend of the river
and send out warbands to plunder the land around Rouen. We use
our drekar to threaten Paris. I have no intention of bleeding upon
that rock but the Franks will draw all of their men to defend it and
Rouen will be isolated. We have a whole summer to raid, ransack
and to ravage. When they are weak I will have the priest build me
machines and I will break down the walls. By the time my son is
born, I will be the lord of Rouen."

"Poppa is with child?"

"She has my seed in her. I plant more each night. She will breed sons and daughters for me. I did listen, grandfather."

Perhaps the Norns were laughing or just weaving webs but, as I left for the campaign, Poppa was still without a child and I had doubts about my manhood. My oathsworn had all fathered children on the first night they had lain with their wives. It was a distraction I could have done without. We rode our horses hard and covered more than seventy miles that first day. My fleet would be sailing up the river to go beyond Rouen. Ragnar's men had the shortest journey from Djupr to Rouen but they would be on foot. It would be my mounted horse band which would alert the Franks and the Bretons. Our thundering hooves would sound like the crack of doom. My aim was to get to the river as soon as I could. Drekar would be waiting at Jumièges to ferry us across but I wanted to make certain that there was no opposition south of the river.

We were opposed at Routot. It was just five miles from the river and, until we reached the small, walled hall, we had only seen farms and hamlets. Every town and hall had been deserted. There was a Frankish lord at Routot. Although we had scouts out they heard our approach. They sounded their bell and by the time Arne and Leif had ridden back to say there was a hall they had gathered men. We dismounted and, after tethering our horses, walked the one thousand paces to their walls. It was hard to see numbers for they were behind the wood of their palisade. It was not a substantial wall. They had a church within the walls; I could see the cross on the small bell tower. Every farmer and his family who had been within hearing had fled to the walls. If we could take this village then there would be no one south of the river to threaten us.

I turned to Sven. "This is an old-fashioned hall let us take it the old-fashioned way. We attack the gate and this wall. Have twenty men with bows keep their heads down and we advance behind shields."

Sven Blue Cheek pointed to the standard which fluttered above the gate. "There is a lord here and he will have oathsworn who wear mail."

"Good, it will save Bagsecg making more! Shield wall!" I was confident. The first blow struck in this campaign would be by me!

With twenty men ready with bows we had three lines of sixty men. That was enough to attack the full frontage of the walls. We had some Danes with us and I placed them so that they could attack the gate with their axes. The rest of us would ascend the walls. Once again Göngu-Hrólfr Rognvaldson would be the human ladder.

I banged my shield and we chanted to get the rhythm.

> *Men of Caen with leader tall*
> *Fight the Frank and his walls do fall*
> *Men of Caen fear no pain*
> *They will fight and a land will gain*
> *Men of Caen we come for you*
> *Men of Caen bring on your doom!*
> *Men of Caen with leader tall*
> *Fight the Frank and his walls do fall*
> *Men of Caen fear no pain*
> *They will fight and a land will gain*
> *Men of Caen we come for you*
> *Men of Caen bring on your doom!*

We marched on the second repetition. Our archers took the men on the walls by surprise when arrows rained down on them. They sent five flights and then ran to rejoin us. As we marched I saw men fall from the walls. Their boys with slings began to hurl stones at us. We had none to counter them and we had to raise our shields and endure the stone storm. One cracked off my helmet. My helmet was well made else it might have caused a wound.

I heard Sven shout, "Kill the slingers!"

The closer we came to the walls the more accurate were our bows and the boys fell. The stone storm stopped. They then began hurling javelins and spears at us. If we had worn open helmets then we might have suffered more casualties. As it was the narrow gap between the nasal and the side of the helmet, aided by our shields, stopped us losing men. The danger lay in the weight of spears on our shields. Some of my more inexperienced men tried to remove them. They paid for their naivety with a spear in the leg. My archers switched targets and the fall of spears slowed. We reached the wall and I dropped my shield and turned my back to the wall. My other men paired up and held a shield between them. Speed was all-important and Leif the Leaper lived up to his name as he jumped into my cupped hands and I threw him upwards. Even as he landed Sven Regnisson followed his friend and the two of them were the first to land on the wall. They wore mail and the men amongst whom they landed did not.

To my right, I heard the sound of Danish axes on the gate. My shield men were rising like wraiths to join the two leapers. I picked up my shield and went with Sven to the gate. The Danes had come from Guthrum and were desperate to impress the friend of the famous Dane. I saw that the gate would fall within a few more blows. I drew Long Sword and held my shield before me. When the last stroke struck the gate, the Danes threw their shoulders at it and it burst asunder. The fighting platform was filled with battling warriors. We would win that battle. Ahead of me, the Frankish lord had his mailed men ready to face us.

Sven flanked me and the Danes with axes joined him. The ten of us, backed by thirty men behind us, began to march towards the Franks. Their shield wall bristled with spears. The front two ranks held their best men. The rest were farmers. I had not seen the two handed Danish axe used much before. I now saw its effect. With their shields around their backs, the six Danes with us swung their axes in a figure of eight. They must have practised this action many times for the six axes were as one. The spears which were jabbed at them became splintered and shattered. The ones which came towards Sven and I were batted away by our swords. As the Frankish lord reached for his sword I punched him in the face with the boss of my shield. At the same time, six Danish axes smashed into helmets, skulls, shields and bodies.

The Frankish lord reeled and before he could gain his balance I lunged. My sword was tipped and sharp. It tore through his byrnie and into his guts. I leaned and twisted before withdrawing my sword and stepping over his body. The Danish axes and the death of their lord were enough for the farmers; they fled. The oathsworn who remained were surrounded and slaughtered. They kept their oath.

The men on the walls secured the second gate but, by then, the defenders and their families had fled. They had taken nothing save their bodies. The church had been abandoned. The food in the lord's hall was still on the table. After dispatching the wounded, we fetched our horses and enjoyed a night in the hall. We ate and drank well. We had time aplenty to search the hall and the church for treasure. We dug in each hut and beneath the altar to find all that the Franks had hidden. The ones who had escaped had nothing save their lives. We buried our own dead and burned the Franks. The smoke of the funeral pyre was a warning to the rest of the land that Vikings were raiding.

The next morning, we loaded most of the horses with the booty and I sent twenty men back with them to Caen. The horses had served their purpose. We had four miles to march and await our drekar. Before we left we burned the hall and the walls. It would be a marker for our ships and a warning to the Franks that they farmed this valley at their peril. There was a trail through the forest. Along it we found bodies of some of those who had fled and succumbed to their wounds. All were farmers and those who served the lord.

Leif the Leaper walked close by me and after the third body said, "Lord why did they not stay to defend their home? They died anyway. Better to have died protecting what they had than trying to save their lives."

"These men are the followers of the White Christ. They do not believe in Valhalla. Do you see how they died with their hands around their wooden crosses?" He nodded. "They hoped to gain forgiveness for their sins. There is no certainty of heaven for the Frank. That is why they chose the chance of life rather than a glorious death. That is why we will prevail and they will fail."

We could smell the river and we hurried the last thousand paces. The river was empty. Our ships had yet to arrive. I was unworried. I could see the abbey at Jumièges on the hillside on the opposite bank. They could see us and knew what it meant. I had no doubt that the smoke to the south and refugees had alerted them. It

185

mattered not. Our arrival made them sound the bell. Riders would be racing to Rouen to summon help. The priests in their bell tower would be counting our spears and helmets. They would see just a hundred and odd men. We were a small warband. This was deliberate for I wanted to tempt the Franks.

We made camp and I sent men hunting. The arrival of our fleet was not a precise event. They had the wind and tides to negotiate as well as the bends in the river. My plan was a good one. My grandfather and Sven Blue Cheek had approved. I took off my mail and went to the river to bathe. I knew not what the priests who peered from their walls, more than a mile away, made of the naked giant.

That night we ate well. My men had found wild boar and deer. We roasted the meat and feasted. We drank the last of our ale. I knew that the monks at Jumièges brewed good ale, wine and fermented apple juice. When our ships arrived, we would be able to refill our skins. Sven had never seen the abbey before. It was an impressive structure although it had been raided many times and burned down once. It was now made of stone. We kept a fire burning by the river. It showed the priests that we had not left and it would be a marker for our drekar.

"Will there be anything left in the church? They know we are here and surely they will send it to Rouen."

"This is why I wanted us to be the first to arrive. They will have enough men to defend against our paltry numbers. When our drekar arrive, that will be a different matter. Then they will flee. Besides, it matters not if they send their treasure to Rouen. When we take Rouen, we will take all that Jumièges contained anyway."

I had not been asleep long when one of the sentries woke me, "Sorry lord but we thought you should know, one of the drekar is here."

This was good news. The Norns had been spinning. "Wake the men but do so silently." I reached the river and saw that it was *'Fafnir'*. Harold Haroldsson was at the steering board. He clambered to the bank and clasped my arm. "You made good time."

He nodded, "I know the river better than most but the Franks tried to stop us downstream. They held us up briefly but I would not call it a battle. Their ships are little more than big knarr. The rest of the fleet will be here by morning. Their captains were not as confident of the river. I confess that I would not have gone much further upstream at night."

I grasped his shoulders, "Then this is fortuitous. I would have you ferry us across in the dark. I would surround the church before they see our fleet. You have a full crew?"

"Aye, lord, we lost none."

"Then I will fetch my mail and I will lead them." I hurried back to the camp and told Sven my plan. I could leave him to organise the men. *'Fafnir'* had more than sixty men on board. I could leave just ten to ferry and take the other fifty and give the priests a surprise. I donned my mail while Harold turned the ship around. We rigged a rope to make it easier to cross the river. Tying it at one end we would secure it to the other bank and then the ten men we left above could ferry the rest of the warband.

The men aboard were eager to raid. They were envious of the ones I had taken with me. As we rowed across the narrow stretch of water I told them what I expected of them. "We are here to stop the priests from taking away their treasures. This abbey will be our home until we have defeated the Franks. We do not destroy the walls and we avoid slaughtering the priests. They will make good hostages and there is little honour in killing a priest." I saw them nod as they strained to pull us against the current.

As soon as we landed the ship's boys wrapped the rope we had carried around a large tree and held the drekar against the bank. I jumped ashore with the fifty men I would lead. Even as the last one landed the drekar was being dragged back across the river for the next fifty men. My grandfather told me how there was a well-worn path which led up to the abbey. They had had walls and gates at one time but they had been thrown down. We hurried up the slope.

We were just five hundred paces from the abbey and the church when the alarm was sounded. I had expected it. They would not leave us unwatched. Some sentry had noticed the movement of the drekar. The strident notes of the bell rang across the valley. Sven Blue Cheek would be already landing and it would spur him on. I waved my sword as I shouted, "Surround the church!"

There would be guards, I knew that. I left my shield around my back and held Long Sword in two hands. The Franks had left men to guard the priests. Some wore mail. The first ones we met were the sentries who bravely raced towards us with spears and shields. Running with a spear down a slippery slope is never easy. We had the advantage that we were travelling slower. The Frank who came at me rammed his spear at my head. In those days I was young. I had quick reflexes and while moving my head to the side I swept my sword in a wide arc to cut him through to his backbone. I threw his body from my blade and hurried up the hill. The Franks came at us in knots of warriors. My fifty men were in a half-circle. Those we met we slew. I waved to Arne Audunsson, "Take twenty men and cut them off. We will deal with these warriors."

"Aye lord."

Down the slope, I heard Sven Blue Cheek, "Move you lazy whores! Our lord needs us!" It told me that help was on its way.

I was able to swing with confidence. My men had spread out. Few Franks relished facing my singing swinging blade. In avoiding me they ran into warriors eager to make their first kill. I saw a light from the church door and I ran towards it. A young Frank ran at me. He was moving too quickly. He threw his spear when he felt himself tumble. I flicked my sword and knocked aside the spear. As he tumbled at my feet I gave him a warrior's death and continued to the church door. The sky to the east was becoming grey.

Sven Blue Cheek appeared next to me. He was out of breath and his sword was bloody, "You could not wait, lord?"

I pointed to the open door. "They are fleeing. I would have their treasure in my drekar and not in Rouen!"

As we burst through the door priests were filling a chest with the candlesticks, altar ware and holy books. They saw the two of us and dropped the chest. Mindful of my words to my men I said, "We let them go." I turned to the two men who had followed us, "Take this chest to the drekar." As more men entered I had them search for more treasure. We hurried out of the church door to the abbey proper. This was where the priests lived. There was a covered walkway around an open square and buildings off to the side. Some would be simple cells but the abbot would have a finely furnished one. We sought that. We found it and it was clear that the abbot had attempted to pack but our sudden attack had made him realise that his life was more important. Leaving my men to continue to search the building we hurried through the abbey.

Sven and I found Arne Audunsson. They had twenty priests kneeling on the ground before them. Six Frankish warriors lay dead and two priests. The priests were holding on to their crosses and mumbling prayers. Arne shook his head, "I am sorry, lord, the two priests we killed came at us with swords."

"You did right." The chanting was annoying. I snapped at them in Frank, "Shut up that chanting or you will die!" They looked up in terror at the fierce blood-covered giant and they obeyed.

"Did any escape?"

"Yes lord, they had horses. Four warriors and four priests rode towards Rouen. They carried nothing. One of the priests was so fat he could barely mount the horse."

I nodded, "That would be the abbot. Take these priests to the church. We may sell them back to the Franks. We will see how much they value them." I took off my helmet and turned to Sven, "That went better than we planned. The Norns were spinning. Had *'Fafnir'* not reached us in the dark we would have had to attack in daylight and they would all have fled."

"Some escaped."

"As we planned, Sven. When our fleet sails towards Rouen and then Paris they will bar themselves in their halls and we can raid and ravage the whole of the valley. By the time they realise that we have no intention of sacking Paris, this will be a wasteland. Our men will have returned from Caen and we will be able to bring them to battle."

When dawn broke we saw just how successful we had been. *'Fafnir's'* hold and decks were filled with treasure. When the rest of our fleet arrived, we could send her back to Caen. There she could pick up the men who had taken back our horses. While we waited for the fleet we made the abbey defensible. It was not hard. We put men in the bell tower. They had a fine view all around. We put sentries around the perimeter. When our whole army arrived, we would fill the hill with warriors.

It was noon when the fleet arrived and disgorged half of their men. They had all been double crewed. They would be able to sail to Paris easily enough. *'Fafnir'* headed back to Caen with the treasure we had captured. There she would pick up the men who had taken back the horses. I gathered my captains to give them their final instructions. "You sail to Rouen and anchor there for the night. They will expect a dawn attack. When they awake you will be gone. You sail to Paris.to see if you can burn one of their bridges. I would have you stay there for two days. I want Charles the Bald to fear another attack on his capital. I want every Frank for miles around inside Paris' walls. Then you return here."

It was a devious plan but I hoped it would help us sow confusion amongst the Franks. The rest of the men were split up into raiding parties. When darkness fell they would head across country. Franks would wake up to Vikings in their homes. Sven and I would wait for the arrival of Ragnar the Resolute. Although he had the shortest journey it would take him the longest to reach us for he was on foot and we knew not how many enemies lay between them and us.

It felt lonely when the fleet set sail and my warbands set off on their raids. I kept just fifty warriors to guard the priests. We had them tethered at night and during the day they prepared our food. They were watched closely for treachery. Ragnar the Resolute and his men arrived the next day. There were just one hundred and eighty of them. They rode twenty horses. Here was a story.

"We met Bretons who barred our way. They were led by a Frankish lord. I took his head and the rest fled. We captured these horses but it cost us, ten men, dead. The other ten were wounded and I sent them back to Djupr. They emptied their stronghold and headed to Rouen."

"You have done well Ragnar and are rightly named Ragnar the Resolute. The horses will be useful and we have set the Count of

Rouen a problem. Your defeated warriors will report a warband from the north. The priests will report our presence and, by now, our fleet will have anchored close to their walls and they will fear an attack. What they will not know is from which direction. We now have enough men here to repulse an attack, should they send one. You truly are Ragnar the Resolute for you have ever been as a rock for me."

The first of our raiding parties had returned when my sentries reported the Frankish army approaching. It was not as large as I had expected. There were less than five hundred men who approached the abbey. We had just over three hundred to fight them but we had the slope and we were well-rested. Our raiding parties drove animals before them and they had captives. I had to allocate twenty valuable men to watch the captives and the animals. The Franks, augmented by some Breton horsemen camped at the bottom of the hill. They had the two banks of the river guarding their flanks. They must have thought that we were trapped.

When *'Fafnir'* returned with sixty men she was hidden from the Franks by the abbey. Their numbers meant that we could attack. We prepared during the night and, in the hours of darkness, we made our way down to their camp. A night attack always frightened the Franks. They liked daylight. We had used seal oil to grease our mail and we moved carefully. They had sentries out. We could smell them but the bulk of their warriors lay asleep with their horses close by. I knew that word would have reached Rouen that my fleet was attacking Paris and we must have seemed like a rear guard. They had not sent out scouts and assumed too much. I had Petr with me. He was desperate to fight in the shield wall but I had impressed upon him how much I needed him to make the signals.

I had not seen the sentries when the alarm was given. One must have been sharper eyed than the rest. His shout of alarm was truncated by a gurgled scream.

"Now Petr, sound the horn!" Even as the three notes were sounded I had drawn my sword and was leading my men into the enemy camp. More than half of the warriors were horsemen. They were not on their horses. They were half asleep and without mail. With over three hundred and fifty warriors we burst amongst them. The sentries tried to make a stand and to slow us down but it was like trying to keep out the sea with a wall of sand. My sword hacked through two men as though they were naked. Sleeping men rose and found axes and swords hacking into their bodies. So swift was the attack that we reached their leader, the Count of Montfort-sur-Risle when he was still donning his mail. When four of his guards were slain by Ragnar, Sven and myself he surrendered.

When dawn broke we had fifty prisoners and over two hundred horses. The Count was angry beyond words when he saw how few men we had. We had only slain sixty of his men and the rest had run away. This was our chance to make some coin. He had with him his son. I sent his son and two other men, on horses, to Rouen. "I want a chest of gold for the priests and these fifty men. I want the chest to be as long as my arm and as deep. It will be filled with gold. A priest and a warrior will die for each coin which is missing. You have two days. After that, we begin to execute your men."

As they rode off we herded the prisoners back up the hill. We had taken a great number of weapons as well as the horses and the supplies. Now, all depended upon my fleet. By my reckoning, they would be leaving Paris the next day. When they appeared in the river by Rouen it would make the collection of the ransom more urgent. Of course, once the ransom was paid and the Count of Montfort-sur-Risle returned they would know how few men we had. That would be when we would face our real battle.

The Count was still angry when he was fed, by the priests later that evening, "You gave your word that you would not attack the land of Brittany!"

"Nor have I. This is the land of West Frankia." I waved a hand at the captured Bretons. "These men came here when Charles the Bald needed protection from Vikings. Do not bleat if your sheepdogs were not up to the task."

"You cannot win, you know! When you are defeated your men will drift back to Caen and, eventually, the King will gather an army and defeat you. This handful of men cannot fight a royal army."

I nodded, "I will not retreat back to Caen. When I defeat whoever your King sends against us I will reduce Rouen and that will be my new home."

For the first time, he saw the scale of my ambition. He had thought me a raider who took what they had and fled. The thought of Vikings as neighbours terrified him. I saw him clutch at his cross, "You are pagans! God will not allow this to happen. The Holy Roman Emperor himself and the Pope will drive you from this land."

I laughed, "Pagans have done just that in the lands of Mercia, East Anglia and Northumbria. There was a time when you aided your Saxon friends. That land is now ruled by Vikings. The time of the Frank is over, Count. Now is the time of the men from the North. Snow and ice make us hard. We have clawed a hold on this land and, unlike the last time, we have learned our lessons. We will make fortresses which you cannot take. Our ships will control every river. Your King will pay tribute to me to use this river you call the Seine. You are living in the past. Welcome to the future."

'Fafnir' returned with our horsemen. It had managed to negotiate the bends in record time. I was pleased for I needed her crew. We now had another sixty men to stand watch and to repel any attack.

Chapter 15

We had more than enough men to guard all of our prisoners. The priests fed us. There was relief on the faces of the followers of the White Christ. The ransom would be paid and they would not become the slaves of barbarians. The next day riders appeared from the south. We now had enough horses to send out thirty or forty of our men to keep them from closing with us. When my men neared they retreated. The last of our warbands returned during the morning. They drove animals before them and had captives too. We would not sell or keep all of them. The old and the infirm would be released. The young women would be kept and the rest sold in Lundenwic.

The number of Franks and Bretons we had captured had grown. When our ships arrived, I would send the captives back to Caen. There they could be watched more carefully. This campaign was far from over. We anxiously awaited the return of our drekar from Paris. The first of them arrived at dawn the next day. Their news was disappointing. Olaf Two Teeth had captained *'Hermóðr'*. When he stepped ashore his face was as black as thunder.

"What is amiss Olaf?"

"We lost a drekar. *'Worm's'* captain was too reckless. We destroyed one bridge without losing a man. *'Worm'* had not taken part in the destruction. She and two others acted as guard ships. When we closed with the second bridge the Franks were ready. *'Worm's'* captain raced ahead of the others without scouting out the danger. They poured boiling fat and oil on the drekar. The others managed to extricate themselves but *'Worm'* and its crew all perished. I abandoned the attempt on the other bridge. I have failed you, lord."

"No, you have done that which I wished. The Franks will fear a second attack. I am sorry that we lost a ship but we have yet to lose many men. Our plan still succeeds. I need to send four drekar back to Caen. I would have you choose the ships. You know which captains need to have time to recover from the loss of a drekar." I could see he was still brooding. It had been his command. "When you command Olaf, you will lose men no matter how well you plan. The Norns spin. The loss of the drekar was *wyrd*. We will mourn them and when we fight the Franks and defeat them then their deaths will be avenged."

Gradually the rest of our fleet returned. The mood amongst the crews was sombre. The deaths of our men had not been glorious. It was unlikely that any of them would have found their way to Valhalla. The hatred in their eyes made the Franks flinch with fear when my men passed them. It guaranteed that there would be no trouble from even the belligerent Count. Our ships took the captives and the booty back to Caen the next morning. There was nothing to be gained from risking the river at night. It was now our river. No ships had passed upstream and the crews of those which sailed downstream were in no mood for ambushes. They would destroy any who got in their way.

The ransom arrived in the late afternoon. The escort was over two hundred mailed horsemen. The Count of Rouen himself led them. Our superior numbers guaranteed that there would be no treachery but my men still fingered their weapons. I went forward with Sven and Sámr Oakheart to examine the chest. The Count glowered at me. He did not dismount. That was discourteous but I let it go. Sven Blue Cheek opened the chest. We had brought one roughly the same size and Sven painstakingly emptied each coin from one to the other.

When he was halfway through the Count said, "What is this? Do you not trust us?"

My height meant that I could look him in the eye. I said, simply, "No."

"You insult me!"

"Good, then you are not as stupid as you look and if you wish to do something about the insult then dismount and I will give you

195

the opportunity to remedy that." He said nothing and remained on his horses as Sven Blue Cheek continued to shift the coins from one chest to the other.

"It is all here, lord."

I took out my sword. I saw the Franks flinch and I laughed. I waved the sword and the priests, the Count of Montfort-sur-Risle and his men, as well as the old and infirm Franks, began to hurry down the hill, released by my guards.

As they passed us the Count pointed at me, "And now you will leave this land! You will never return."

I laughed whilst shaking my head, "I did not agree to that. I agreed to sell you back those that we captured. I have done so. I made no promise to quit this pleasant valley."

He looked dumbfounded. He looked around at his men as though they might give him inspiration. "But you have raided the land hereabouts. What else is there?"

"Rouen."

He looked as though I had slapped him across the face. "Rouen is my city."

"It was. I give you notice, Count, that it will be mine. If you want to avoid your people being slaughtered then abandon it now for one day it will be Norse!"

I wondered if he might ignore the conventions of a truce and strike me. He managed to get control of himself and, jerking his horse's head around, led his men back to Rouen.

Sven Blue Cheek laughed, "I think he thought the ransom was the biggest insult he would have to suffer. Was it wise to warn him?"

"I did not say when and my words were intended to spur him to battle." I swept an arm out. "This is a perfect place for us to do battle. We can fill drekar with archers and use the river to outflank them. It is as though the Allfather has placed this battlefield here just for us."

Sámr said, "But if he does not come?"

"He said that we had all that there was to have. He is wrong. There are many places which lie closer to Rouen. We are but thirteen miles from Rouen. With our ships, we can raid almost to their gates. Our men can go across land and take whatever remains. His men will be behind Rouen's walls waiting for our attack. He will tire of us." I pointed north. "The gap between the two arms of the river is just over one and a half miles. That is where we will force him to attack. When he has bled enough and trudged back to Rouen with the wreckage of his army then we send for the priest. We build machines and we take Rouen. This is a pleasant part of the world. We are well fed and we can hunt. Our men can raid at will. Time is on our side and not the Franks. How will they harvest their fields if there are over a thousand Vikings attacking them?" I turned, "Let us divide the coin. Our men deserve a reward!"

We spent the next three days preparing a battlefield we might not need for some time. I was awaiting the return of my four drekar. The next part of my plan needed coordination between my ships and my men on horses. Olaf brought not only the ships but another one hundred men. The war in Wessex was almost over. King Alfred was still besieged in his swamp and Danes were becoming restless. Guthrum encouraged them to join me. I did not mind. We would need great numbers when the last battle came. I made them swear an oath to me. When I won then I would be the lord they followed.

All was ready. I had no horse which was large enough to carry me and so I went aboard *'Hermóðr'* with Sven Blue Cheek. We had two hundred horsemen led by Stephen of Andecavis and Erik. While we landed and attacked the towns on the river east of Rouen, they would attack the towns and villages north of Rouen. I took ten drekar and each one was fully crewed. The land which lay to the west of Rouen had been raided extensively. There was nothing there to take. Apart from the attack on the bridges of Paris, the land to the east of Rouen was untouched. That was going to change. My plan was simple. While still within sight of Rouen I would land five ships on each bank and send the three hundred men to take as many animals as they could. Their task was to ransack and then burn halls and churches and to kill every warrior that we could find. The fact that we would do so in sight of Rouen would further enrage the Count. It would also fill our larders.

Lord of Rouen

We had to row for the river twisted and turned. I did not mind. We could use the sails on the return voyage and the current would take us. As we passed Rouen, just after noon, the men on the walls hurled stones at us from war machines. They missed but, crucially, they told me where the machines were placed. We split into two and landed at the two villages we saw. The people fled. There had been armed warriors but when they saw our numbers they mounted their horses and they ran. There were too few of them to contest the ground. None had been expecting us to land. They must have thought we were going to Paris again. The churches were filled with precious metals, fine linens, holy books and, hidden beneath the altars, coins. The Franks had run so fast that they left their animals. We loaded them and then fired the buildings. As darkness began to fall we set sail and allowed the current to take us back to Jumièges. It was in the middle of the night when we reached our camp. My horsemen had returned with even more success. We had milk cows, pigs, sheep and sacks of cereal. We could see the fires burning in the distance. The Count now knew what we intended. How long would he endure it?

We sent *'Fafnir'* back with the booty and a small crew. Our knarr could still trade. The coin would buy stone. Stone would make our people safer. We made preparations for our defences. With just over a mile to prepare we had much work to do. We cut into the two banks of the river to make the frontage even narrower. The enemy would have horsemen and so we dug a ditch and planted stakes. We watered the ground before the ditch to make it muddier. We used pails of river water and my men enjoyed making water. The soil from the ditch gave us a fighting platform. We used river pebbles to make the fighting platform we would defend higher and drier. With a ditch before us and stones upon which to stand we were making a small fort. Our ships moored in the river. The ships' boys, on the mast tops, had a view far to the east and the north. The bends in the river meant that we would see the Franks long before they reached us. With no bridges over the river, they would have a long march to reach us.

'Fafnir' had not returned when they did attack. Their scouts had approached for a number of days although it must have been

obvious that we were going nowhere. Other raiders had ransacked and then, satiated, left for home. We had been there all summer. It was a mighty army. The Franks had gathered every horseman that they could. There were many banners which suggested nobles. I guessed there were over three hundred horsemen. They had raised the levy. There could have been in excess of fifteen hundred but it was hard to count and that was an estimate.

We had five hundred men spread across the mile between the necks of the river. We had but a single line for the rest of my men were in the drekar with bows and slings. Sven Blue Cheek and I thought it unlikely that they would attack across the whole front. I intended to switch to a two-line as soon as we knew the focus of their attack. As a reserve, we had a hundred and fifty men just four hundred paces up the slope from us. Led by Ragnar the Resolute their task would be to anticipate threats and plug the gaps almost as soon as they appeared.

It took half a day to reach us. I now knew the banner of the Count of Rouen and I saw it in the front rank. Would he lead their attack? They would be able to see the stakes but not the ditch and not the muddy ground on the flanks. When they formed their horsemen up then I knew that they had not learned from the Breton failed attack at Caen. They seemed to ignore the drekar which were drawn up in double lines. With their sails down the men within would be able to release arrows over the drekar before them. The willows by the river had given us plenty of arrows. The sky would be black when they began to rain upon them.

It took some time for them to organize and then their horns sounded and their horsemen came. They came in three lines with one hundred men in each line.

I shouted, "Shield wall!" We would be able to match them. Our line would be one hundred and sixty men wide. There was a risk that they would overlap us but my secret archers would deal with them. I had my sword raised as men raced to fill in the lines behind us. It did not take us long. I confess that it felt to be a small number who faced the Franks for there were large gaps on our flanks. The ditch lay forty paces from us. As my men arrived they shuffled their seal skin boots into the pebbles to give them a good base upon which to fight. We had a wall of spears before us. The pebbles and the raised ground meant we would be at head height when we fought. Their horses would have to brave our spearheads to get at us.

The stakes before the ditches caused some of the horsemen to slow and that made their approach a little more ragged. I dropped my sword when the horsemen neared the ditch and arrows and stones suddenly dropped from the sky. Those on the left of the Frankish line fared best for they had shields on their left arms. The ones on the right had no such protection. Horses and men on their right fell in great numbers. Even on the left, they took casualties. The centre remained untouched.

"Brace!" With shields locked and spears held over their shields, my men awaited the crash of horses. I relied upon Long Sword. It was then that I saw that the Count had not led the attack. His banner was not to the fore. I also saw Arne the Breton Slayer's brother and his oathsworn. They looked to be the Count's bodyguards. Then the Franks hit the ditch. Those at the front tried to jump. The muddy ground did not help them and some struck the ditch. Even the ones who were successful were almost unseated and when they reached us they were not seated well. Those in the second and third ranks only saw the ditch when they reached it. Many horses baulked and others turned around. All the time our arrows and stones reaped an early harvest.

Twenty horsemen made our lines. Around me, spears darted at heads. I was ruthless. I swung my sword before me. It bit into the skull of a horse. It died instantly and rolled down, crushing the leg of the horseman who was then trampled by a Frank following up. Many of those who faced us were nobles. Their horses were of great value to them and when those of my men armed with Danish axes began to hew horses' heads they turned and fled. The attack of their horsemen ended when the nobles left. Less than one hundred horsemen made their way back to the main army on the backs of their horses. Another fifteen who had been unhorsed trudged slowly and disconsolately back. My archers and slingers gave them no respite. Their vaunted horsemen were finished. A few horses wandered disconsolately across the body littered neck of land.

Sven Blue Cheek shouted, "Have our dead removed and any wounded join the reserve." He turned to me. We had thirty casualties lord." I nodded. It could have been worse.

The Count now sounded his horn and this time the levy began to attack. Sámr asked, "Do we go into a single line, lord?"

"No, we trust to our shield wall and that Ragnar the Resolute will strike when the time is right." When the men on the drekar had exhausted their arrows, they would also land and join us. My plan depended upon my best warriors holding down the flow of Franks to allow my archers and slingers to kill them. Unlike many of the horsemen who had come to do battle, the ones on foot had little mail. Every arrow and stone which struck would eliminate a warrior from the battle.

The approach was, perforce, slower. There were bodies to negotiate and they were walking. My ships began releasing their slings and arrows at the great mass of men as the enemy plodder ponderously towards us. To many, armies the sight of such an overwhelming force would be intimidating but my warriors all knew how to fight. Large odds did not worry them. Our greatest danger came from blunted weapons. Bone tended to do that!

The Franks had lords in mail leading the men on foot. Their mail, helmets and large shields meant that they were safer from the arrows. We had to kill them first. The ditches had been partly filled by their dead. Some were able to step over on the bodies of the dead men and horses. They still had to face the wall of steel. Even as they crossed towards us our archers and slingers took men down. It was only once they reached our spears that they were safe and so they hurried the last few steps to be away from the withering rain of death. I used my sword like a spear and my front line thrust our spears forward. The Franks did the same but, thanks to their hurried approach, they were not a continuous line. The spears found shields, helmets and mail. My sword found the open face of the Frankish lord. My sword ripped out of the back of his skull. I twisted and pulled. His body tumbled to the ground.

Sámr Oakheart was in the third rank. I heard him shout, "Rear rank split and support the front rank!"

I could not see what was happening but the command told me that we were in danger of being swamped on our flanks. Ragnar the Resolute would be watching to choose his moment to launch the reserve. On my drekar, my archers would be sending their arrows towards our vulnerable flanks. The result would be more pressure on the centre. Bergil and Sven's spears darted out and then shattered. To help them draw their swords I punched with my shield, stepped forward and swept my sword in a wide arc before me. It takes a brave man to face Long Sword. My long arms and my height mean that their weapons, mainly short swords and axes, could not reach me. My blade tore across the jaw of one man and into the shoulder of a second. The others recoiled and I was able to step back into the line knowing that Sven and Bergil had their swords out.

The battlefield was filled with the crash of metal on metal and wood. The screams of warriors with blood in their head filled the air. The cries and screams of the wounded and the dying were all around us. Then, from the second rank, the warriors who had yet to be engaged came the chant of my grandfather.

The horseman came through darkest night
He rode towards the dawning light
With fiery steed and thrusting spear
Hrolf the Horseman brought great fear

Slaughtering all he breached their line
Of warriors slain there were nine
Hrolf the Horseman with gleaming blade
Hrolf the Horseman all enemies slayed

With mighty axe Black Teeth stood
Angry and filled with hot blood
Hrolf the Horseman with gleaming blade
Hrolf the Horseman all enemies slayed
Ice cold Hrolf with Heart of Ice
Swung his arm and made it slice

Lord of Rouen

Hrolf the Horseman with gleaming blade
Hrolf the Horseman all enemies slayed

In two strokes the Jarl was felled
Hrolf's sword nobly held
Hrolf the Horseman with gleaming blade
Hrolf the Horseman all enemies slayed

They banged their shields as they sang. I saw the fear in the faces of the Franks. They did not understand the words and that increased their terror. What did the song mean? Was it our death song? When the rest of us took it up it made the Franks slow. Now was the time, "Petr, sound the horn three times. Let us push them into the ditch!"

Ragnar the Resolute had not been needed and now was the chance to use him and those in the second rank with sharper weapons to finally break the spirit of the men of Rouen. As the last notes faded I stepped forward smashing my shield into the face of the lord who was trying to rally his men. As he slipped on a piece of bloody ground I swung my sword in an arc and hacked through his thigh. Bright blood sprayed those around him. I stepped over his body. We had momentum although we did not have numbers. There were still many more Franks before us but my archers and slingers harried them and when we struck those near to the ditch and killed them then the rest halted. There was some discussion and then they turned to flee. They had broken upon our shields and now that wall of warriors threatened to engulf them. These were farmers, not warriors. These were Christians with families. If the Vikings wanted this land there was more to be had further east. They ran.

I held up my sword and halted us by the ditch. Sven Blue Cheek shouted, "Have the wounded taken back. Give a warrior's death to the enemy and take the mail from their bodies." He turned to me, "We eat horsemeat tonight lord."

I looked at the sky. The sun was setting. "Let us wait. Have the men reform. They still have more than a thousand men. The Count did not commit all of his lords. He has his Viking oathsworn. They have a hundred horsemen who could charge us."

"The Franks do not fight at night, lord!"

"Perhaps. This is almost a great victory. Let us not be so foolish that we lose the battle by being careless. Take charge here and I will go to speak with our drekar captains. Come, Petr."

I sheathed my sword and slung my shield over my back. I took off my helmet and felt the refreshing late afternoon air. I needed to bathe. My mail was bespattered with blood. I could taste it in my mouth. We were closer to victory but I would be happier when the Franks quit the field.

I neared *'Hermóðr'*. Olaf Two Teeth leaned over the side, "Is it over, lord?"

I shook my head, "I am not certain. Have Arne go to the top of the mast and tell me what he can see before darkness falls."

He ordered the ship's boy up the mast and then said, "You slew far more of their men than they did of us."

"They had more to start with."

"You sound disappointed, lord."

"No Olaf, merely cautious. We killed more of their horsemen than I expected but they had more men than we anticipated. When they have quit the field, we can see the true cost they have paid. Those numbers will determine when we attack Rouen. If we have to we will winter here but I would rather attack the walls while it is still clement weather. The winter aids them."

Arne shouted down from the masthead, "Lord there is a meeting of the lords with the banners. There is much pointing and shouting."

"What of the men on foot?"

"Many are leaving lord. They look to be drifting in small groups."

"How many remain?"

I knew that not all of my ship's boys could count; at least not in the way that most people did. There was a pause and then he shouted, "Nine or ten drekar crews lord."

That was all that I needed to know. With the men on the drekar, we now outnumbered them. The Count was trying to save face.

Lord of Rouen

The sun had almost set when Arne shouted, "Lord, they are leaving! They are heading for the road!"

"Olaf, take your drekar and sail to Rouen. When the Count arrives there, return and tell me."

"Aye lord. He grinned. His almost toothless mouth looking like a black cavern, "Now do you have your victory, lord?"

I nodded, "Now we have our victory and I will bathe!"

Lord of Rouen

Chapter 16

We burned the Frankish bodies in the gap where they had fought and died. The blackened earth would serve as a reminder of our victory. Our own dead were buried in the abbey grounds. That would annoy the priests. We butchered the dead horses and we ate well. We had lost over sixty men. Some had come from Norway and there were others who had come from the Haugr. A third of the dead were Danes who had come from Guthrum. All had fought and died for the tribe and we would remember them.

That night as I sat with my captains and leaders around the fire enjoying the choice cuts of horse I laid out my plans. "Harold, I want you to fetch the priest. Our wounded can be taken home. When Olaf returns I will know the situation at Rouen. We hew down wood to make war machines and when the priest comes we sail to Rouen."

"We will try to take a fortress?"

Sven Blue Cheek said, "We have broken their spirit. We have fought two battles and killed many. More importantly, we killed many of their lords. The ordinary farmers will head home to harvest their fields. Our lord is clever. We have made them bleed and they will have few to defend their walls."

I was not so sure. I had hoped that my attack on Paris would make Charles the Bald fear an attack there. It was now out of my hands. We had done all that we could. When my priest arrived, we would sail to Rouen and begin our attack. *'Fafnir'* returned with the priest and more men. It was seven days after the battle. The smell of death had gone. Our hurts were healed and our mail repaired. We were ready. We had timber ready to tow upriver to build the war machines. Æðelwald of Remisgat was, at first, reluctant to help us to build the machines.

"Lord these are Christians who live in Rouen. How could I face my God if I helped you to destroy them?"

I nodded and then spoke quietly, "I suffer your presence priest out of respect for my grandfather and because you seem to please my wife. I could have you killed in the blink of an eye and I would lose no sleep over it. My father died because of you. I hold you culpable. Do we understand each other? This is not a request; this is a command. When you have built the machines, if you no longer wish to live amongst my people, you may leave my land unharmed. That will be your choice but you will either build the machines or you will die."

He stared into my eyes, "You are a hard man but you are a man of your word. I will build your machines but I do so in the hope that one day your people will become Christian."

I laughed, "There is little hope of that." I did not know it but the Norns were spinning.

We were loading the ships the next day when one of the ship's boys shouted, "Sails, lord! A fleet!"

I looked at Sven Blue Cheek who shrugged, "Men who wish to fight with us?"

"We will discover that soon enough."

We went down to the river. It was a fleet of Danish ships. A young Dane stepped from the leading drekar. "I am Sigfred Lodbrokson. Guthrum has sent me with a request. He knows that you are the lord of this valley. I seek permission to take my ships and my men to attack Paris. We heard that you had destroyed part of their defences."

I nodded, "It is good of you to ask my permission."

"And if you grant us permission then we would give you one-tenth of all that we take."

Sven Blue Cheek said, quietly, "These men would be a great addition to our attack on Rouen."

I shook my head, "Do you not hear the Norns spinning? I worried about King Charles. If he fights these Danes then there will be no support forthcoming. Besides, when we take Rouen I want no dispute with a Dane over who is Lord of Rouen." I turned back to the Dane, "You have my permission but I should warn you that when my men and ships were attacked they used fire and we lost a whole drekar crew."

"It is true what they say about you, Göngu-Hrólfr Rognvaldson, you speak the truth and your tongue is not twisted with lies and deception. We will take our chances and whatever the result you shall have one-tenth of whatever we take. My Lord Guthrum holds you in high esteem."

We allowed the Danes to sail upstream first. They had a fleet of a hundred ships. They dwarfed my drekar. I wondered what the Count of Rouen would think when they sailed past his fortress. Leaving fifty men to guard the horses and the camp we left later in the day. We would reach Rouen after dark. That suited me for I wanted the shock of a fleet of ships on the Count's doorstep. Our journey was slow for we towed timber. Æðelwald of Remisgat had eventually agreed to build us three rams and three stone-throwers. I had asked for bolt throwers but he assured me that they were more complicated and time-consuming to build. He promised me the six machines within four days if I would provide the labour. I believed him. There was an island opposite the walls of the citadel and I planned on having one of the stone-throwers sited there along with four drekar. Their arrows and the onager's stones would wear down the defenders there.

The rest of us would camp to the west of the town on a piece of higher ground we had seen on our voyages up the river. We faced the main gate in the wall. They had a stone tower behind the wall. Rouen had been attacked many times and each time the defences had been weakened. A strong ruler would have made them better after each attack but all that they had done was to repair them. The result was that the town walls, though high, had a stone base topped with a wooden palisade. The gates were substantial but they were wooden and set in wood, not stone. The bottom half of the round tower was made of stone but there were no buttresses along the wall and the entrance was at ground level. When we breached the main gate, we would be able to use a ram to gain entry to the citadel. All of our efforts would be on the western side. They would be able to flee or to reinforce through the east gate but now that the Danes had sailed to attack Paris I was confident that no help would be forthcoming.

We had brought twenty horses with us and I had mounted men riding around the walls during the day. My intention was to wear down the defenders. When dawn broke and we were seen there was a clamouring of bells. They were warning those who lived nearby of our presence. My drekar captains reported people flooding towards the north and east gate. I allowed them in. They were farmers and their families. They were mouths which would need feeding and they would add nothing to the defence save bodies to be hacked.

Until we attacked there was no need for mail. We set up our lines two hundred paces from the walls. I saw that they had a ditch but it was in a state of ill repair. Many of those who lived close by had used it to throw in rubbish. That would not stop us. I knew that we could simply assault the walls and we would probably win but in that attack, we would lose men. We had time for we had supplies and we had the weather. Æðelwald of Remisgat's machines would save us lives and show the Franks that we were not the barbarians they thought we were. I was tireless. I was the first up and the first to break my fast. I chivvied the builders and oversaw the construction of the machines. I would be able to build the next ones and I would have no need of Æðelwald of Remisgat. I would send him back to Caen, on foot.

When I was sure that the men were working as hard as they could I walked to the lines around the walls and strode all the way around. My men were thinly spread in places but the Franks had shown no desire to risk confrontation. Perhaps they thought to wait for relief from Paris. By the time I returned to the west gate it would be time for food and for me to speak with my leaders. All were keen to begin the assault for we had had nothing but success. It took all the efforts of Sven Blue Cheek and myself to dissuade them from premature attacks.

The rams took shape the quickest. The cattle we had slaughtered gave us the hides to cover the roof. Their hooves provided the point for the ram's tip. The stone-throwers were more difficult to build. I had Æðelwald of Remisgat make all the component parts for all three. We watched him assemble the first one so that we could take the third and assemble it on the island. My men's skill with ropes impressed the priest for it was the arrangement of ropes and the tension they created which gave the stone-throwers their power. When the first one had been built I took the third to the island.

My men who were based there had not been idle. They had constructed large willow shields behind which they could shelter. They had also built up the ground so that it was three paces higher than it had been. We were two hundred paces from the walls. I was unsure of the range but Æðelwald of Remisgat had told me that a good crew could send stones up to three hundred paces. Our archers would be at extreme range. We began to build the stone thrower on the raised platform. The defenders saw us and began to use their bows. The Franks have poor bow skills and the arrows fell woefully short.

I turned to Leif Eriksson, "Leif show them a real archer!"

He chose a good arrow and nocked it. He pulled back and it sailed high into the air. It struck a sentry on the arm and immediately shields came up and heads disappeared. He grinned at me, "Now if you were to send an arrow, Göngu-Hrólfr Rognvaldson, then the men in the tower would not be safe."

"You flatter me, Leif. It is some time since I drew a bow." It was a good sign that they were so relaxed.

While we toiled to build the machine, my men searched the island for rocks which would be big enough to use when the machine began to assault the walls. I wanted all of my machines to be used at the same time. They would have a shock effect. It was almost dark when the machine finished. The men were keen to use it. I shook my head. "You will wait until the others are ready. When all three machines throw stones then the archers can begin to pick off the defenders. I have planned and the Allfather will reward us if we stick to the plan."

I went back to the main camp. I saw that the third stone-thrower would be ready by the next day and the rams a day later. Although they were quicker to build we needed the stone-throwers ready first. We were almost ready to attack.

"We have plenty of stones?"

Ragnar the Resolute nodded, "Aye lord we found a small chapel. The stones are all the same size and the priest assured us that if we had the same sized stones we could predict the fall of stone more accurately."

"Bergil, do we have the men for the rams? They must be strong and if they can use axes then so much the better."

"The Danes were keen to use them. We have water ready to soak the hides and the wood. The men who were at Paris remember '*Worm's* fate."

"Sámr Oakheart you will need archers to follow the ram. Have them make willow pavise. Ships' boys can carry them to protect the archers."

Sven Blue Cheek handed me a horn of ale, "Lord you are like a father expecting the birth of his first son. You have done all that you can. We know what we are doing. Trust us."

I laughed and quaffed the ale, "You may be right but when we take Rouen it will fulfil the prophecy the witch told my grandfather. My father will be watching from Valhalla and I would have him be proud of me."

Sven Blue Cheek shook his head, "There is no doubt that he will be lord. You were dead and reborn. You had nothing and now you are the lord of this land. You rule a land which is greater than that which your father controlled and the great and the good, like Guthrum and the sons of Ragnar Lodbrok seek your favour. For one so young you have achieved much."

He was right and yet it was not enough. It would never be enough until I was Lord of Rouen and my lands were safe.

We were ready before dawn. Petr was ready with the horn. That would be the signal for the men on the island to begin their attack. Despite his pacifist tendencies, the engineer in our priest was interested to see how his machines of war would work. We had built a solid platform for the two stone-throwers and Sven Blue Cheek had supervised the selection of the stones. We had named the two machines Freya and Hel respectively. It made them seem alive but it would allow us to use them separately to check their range. When the men were ready I said, "Petr, sound the horn." As the horns sounded I said, "Launch Freya!" The six men pulled hard on the rope. It was too hard. The stone sailed over the walls. We heard a crash and screams from within Rouen. The six men looked shamefaced.

I smiled, "That proved that the machine works!"

Sven said, "Let us see if Hel can do better."

The six men had watched the other team. It did not fly as high and it crashed into the bottom of the wall. I nodded. "Somewhere between the two and hitting the gate and the supports would be better." They reloaded. I allowed them to choose the stones. "Freya!"

This time it was more accurate and it struck the wall just to the right of one of the supports. The crack and the dust told us that damage had been done, Hel had even more success. It managed to hit the centre of the gate which shivered with the impact. They would brace the gates but every hit would weaken the whole structure. I said, "Carry on. Sven, change the crew every ten stones. I will go and see how Thor is doing."

I walked down to the river. The men had named the machine on the island Thor and they had had the same experience as the other two crews. They now had the range and the technique. Their task was easier. So long as they hit the wall then they had success. They could move up and down as they saw fit. The archers were already scoring hits. I waved at them. They cheered, "Göngu-Hrólfr Rognvaldson!"

The archers with Freya and Hel were also scoring hits. The willow shields were effective. Some of the more reckless ship's boys even plucked the arrows from the shields to hand them to the archers. We sent the Franks their arrows back. Each time a stone made a good hit the watching warriors cheered. I saw parts of the palisade, hit by rogue rocks, destroyed. The Franks quickly replaced them with wood which was crudely hammered into position. They would have a limited amount of timber. By noon the men were tired and one of the machines, Hel, had broken ropes. I called a halt so that we could repair the machine and assess the damage. The gate had been hit many times but the gate supports were more badly damaged than we could have hoped. We heard hammering in the silence which followed the cessation of stones.

As we ate and watched Hel being repaired Sven Blue Cheek said, "The rams will be ready tonight. Do we try a night attack?"

I shook my head, "These machines can keep the enemy's head down until the last moment if we use daylight."

Bergil said, "The men are all keen to attack."

"And they will obey orders. We are not the barbarians the Franks think that we are. We have discipline. The prize is so close that I can taste it." I waved the duck's leg like a sword, "You have seen what we did with Caen. What more could we do here? We will make the walls and the tower of stone. We will divert the river to encircle the town. When we take it then it will be forever! I would not lose this prize!"

With the machine repaired and the crews refreshed, we continue our barrage of stones. The power of the machines was shown when one rock flew a little too high and a Frank lost his head to the stone. After that, they stopped standing where they could be hit. By the time darkness fell, there were many holes in the walls next to the gate. The gate and its supports had been badly damaged and we heard them repairing it during the night. Thor had breached the wall in a number of places. We knew they lacked timber for they did not try to repair it. They would pay for that. When our rams attacked I would take in four drekar and scale the breach.

That night I divided my leaders. "Sven Blue Cheek, Sámr Oakheart, you will come with me and we will assault the river wall. Bergil and Ragnar the Resolute you will supervise the rams. I hope that the wall will fall to one ram but it may not. Once the gate is breached you lead your men through it. I will have Petr with me. If you hear the horn sound four times then we are within Rouen."

Sven and I then selected the men for the attack on the breach. We rowed to the island and anchored where the island hid us from view. We slept on the island. The two of us spoke with our men so that they knew exactly what we intended.

We were awake before dawn and we soon had the four drekar loaded. I went to Thor and its crew. "You keep up the stones until you see me almost at the walls."

"But what if we hit you?"

"Then it will be *wyrd*. But you will not hit me. I have confidence in you!"

I headed for **'Hermóðr'**. Once I was aboard my men began to row. We had the mast stepped and, in dawn's early light would be hard to see. I heard the twang of arrows as Leif and his archers cleared the fighting platform. Then I heard the crack as the first stone hit the walls. We could see nothing for we were making our way around the island. Dawn broke and a sudden shaft of sunlight lit the walls as we turned west. I saw a stone hit two of the wooden timbers on the wall. There were now gaps all along the wall. I could see that the fighting platform had been destroyed in places. My men were keen to make our task as easy as possible and they worked their way along the wall.

We ground on to the shingle and I leapt ashore. The bank was steep and I left my swords sheathed so that I could use the scrubby undergrowth to pull me up. I heard a cry from above me and saw a Frank skewered by an arrow. I pressed my body close to the ground as his corpse fell. My height came to my assistance. I reached the breach and put my hand onto the stumps of wood to pull myself up. A Frank with a spear appeared above me. If he struck me I would be dead. Two arrows sprang from his chest and he fell back. Spurred on by my near-death experience I hauled myself up.

Before I had time to draw a sword a Frank ran at me with a spear. I grabbed it with two hands and threw him to the ground. I heard his back crack as he struck. I reversed it and ran down the fighting platform to the Frank who had a spear raised to strike Sven Blue Cheek. Sven had his hands full trying to pull himself up. The spear went through him. I reached down and pulled Sven onto the fighting platform.

I could hear the sound of the ram as it struck the gate. I drew my sword as Sven helped up Sámr Oakheart. I looked around and saw that we had ten men on the fighting platform. I swung my shield around. "Petr!"

A hand appeared above the stumps of the timbers. I reached down and hauled up the youth. "Sound the horn! Sámr Oakheart you stay here and consolidate our breach. Send men to support us and use the rest to clear the walls."

"Where will you be, lord?"

"Sven and I go to the gatehouse."

The Franks had thought there was no danger on the river wall and it was poorly held. Sámr would have over three hundred men with no one to oppose us we could take this part of the town. As we ran down the walkway I held my shield on my right side. The archers in the tower were sending their arrows at us. One struck the fighting platform before me and I saw that they were hunting arrows. They could not pierce mail.

The men on the gate turned as they heard our feet thundering on the wooden walkway. They turned to face us. The Franks had only built it wide enough for two men and Sven Blue Cheek and I were far bigger than the two Franks. I held my sword across me and it sliced deep into the neck of one of them. Sven gutted the other. Sámr was sending men to join us. We had support. There was a door to the gatehouse but it was closed. I doubted that it was barred. I went to the wall and raised my sword. Bergil and Ragnar were there with my men. They were already in a wedge awaiting the crash which would herald the breaching of the gate.

Ulf and Olaf joined us. Slipping my shield around my back I pointed to the door. "Break that down and we will follow."

The two of them took two steps back and, holding their shields ran at the door. It almost disintegrated. I ducked beneath the lintel and lunged with my sword at the Frank who ran at me. It was a tight space. His sword grazed my cheek and I impaled him. The other three were quickly slain. I saw a ladder. Picking up the body of the man I had killed I dropped it through the hole. I heard a cry as the body knocked the man who was already ascending the ladder. I quickly turned and slid down the ladder. I landed on two soft bodies. Two blows hit my back but my shield saved me. I swung my sword blindly and was rewarded by a cry. I saw a

Frank's face and, grabbing his beard, pulled him into my helmet. He fell unconscious. Sven joined me and we hurried to the door which led to the gateway.

We should have waited but sometimes the blood rushed in your ears and you felt that you were immortal. That was one such moment. I opened the door and Sven charged through. I followed. Our ram had almost broken through and the twenty Franks who were there were trying to bolster the gate with beams. The first four died without evening knowing that their wall had been breached. I drew my second sword and hacked and chopped into bodies. All before me were enemies. When Ulf and Olaf joined us, it became a slaughter.

When the Franks were all dead I turned to the men who descended the ladder to join us. "You men take down the braces. Let the rams come through. We have not yet finished. There is a tower to destroy. Sven let us go and announce our arrival to the Franks!" I sheathed my second sword and held Long Sword in two hands. I shouted, "Clear the gateway and bring both rams through! We have a tower to take!" My men cheered. The Franks had used the second gate to brace the first and we walked into the open.

We stepped out into the light. Sámr Oakheart and my men had cleared the walls. The Count had abandoned all but his warriors and his family. Women and children cowered with the wounded. There were homes and workshops. They sheltered the surviving Franks. I raised my sword and pointed to the east gate, "Go, flee to your King and tell him that Göngu-Hrólfr Rognvaldson now rules this valley."

They looked dumbfounded, Sven shouted, "Boo!" and they ran. Others left the buildings in which they had been hiding and they fled. It was a rout. They would flee through the east gate.

My men wasted no time in demolishing the gates. I heard the rumble of the ram as it was pushed through the narrow entrance. Sven Blue Cheek asked, "Should we see if they will surrender?"

"You and I know that he will not but we will try." I cupped my hands, "Count, we have your walls. It will take but a short time to punch a hole in your wall. Surrender and I will allow your men to go free. Resist and you die." Their response was a series of badly thrown spears, all of which missed me.

Sven nodded and shouted, "Bergil, Ragnar the Resolute bring the men. Clear the top of the tower with our archers."

It was then I noticed that this was a tower as big as that in Caen. Was there another entrance? Even as I turned to shout to Bergil to surround the tower I heard the clatter of hooves. "With me!" I drew my sword and I ran. I have long legs and I covered the ground quickly. There was another entrance. It came from a cellar. It was where they kept their horses. Even as I looked I saw that the Count had evaded me. He and two others were already galloping towards the open east door. I swung my sword and hacked into the chest of the Frank who tried to follow them. Sámr and Sven were with me and they hacked into the next two horsemen. More warriors had followed them and I led them down the ramp into the cellar. There were other lords trying to mount horses. There was no light and it was hard to see who we were fighting but we hacked slashed and stabbed until there were Vikings and horses, only, left alive in the cellar.

Sven said, "We do not need the rams now!" He led us towards the door which had been opened. Once we reached it there was light from the sconces along the wall. I guessed that the Count had not told his men that he was leaving. They would all be on the upper floor. We climbed up the stairs and heard the murmur of voices. It sounded to me like the Great Hall. Sven and I found the door and opened it. Inside were the women the Franks had abandoned. When the door was opened they screamed.

"Bergil silence and then watch the women. The men above us will know that we are here."

We met them on the next floor. This was the Count's sleeping quarters. Men poured down from the fighting platform. The screams had alerted them to the fact that the fox was in the henhouse. Abandoned by their lord they had no option. They had to fight to the death. I did not bother with my shield. This was close-quarter fighting. I drew my seax. My Long Sword allowed me to sweep and keep my enemies at a distance. Then Sven, Sámr and Bergil were able to dart in and slay the mailed warriors of the Count of Rouen.

I saw Audun Leifsson slain by a warrior who was almost as tall as me. He saw me at the same time, "Come giant! I am the Count's champion and I have never been bested. This is the day I hew down a mighty oak."

He had a long narrow shield and a long sword. Mine was longer. He swung his sword at my left side. With no shield, he thought me weak. Rowing a drekar had made my left arm as strong as my right. I blocked his sword at the hilt and he pushed. I held him. I watched as he strained. I thought his eyes might pop from his head. I brought back my head and butted him. As he reeled backwards my right hand darted forward and the tip tore into his thigh. I stepped closer to him and ripped my seax behind his right arm. I severed his tendons. His sword fell from fingers which could no longer grip. He stepped backwards. Blood was pumping from his thigh. I lifted my leg and kicked him hard in the stomach. He fell backwards.

"You are the champion of a coward. You will die slowly as your lifeblood seeps from you. I will not give you the warrior's death for you do not deserve it."

I sheathed my sword and looked around the chamber. All the Franks were dead. What I could not see was Ailmær the Cruel. We had killed no Vikings and they had not fled. Where were they?

"Sven Blue Cheek, bring my best warriors. We have a snake to find and to kill!"

I walked to the stairs and climbed to the fighting platform. The skill of my archers could be seen by the number of dead bodies. A spear was hurled at me. Some instinct made me move my head and it thudded into the door behind me. Ailmær the Cruel and ten of his men stood there. They had a crude shield wall.

I nodded, "Your master abandoned you like the worthless dog that you are."

He smirked, "There are eleven of us and you are alone!"

Bergil's voice came from behind me, "Not for long! We do not leave our leader to fight alone."

I still had my shield around my back. I used a two-handed stance and approached Ailmær the Cruel. I could rely on my other men to deal with the rest. He had a good shield and a good sword but it was shorter than mine. He lunged at me with his sword. Sparks flew and the blades rang as I blocked the blow. I was much taller than Ailmær the Cruel and I used my height. I brought my sword down from on high. He could have risked a lunge at my middle but his blade had no tip and so he used his shield to block the blow. It was a well-made shield but my sword split it in two. He rolled away, drawing a seax as he did so.

One of his oathsworn leapt towards me. Bergil had anticipated the blow and his sword came down to take the Viking's arm at the elbow. The attack had given Ailmær the Cruel the chance to rise to his feet but he now had fear on his face. He slashed his sword at my head and, as he did so tried to gut me with his seax. Long Sword caught the seax and knocked it from his hand. He now tried a two-handed grip. He was at a distinct disadvantage. I feinted as I approached and he reacted each time. He was in my power.

Behind me, I heard Sven Blue Cheek shout, "End it lord. He is the last of the treacherous ones."

I feinted at his middle and, as his sword came up, swung my own blade and took his head. It flew from his shoulders and over the parapet.

I took off my helmet and walked to the side of the tower facing the gate. My men saw me and cheered. I raised my hands and they began to chant.

"Göngu-Hrólfr Rognvaldson
Göngu-Hrólfr Rognvaldson
Göngu-Hrólfr Rognvaldson!"

Then Sven Blue Cheek, Sámr Oakheart, Ragnar the Resolute and Bergil joined me. Sven held up his hands and shouted, "All hail, Göngu-Hrólfr Rognvaldson, Lord of Rouen and ruler of the Seine!"

The cheers rang out. We had won.

I turned to Bergil, "That was bravely done, Bergil. You have quick hands! I owe you a life. From this day you are Bergil Fast Blade."

219

Lord of Rouen

"Thank you, lord! And you owe me nothing. You have given us all. You are Göngu-Hrólfr Rognvaldson, Lord of Rouen and ruler of the Seine!"

Epilogue

This time we did not ransom the captives; not all of them at least. We kept the Count's family as our guests. It was to make certain that he did not attempt to wrest the land from us. He blustered and threatened us with a war against the church. It did not sway us. Eventually, he had to agree that we held Rouen and, while his family lived, he would not attempt to retake it. We had bought time to build up our army. When Sigfred returned from his raid on Paris it was the end of the Count of Rouen. The Danes had managed to capture and sack many churches. They had lost ten drekar but the Franks were in no position to wage a war against us. When we entertained the Danes, they told us how they had heard that Charles had had to send to his allies in Italy and Germany for help. It had not been forthcoming. With the end of Saxon power in the land of the Angles King Charles, the Bald had lost his major ally. Sigfred was true his word and we received a tenth of his booty. With what we had captured in Rouen and the ransom for the captives we allowed to go we were rich.

It was Ýlir by the time that we had repaired the stronghold and added new gates. It was more secure than when we had attacked. I had had buttresses built and the timbers I used were backed by extra wood on the town side. I built a tower on the island and left Thor there. We could control the river!

I sent my drekar for my family. My counts returned to their homes. My grandfather, Gefn and Lady Poppa arrived twenty days after I sent *'Fafnir'* and *'Hermóðr'* for them. My men had toiled tirelessly to make sure that their quarters were as fine as they could be. I waited anxiously at the quay for them. I had hoped to see my wife heavy with child but she was still slim. I hid my disappointment.

Gefn looked at the mighty walls and tower, "This is all yours, my son?"

"It is, I am Lord of Rouen."

My grandfather nodded and patted the solid stone walls, "And the Franks are happy about that?"

I laughed, "I care not. They are in disarray. I have the Count's family hostage. Until he is replaced he will not try to take my land. King Charles is equally bereft of friends. We have time to build and to consolidate. I have lords who wish land to rule. We have five towns. Soon there will be many more!"

He took Gefn's arm, "Come, let us explore this palace. For one who grew up as a thrall, this is a mighty leap."

I was left alone with Poppa. She threw herself in my arms and burst into tears, "I have failed you, lord! I am not with child!"

I could not trust my voice and so I held her tightly in my arms. When my voice came I said quietly, "I promise that I will not go to war until the new grass. Until then I will devote my time to you and to making our children."

She pulled away from me, "You are too good to me." She looked at the mighty tower. "And this is my home?"

"This is our home. You are the Lady of Rouen. I know that your father was a Count but I like the title Lord of Rouen. This bastion has held out against Vikings since my grandfather was younger than me. What we have achieved is the stuff of legend. I am content!"

The End

Norse Calendar

Gormánuður October 14th - November 13th
Ýlir November 14th - December 13th
Mörsugur December 14th - January 12th
Þorri - January 13th - February 11th
Gói - February 12th - March 13th
Einmánuður - March 14th - April 13th
Harpa April 14th - May 13th
Skerpla - May 14th - June 12th
Sólmánuður - June 13th - July 12th
Heyannir - July 13th - August 14th
Tvímánuður - August 15th - September 14th
Haustmánuður September 15th-October 13th

Glossary

Ækre -acre (Norse) The amount of land a pair of oxen could plough in one day

Addelam- Deal (Kent)

Afon Hafron- River Severn in Welsh

Alt Clut- Dumbarton Castle on the Clyde

Andecavis- Angers in Anjou

Angia- Jersey (Channel Islands)

An Oriant- Lorient, Brittany

Áth Truim- Trim, County Meath (Ireland)

Baille - a ward (an enclosed area inside a wall)

Balley Chashtal -Castleton (Isle of Man)

Bárekr's Haven – Barfleur, Normandy

Bebbanburgh- Bamburgh Castle, Northumbria. Also, known as Din Guardi in the ancient tongue

Beck- a stream

Blót – a blood sacrifice made by a jarl

Blue Sea/Middle Sea- The Mediterranean

Bondi- Viking farmers who fight

Bourde- Bordeaux

Bjarnarøy –Great Bernera (Bear Island)

Byrnie- a mail or leather shirt reaching down to the knees

Brvggas -Bruges

Caerlleon- Welsh for Chester

Caestir - Chester (old English)

Cantwareburh- Canterbury

Casnewydd –Newport, Wales

Cent- Kent

Cephas- Greek for Simon Peter (St. Peter)

Cetham -Chatham Kent

Chape- the tip of a scabbard

Charlemagne- Holy Roman Emperor at the end of the 8th and beginning of the 9th centuries

Cherestanc- Garstang (Lancashire)

Ćiriċeburh- Cherbourg

Condado Portucalense- the County of Portugal

Constrasta-Valença (Northern Portugal)

Corn Walum or Om Walum- Cornwall
Cymri- Welsh
Cymru- Wales
Cyninges-tūn – Coniston. It means the estate of the king (Cumbria)
Dùn Èideann –Edinburgh (Gaelic)
Din Guardi- Bamburgh castle
Drekar- a Dragon ship (a Viking warship)
Duboglassio –Douglas, Isle of Man
Djupr -Dieppe
Dyrøy –Jura (Inner Hebrides)
Dyflin- Old Norse for Dublin
Ein-mánuðr- middle of March to the middle of April
Eopwinesfleot -Ebbsfleet
Eoforwic- Saxon for York
Fáfnir - a dwarf turned into a dragon (Norse mythology)
Faro Bregancio- Corunna (Spain)
Ferneberga -Farnborough (Hampshire)
Fey- having second sight
Firkin- a barrel containing eight gallons (usually beer)
Fret-a sea mist
Frankia- France and part of Germany
Fyrd-the Saxon levy
Gaill- Irish for foreigners
Galdramenn- wizard
Glaesum –amber
Gleawecastre- Gloucester
Gói- the end of February to the middle of March
Greenway- ancient roads- they used turf rather than stone
Grenewic- Greenwich
Gyllingas - Gillingham Kent
Haesta- Hastings
Haestingaceaster -Hastings
Hamwic -Southampton
Hantone- Littlehampton
Haughs/ Haugr - small hills in Norse (As in Tarn Hows) or a hump- normally a mound of earth

Lord of Rouen

Hearth-weru- Jarl's bodyguard/oathsworn
Heels- when a ship leans to one side under the pressure of the wind
Hel- Queen of Niflheim, the Norse underworld.
Herkumbl- a mark on the front of a helmet denoting the clan of a Viking warrior
Here Wic- Harwich
Hetaereiarch – Byzantine general
Hí- Iona (Gaelic)
Hjáp - Shap- Cumbria (Norse for stone circle)
Hoggs or Hogging- when the pressure of the wind causes the stern or the bow to droop
Hrams-a – Ramsey, Isle of Man
Hrīs Wearp – Ruswarp (North Yorkshire)
Hrofecester-Rochester Kent
Hywel ap Rhodri Molwynog- King of Gwynedd 814-825
Icaunis- a British river god
Ishbiliyya- Seville
Issicauna- Gaulish for the lower Seine
Itouna- River Eden Cumbria
Jarl- Norse earl or lord
Joro-goddess of the earth
Jǫtunn -Norse god or goddess
Kartreidh -Carteret in Normandy
Kjerringa - Old Woman- the solid block in which the mast rested
Knarr- a merchant ship or a coastal vessel
Kyrtle-woven top
Laugardagr-Saturday (Norse for washing day)
Leathes Water- Thirlmere
Ljoðhús- Lewis
Legacaestir- Anglo Saxon for Chester
Liger- Loire
Lochlannach – Irish for Northerners (Vikings)
Lothuwistoft- Lowestoft
Louis the Pious- King of the Franks and son of Charlemagne
Lundenwic - London

Lord of Rouen

Lincylene -Lincoln
Maen hir – standing stone (menhir)
Maeresea- River Mersey
Mammceaster- Manchester
Manau/Mann – The Isle of Man(n) (Saxon)
Marcia Hispanic- Spanish Marches (the land around Barcelona)
Mast fish- two large racks on a ship for the mast
Melita- Malta
Midden - a place where they dumped human waste
Miklagård - Constantinople
Leudes- Imperial officer (a local leader in the Carolingian Empire. They became Counts a century after this.)
Njoror- God of the sea
Nithing- A man without honour (Saxon)
Odin - The "All Father" God of war, also associated with wisdom, poetry, and magic (The ruler of the gods).
Olissipo- Lisbon
Orkneyjar-Orkney
Portucale- Porto
Portesmūða -Portsmouth
Penrhudd – Penrith Cumbria
Pillars of Hercules- Straits of Gibraltar
Qādis- Cadiz
Ran- Goddess of the sea
Remisgat Ramsgate
Roof rock- slate
Rinaz –The Rhine
Sabrina- Latin and Celtic for the River Severn. Also, the name of a female Celtic deity
Saami- the people who live in what is now Northern Norway/Sweden
Saint Maclou- St Malo (France)
Sandwic- Sandwich (Kent)
Sarnia- Guernsey (Channel Islands)
St. Cybi- Holyhead
Sampiere -samphire (sea asparagus)

Lord of Rouen

Scree- loose rocks in a glacial valley
Seax – short sword
Sheerstrake- the uppermost strake in the hull
Sheet- a rope fastened to the lower corner of a sail
Shroud- a rope from the masthead to the hull amidships
Skeggox – an axe with a shorter beard on one side of the blade
Sondwic-Sandwich
South Folk- Suffolk
Stad- Norse settlement
Stays- ropes running from the mast-head to the bow
Streanæshalc -Whitby
Stirap- stirrup
Strake- the wood on the side of a drekar
Suthriganaworc - Southwark (London)
Svearike -Sweden
Syllingar- Scilly Isles
Syllingar Insula- Scilly Isles
Tarn- small lake (Norse)
Temese- River Thames (also called the Tamese)
The Norns- The three sisters who weave webs of intrigue for men
Thing-Norse for a parliament or a debate (Tynwald)
Thor's day- Thursday
Threttanessa- a drekar with 13 oars on each side.
Thrall- slave
Tinea- Tyne
Trenail- a round wooden peg used to secure strakes
Tude- Tui in Northern Spain
Tynwald- the Parliament on the Isle of Man
Úlfarrberg- Helvellyn
Úlfarrland- Cumbria
Úlfarr- Wolf Warrior
Úlfarrston- Ulverston
Ullr-Norse God of Hunting
Ulfheonar-an elite Norse warrior who wore a wolf skin over his armour

Uuluuich- Dulwich
Valauna- Valognes (Normandy)
Vectis- The Isle of Wight
Veðrafjǫrðr -Waterford (Ireland)
Veisafjǫrðr- Wexford (Ireland)
Volva- a witch or healing woman in Norse culture
Waeclinga Straet- Watling Street (A5)
Windlesore-Windsor
Waite- a Viking word for farm
Werham -Wareham (Dorset)
Wintan-ceastre -Winchester
Withy- the mechanism connecting the steering board to the ship
Woden's day- Wednesday
Wyddfa-Snowdon
Wyrd- Fate
Yard- a timber from which the sail is suspended on a drekar
Ynys Môn-Anglesey

Lord of Rouen

The Norman dynasty

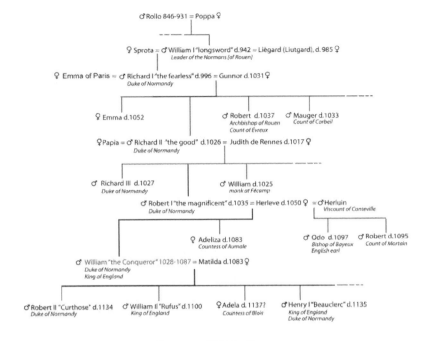

Courtesy of Wikipedia.

Historical note

The Franks used horses more than most other armies of the time. Their spears were used as long swords, hence the guards. They used saddles and stirrups. They still retained their round shields and wore, largely, an open helmet. Sometimes they wore a plume. They carried a spare spear and a sword.

One reason for the Normans success was that when they arrived in northern France they integrated quickly with the local populace. They married them and began to use some of their words. They adapted to the horse as a weapon of war. Before then the Vikings had been quite happy to ride to war but they dismounted to fight. The Normans took the best that the Franks had and made it better. This book sees the earliest beginnings of the rise of the Norman knight.

I have used the names by which places were known in the medieval period wherever possible. Sometimes I have had to use the modern name. The Cotentin is an example. The isle of sheep is now called the Isle of Sheppey and lies on the Medway close to the Thames. The land of Kent was known as Cent in the early medieval period. Thanet or, Tanet as it was known in the Viking period was an island at this time. The sea was on two sides and the other two sides had swamps, bogs, mudflats and tidal streams. It protected Canterbury. The coast was different too. Richborough had been a major Roman port. It is now some way inland. Sandwich was a port. Other ports now lie under the sea. Vikings were not afraid to sail up very narrow rivers and to risk being stranded on mud. They were tough men and were capable of carrying or porting their ships as their Rus brothers did when travelling to Miklagård.

The Norns or the Weird Sisters.

"The Norns (Old Norse: norn, plural: nornir) in Norse mythology are female beings who rule the destiny of gods and men. They roughly correspond to other controllers of humans' destiny, the Fates, elsewhere in European mythology.
In Snorri Sturluson's interpretation of the Völuspá, Urðr (Wyrd), Verðandi and Skuld, the three most important of the Norns, come out from a hall standing at the Well of Urðr or Well of Fate. They

draw water from the well and take sand that lies around it, which
they pour over Yggdrasill so that its branches will not rot. These
three Norns are described as powerful maiden giantesses (Jotuns)
whose arrival from Jötunheimr ended the golden age of the gods.
They may be the same as the maidens of Mögþrasir who are
described in Vafþrúðnismál"
  Source: Norns - https://en.wikipedia.org

Viking Raid on the Seine
  At some time in the 850s, a huge Viking fleet sailed up the
Seine to raid deep into the heart of Frankia. Some writers of the
period speak of over a hundred ships. The priests who wrote of the
plague that they believe the Vikings to be tended to exaggerate. I
have erred on the side of caution.
  Guthrum, founder of the Danelaw
  It is not known how Guthrum consolidated his rule as king over
the other Danish chieftains of the Danelaw (Danish ruled territory
of England), but we know that by 874 he was able to wage a war
against Wessex and its King, Alfred.
  In 875 the Danish forces, then under Guthrum and Halfdan
Ragnarsson, divided, Halfdan's contingent returning north to
Northumbria, while Guthrum's forces went to East Anglia,
quartering themselves at Cambridge for the year.
  By 876, Guthrum had acquired various parts of the kingdoms of
Mercia and Northumbria and then turned his attention to acquiring
Wessex, where his first confrontation with Alfred took place on
the south coast. Guthrum sailed his army around Poole Harbour
and linked up with another Viking army that was invading the area
between the Frome and Piddle rivers which was ruled by Alfred.
According to the historian Asser, Guthrum won his initial battle
with Alfred, and he captured the castellum as well as the ancient
square earthworks known as the Wareham, where there was a
convent of nuns.
  Alfred successfully brokered a peace settlement, but by 877 this
peace was broken as Guthrum led his army raiding further into
Wessex, thus forcing Alfred to confront him in a series of
skirmishes that Guthrum continued to win. At Exeter, which

Guthrum had also captured, Alfred made a peace treaty, with the result that Guthrum left Wessex to winter in Gloucester.

Poppa and Rollo

There is some dispute as to the true identity of the woman called Poppa. Most agree that she was the daughter of a Breton count but the sources dispute which one. I cannot believe that a legitimate daughter of a Count would have been left with a Viking and so I have her as illegitimate. *More danico* was the term used by the Franks to speak of a Danish marriage. The heirs were considered legal, at least in the world of the Norse. William was famously William the Bastard.

Rollo did make Jumièges his base and captured Rouen. My version is a fictitious one. The French king did put bridges across the Seine but it continued to be raided.

This is not the end of the story. There are still twists and turns. Alfred does defeat Guthrum who becomes a Christian! It is not until 911 that Rollo is finally accepted as Lord of Rouen by the French.

Books used in the research

- British Museum - Vikings- Life and Legends
- Arthur and the Saxon Wars- David Nicolle (Osprey)
- Saxon, Norman and Viking Terence Wise (Osprey)
- The Vikings- Ian Heath (Osprey)
- Byzantine Armies 668-1118 - Ian Heath (Osprey)
- Romano-Byzantine Armies 4th-9th Century - David Nicholle (Osprey)
- The Walls of Constantinople AD 324-1453 - Stephen Turnbull (Osprey)
- Viking Longship - Keith Durham (Osprey)
- The Vikings in England- Anglo-Danish Project
- The Varangian Guard- 988-1453 Raffael D'Amato
- Saxon Viking and Norman- Terence Wise
- The Walls of Constantinople AD 324-1453-Stephen Turnbull
- Byzantine Armies- 886-1118- Ian Heath
- The Age of Charlemagne-David Nicolle
- The Normans- David Nicolle

Lord of Rouen

- Norman Knight AD 950-1204- Christopher Gravett
- The Norman Conquest of the North- William A Kappelle
- The Knight in History- Francis Gies
- The Norman Achievement- Richard F Cassady
- Knights- Constance Brittain Bouchard

Griff Hosker
June 2017

Other books by Griff Hosker

If you enjoyed reading this book, then why not read another one by the author?

Ancient History

The Sword of Cartimandua Series
(Germania and Britannia 50 A.D. – 128 A.D.)
Ulpius Felix- Roman Warrior (prequel)
The Sword of Cartimandua
The Horse Warriors
Invasion Caledonia
Roman Retreat
Revolt of the Red Witch
Druid's Gold
Trajan's Hunters
The Last Frontier
Hero of Rome
Roman Hawk
Roman Treachery
Roman Wall
Roman Courage

The Wolf Warrior series
(Britain in the late 6th Century)
Saxon Dawn
Saxon Revenge
Saxon England
Saxon Blood
Saxon Slayer
Saxon Slaughter
Saxon Bane
Saxon Fall: Rise of the Warlord
Saxon Throne
Saxon Sword

Medieval History

The Dragon Heart Series
Viking Slave
Viking Warrior
Viking Jarl
Viking Kingdom
Viking Wolf
Viking War
Viking Sword
Viking Wrath
Viking Raid
Viking Legend
Viking Vengeance
Viking Dragon
Viking Treasure
Viking Enemy
Viking Witch
Viking Blood
Viking Weregeld
Viking Storm
Viking Warband
Viking Shadow
Viking Legacy
Viking Clan
Viking Bravery

The Norman Genesis Series
Hrolf the Viking
Horseman
The Battle for a Home
Revenge of the Franks
The Land of the Northmen
Ragnvald Hrolfsson
Brothers in Blood
Lord of Rouen

Lord of Rouen

Drekar in the Seine
Duke of Normandy
The Duke and the King

New World Series
Blood on the Blade
Across the Seas
The Savage Wilderness
The Bear and the Wolf

The Vengeance Trail

The Reconquista Chronicles
Castilian Knight
El Campeador
The Lord of Valencia

The Aelfraed Series
(Britain and Byzantium 1050 A.D. - 1085 A.D.)
Housecarl
Outlaw
Varangian

**The Anarchy Series England
1120-1180**
English Knight
Knight of the Empress
Northern Knight
Baron of the North
Earl
King Henry's Champion
The King is Dead
Warlord of the North
Enemy at the Gate
The Fallen Crown
Warlord's War
Kingmaker

Lord of Rouen

Henry II
Crusader
The Welsh Marches
Irish War
Poisonous Plots
The Princes' Revolt
Earl Marshal

Border Knight
1182-1300
Sword for Hire
Return of the Knight
Baron's War
Magna Carta
Welsh Wars
Henry III
The Bloody Border
Baron's Crusade
Sentinel of the North
War in the West

Sir John Hawkwood Series
France and Italy 1339- 1387
Crécy: The Age of the Archer

Lord Edward's Archer
Lord Edward's Archer
King in Waiting
An Archer's Crusade (November 2020)

Struggle for a Crown
1360- 1485
Blood on the Crown
To Murder A King
The Throne
King Henry IV
The Road to Agincourt

Lord of Rouen

St Crispin's Day

Tales from the Sword

Modern History

The Napoleonic Horseman Series
Chasseur à Cheval
Napoleon's Guard
British Light Dragoon
Soldier Spy
1808: The Road to Coruña
Talavera
The Lines of Torres Vedras
Bloody Badajoz
The Road to France

The Lucky Jack American Civil War series
Rebel Raiders
Confederate Rangers
The Road to Gettysburg

The British Ace Series
1914
1915 Fokker Scourge
1916 Angels over the Somme
1917 Eagles Fall
1918 We will remember them
From Arctic Snow to Desert Sand
Wings over Persia

Combined Operations series
1940-1945
Commando
Raider
Behind Enemy Lines
Dieppe

Lord of Rouen

Toehold in Europe
Sword Beach
Breakout
The Battle for Antwerp
King Tiger
Beyond the Rhine
Korea
Korean Winter

Other Books
Great Granny's Ghost (Aimed at 9-14-year-old young people)

For more information on all of the books then please visit the author's web site at www.griffhosker.com where there is a link to contact him or visit his Facebook page: GriffHosker at Sword Books

Printed in Great Britain
by Amazon

67049573R00147